Australian Stories
Then and Now

Edmund Fitzgerald
Illustrated by Geoff Pryor

RACK & RUNE
publishing

In memory of my son Geoff

Contents

II Cricketore

Norman is a pompous bastard. He always looks as if he should be sitting on a shooting stick waiting for the polo to start. He phoned me just before midday on the Friday and he spoke in the affected voice he uses on the telephone.

"Hullo?" I said when I picked up the phone.

"Is that you, Ken?" Norman knew it was me but he waited until I assured him that it was before he continued.

"Richard Carrington can't make it for the match on Sunday," he said.

"So?" I made it sound casual but I was waiting for the crunch.

"Actually"—in fact, Norman said 'ectually'—"I think he's got a girl he visits up in Sydney. A bit rough on the team, though, I suggest. Not much of the old esprit de corps, eh?"

"Yeah," I said. "Well?"

Norman got down to tintacks. "That leaves our team a man short, old son. I'm rather relying on you to rout out another player for us. He doesn't have to be a batsman or a bowler, we can handle that"—Norman meant that he could handle those aspects—"but we need him for the fielding."

I listened in silence as he went through it all. And it came, as I knew it must—and as only Norman can.

"I know you've got more friends than I could shake a stick at, you lucky fella!" He radiated charm at that point. "I'd be greatly obliged— that is, the team would be greatly obliged—if you could see your way clear to rounding up another player. We're depending on you, Ken."

"O.K. Norman," I said, and hung up.

To give Norman his due, he was doing the right thing. His dictum, that cricket should be left to the cricketers and organising to the organisers, is probably sound. I'm an organiser. It's me that arranges the ground when it's our turn to be host and it's me that checks the cricket bags and the gear and, most importantly, it's me that sees to the beer and ensures that it's cold. Seeing that I've only averaged seven runs a game this year, I have concluded that I am indeed a better organiser than a cricketer. Norman has me to rights, I guess.

On the other hand, Norman is a cricketer. He is the only one of us who really takes our social game seriously. He is our star bat and our star bowler. The rest of us don't mind him batting on and on because, if he was out quickly, we might not have enough time to drink the beer.

Norman always looks the part too, which is irritating. No grubby sneakers for Norman. Oh, no. Genuine cricket boots and immaculate cream trousers held up, seemingly casually, by an old school tie which serves as a belt. And he wears a cream shirt with the sleeves rolled up to the elbow and a cricket cap with a badge on it. He's a picture. Norman even wears a box when batting and I wouldn't be surprised if he had a badge on that too. As a joke, our wicket-keeper, Harry Wilson, once asked if he could borrow it to keep his sandwiches cool but Norman said NO. I'm sure he thought that he might catch something.

I could not think of anyone who might be willing to fill in at a day's notice and time was short. Driving home from work that evening I swung into the street and there was Roberto, mowing the lawn. I knew Roberto only vaguely. He's twenty or so and he lives opposite me with his parents and two sisters. They all speak good English though I don't think they've been out in Australia all that long. Roberto has black curly hair, a friendly brown face and he's solidly built. He looks athletic. I pulled the car into the curb and got out. Roberto turned off the mower as I approached.

"G'day, Roberto," I said, all casual. "Would you fancy a game of cricket on Sunday? Our team is a player short."

Roberto looked a bit nonplussed. "It's no great hassle," I told him quickly. "It's just a social game and we all stand around and have a few beers, friendly-like, you know."

I could see he was not convinced so I kept talking. "It's a bat and ball sort of game. Someone tries to knock the stumps over with a little leather ball which the batter tries to hit. If he does, he can run up and down the pitch as many times as he can until the players standing around throw the ball back. When one team has made as many runs as it can, the other team has a go."

I think Roberto had been ready to say no until I explained the rules, but when I finished, he laughed and I knew he'd play.

"It sounds fun," he said, and he made a small gesture with his hands. "Thanks, Ken. I'd like to give it a try."

Inwardly, I breathed a sigh of relief. "Great, Roberto," I told him. "I'll collect you. The game starts at ten and we've got to drive out to Garret's Gap, so I'll pick you up around nine. We're playing the Foresters—the Forestry Commission team, that is—the Gap is their home ground."

Roberto nodded and grinned. "O.K. then, mate," he said. "I'll see you at nine on Sunday. I look forward to it."

I smiled too as I turned away. I liked the "O.K. then, mate."

Sunday. A blue sky and a light breeze. Glorious it was. I collected Roberto as arranged. He wore jeans and a yellow shirt and a cap advertising beer, so he was not overdressed against most of the rest of us.

We arrived at Garret's Gap with ten minutes to spare and I parked the car in the shade of one of the pine trees.

Garret's Gap is an old mining town. It is set in the foothills of the Dividing Range, about an hour's drive from town. The copper mine hasn't been worked for around forty years and all there is now is a sad straggle of old weatherboard houses, a couple of shops, a post office, a pub and a one-man police station. That's about it, and the population is way down on what it was once. However, there's a million hectares of forest behind the town to be logged so it's a good location for the Foresters.

The cricket ground is part of the sports reserve. There are two derelict tennis courts mouldering among the pines, a couple of swings and a slide, and there's the cricket ground. It has a concrete wicket and a dry, baked outfield that receives neither water nor top-dressing.

The cricket ground fronts the road and the shops on one side, while its other border is delineated by the salubriously named Dead Dog Creek which contains water only after rain. Behind the creek the hills are heavily timbered and, if you play late in the day, the kangaroos are likely to be out in force at long-on.

Our team was all there so I introduced Roberto. Norman jerked his head at me after the introductions were made and I followed him over to one of the slab seats. He looked searchingly at me and shook his head slowly from side to side. His face expressed pretended bewilderment. "Why did you have to recruit a bloody Italian? What would he know about cricket? He probably can't even catch! Couldn't you find a bloody Australian?"

I resisted the impulse to answer Norman. What's the use of arguing with someone like that? I just walked away to where Reynolds was showing Roberto the bats and the pads. Roberto was asking questions and I could see that they were comfortable with each other.

The Foresters were a good bunch but there was a bit of needle between our teams. We ran a six-team competition and we were a win up on them, though, to be honest, I think they were a better side. Some of our chaps came as much for the beer as for the cricket but the Foresters were a bit more serious than that.

Norman won the toss. "We'll bat," he said. Norman liked to go in at number four after the opening bats had taken the sting out of the bowlers and the shine off the ball—on the rare occasions that we used a new ball, that is. Such a practice is all very well when the openers make a few runs, but the Foresters had got themselves a new demon bowler and he had our side in all sorts of trouble.

When Norman took his stand at the wicket there were fifteen runs on the board for two wickets down and it looked unlikely that our side would see out twenty overs—far less the forty allotted.

Poor Norman couldn't handle the speedster either, in spite of the confidence we supposed his box must give him. He managed to block most of the balls but he wasn't able to score effectively and, meanwhile, the rest of our team was spending so little time at the crease that it was hardly worth the bother of walking out to the wicket. It was a disaster.

When I went in after eight wickets had fallen, Norman was still there—stuck on sixteen, and our grand total was forty-two runs. He came down the wicket with some sage advice for me. "Just play a straight bat," he said tersely, "and leave the scoring to me." He must have remembered what sort of a batsman I am.

As it happened, it didn't matter. The previous dismissal had come on the last ball of the over, so it was Norman who faced the next ball and it was Norman who was out leg before wicket.

"That wasn't out," he shouted in answer to the umpire's decision. "My leg was nowhere near the bloody wicket."

The umpire, standing behind the wicket alongside me, rocked gently back on his heels. He served the Gap as postmaster and he umpired any local matches in which the participants agreed to keep him supplied with cold cans of beer during the match.

"Oh yes you were," he said cheerfully. "Out LBW. On your way, twinkletoes."

Norman blew his cool. "I WAS NOT OUT," he insisted, striding furiously down the wicket. His face was pink with rage. "I was NOT out, was I, Ken?"

"Yes you were, Norman old buddy," I told him. "Leg before wicket—like the man said."

I knew he felt I was being disloyal so, out of the goodness of my heart, I added, "You wouldn't want me to tell a fib, would you, Norman?"

Then he walked, but I could see he was fuming.

That left me in and only Roberto to come. "Poor Roberto," I thought. "What a way to learn about cricket."

Roberto took his place at the wicket. He watched the first ball go by. The next ball he hit for two and the one after that for four. Thereafter, Roberto got stuck into the bowling. He hit three sixes and I don't know how many fours. "'Ave a go, ya mug," called the Foresters from the boundary.

What was more, Roberto kept me away from the bowling and he only took singles from the last ball of overs so that he could keep the strike. He was seventy-three when I tripped over while looking over my shoulder to see if a ball he hit had reached the boundary. There was a good return, and I was out—for none—and our innings ended.

Roberto was a hero. We'd scored a hundred and fifteen and he had saved us from disgrace.

Roberto and I managed a couple of beers each and a steak from the barbie before we were called to take our places in the outfield. Norman was our main bowler and he usually thinned out the opposition batsmen without too much trouble. Not this time, though. The Foresters belted Norman all over the paddock and our bowler at the other end did no better.

The opposition were none for forty-six when one of their openers lofted a ball to the boundary where Roberto caught it. There were sighs of relief from our lot but the new batsman proved just as hard on Norman as had his predecessor.

The Foresters really had their tails up by then and a piece of fielding by me further lowered our spirits to around rock bottom. A ball I was chasing ran down a gully in the outfield and into the dry bed of Dead Dog Creek.

"Look out for the tigers down there, mate," called one of the Foresters on the sideline. "They're everywhere." When I saw the blackberries and the swamp grass, I could see that it very likely was tiger snake country and I went down there very warily.

By the time I got back up, the batsmen had run nine and the Foresters were demonstrating their amusement.

Then one of them belted the ball for what looked like a certain boundary. The two batsmen stopped in mid-wicket to exchange a word as they waited for it to cross the line. Roberto, however, intercepted it in the nick of time, threw it back fast and low and lifted the middle stump out of the ground. The batsmen were flabbergasted, and so were the rest of us.

Norman took off his cap with the badge on it and rubbed a perspiring forehead. "Here, Roberto. You may as well try your arm as a bowler too. You've done everything else in this bloody match," and he tossed him the ball.

Well, I'm not going to give you a ball-to-ball description. Suffice to say that Roberto turned out to be a fair bowler. He was responsible for the capture of all the remaining wickets—bowled, run-out, stumped, whatever—for a total of nineteen runs.

After the last wicket fell and the batsmen headed reluctantly back towards their teammates, our lot sort of gravitated together in an aimless huddle. We couldn't believe it. We'd won by forty-two runs. Well, Roberto had won by forty-two runs.

We all congratulated him but he just grinned. I could see he was pleased.

"What about joining our team?" asked Norman humbly. There was no mention this time about him being Italian.

Roberto was nice about it. He said he'd enjoyed the game but that he worked most weekends and, besides, he was trying to study.

Norman finally gave up. "Well, you can certainly play cricket," he said. "Where did you learn?"

It was the first time I had seen Roberto look embarrassed. "Oh," he said, "we used to play a game something like that when I was a little kid back in Italy."

I took him home afterwards. We pulled up at his place and he said thanks and that he'd enjoyed the day. He got out of the car and turned to walk up the drive but I saw him hesitate so I waited. And he came back. He put his hands on the door where I had wound the window down.

"When that chap, Norman, took you aside after we arrived at the Gap, that was about me being Italian wasn't it?"

I nodded.

"Then tell me, Kenowski, you must know—when do you stop being a Pole or an Italian in this country?"

I thought for a moment before I answered. "It takes a while. For some it takes forever. I came out as a little kid and mostly I pass as a local—but not quite. As for you? You can play cricket—you've got it made, mate!"

Come In Number...

Had Old Robbie been able to look down on the three of them sitting around his bed in the Budawang Hotel waiting for him to die, he would have been amused.

Those sharing the death-watch were Mavis Phillips, licensee, cook and barmaid, and Robbie's two fishing mates, Johnny Pell and Con the Greek. Mavis sat quietly, patiently, but Johnny Pell and Con were uneasy and restless.

Robbie was the hotel's only permanent guest. His room, one of three on the street side of the upstairs corridor, also opened onto the verandah which ran the length of the hotel.

The room was small and sparsely furnished. It contained a wardrobe, bed and a cluttered bedside table. On one wall, brackets supported a fly rod and a spinning rod in the place where a mantelpiece had once provided ornamentation above a now-blocked-off fireplace. On the old hearth, a pair of hip waders lay alongside a canvas satchel with a cotton hat pushed carelessly beneath the flap and an open metal box with shelves full of flies and lures, hooks and lines and, indeed, all the paraphernalia of a long-time fisherman.

A curtain covered the door to the verandah and a holland blind hid a window. Outside, rain drummed on the galvanised iron roof of the old weatherboard hotel and a gusting wind drove flurries of rain against the window of Robbie's room. Distant thunder grumbled and somewhere a door banged, and banged again.

The curtains also hid the late afternoon view of the deserted main street with its straggle of shops and the row of gnarled and twisted peppercorn trees which provided the town centre with summer shade. Also hidden by the driving rain were the fields of stubble behind the huddle of houses and, further away, the heavily timbered flanks of the main upland range.

Downstairs in the bar, a few regulars enjoyed the warmth from the log fire and the relative peace that would last only until the workers from the timber mill beyond the stockyards ended their day's toil. They would pour into the bar rough and loud, bringing the smell of wet woollens and sweat and the bitter cold of a high-country winter evening, their mouths full of oaths and laughter.

Reg Phillips, the barman and husband of Mavis, moved a desultory cloth slowly over a beer ring on the counter. Above his head, a few hardy flies moved casually to avoid the four blades of the ceiling fan as it cut slow swathes through tendrils of cigarette smoke. He was hoping that Mavis would be back in the bar before the rush.

Mavis sat in a cane chair beside Robbie's bed, holding his thin, brown hand and watching his shadowed face, lit by the meagre efforts of the single bulb suspended above the bed, as the life drained from him.

A woman of late years, she had known Robbie from before the war. He had returned to Budawang with a small pension and had moved into the hotel, supplementing his income with odd jobs around town. He was liked by everyone: a nice old man whose passing would be regretted for a moment and then forgotten.

On the other side of the bed, Johnny Pell and Con sat uncomfortably and unwillingly on chairs brought up from the kitchen. Both were long-time residents of Budawang and long-time intimates of Old Robbie by reason of a shared passion for fishing the beautiful and largely untouched rivers and creeks of the high country behind the town.

Mavis's eyes strayed to the companions with whom she was to share Robbie's death and, not for the first time, wondered at the quirk of circumstances that drew the three of them together: Old Robbie, courtly and civilised, while Johnny and Con were a pair of disreputable, drunken layabouts whose only saving grace was Robbie's acceptance of them. She knew that they were as fond of Robbie as she was and that his death would leave a gap in their lives that they, probably, would never be able to fill. Con glanced up and caught her eye. He shrugged broad shoulders. "Poor old Robbie," he said softly, making a spare gesture with his hands. "D'you think anyone will mind if I take his fishing rods?"

Johnny Pell, stirred by Con's declaration of intent and to avoid being deprived of his share, sat forward on his chair, eyes narrowed and voice belligerent. "Yeah, and I want his waders and his lures."

Mavis looked at them over the still figure in the bed. She knew they were trying to express feelings for which they did not have words. "He'd want you both to share his things," she said. "You were his best friends."

She looked down at Robbie, wondering if he even knew that they were there. Death was very close.

Robbie had not heard the interchange. He was walking down the grass slope just above the sheep track that skirted Black Wattle Hill. The air was crisp and there was the smell of earth left wet by overnight spring showers.

Above him, the new-risen sun was golden through the mist.

The day held promise and he glanced about him as he walked, full of the pleasures of the bush and in anticipation of the river below. It ran darkly, part-hidden by overhanging ti-tree, but soon the water would catch the sun and the river would come alive. He dropped down the hill through wet grass, avoiding blackberries and using the proliferation of wattle saplings to slow his descent. He emerged from the shadow of the hill into sunlight and there, ahead, was the first of the pools he planned to fish.

A massive boulder, lichen-covered, narrowed the river at its upstream end and slate-gray water swung clear and fast around it. The bank had been deeply undercut and somewhere in that deep, dark water, sheltered from the current, there would be a trout, its fins barely moving as it watched the big slow swirl of water as the river shelved over gravel towards the sedges on the opposite bank.

Beyond the boulder, Robbie could see the sunlight spreading across the next pool upstream and shafts of light through the ti-tree etched patterns on the grass and water-weed in the shallows. Fish were rising in the still waters to insects moving from the weed that prospered in an area where the bank had collapsed.

Robbie squatted in a hollow behind the bank while he studied the pool and prepared his rod. Then he moved slowly and carefully towards a clearing well below the big rock where there was room to cast.

His first effort was a ranging shot and his line fell across the edge of the big rock. He cast again—feeding out the line as the rod flexed under his hand and the tiny brown and red fly soared beyond the rock to land delicately in the swirl of water waiting its turn to run the narrows.

Once, twice, it circled before joining the current to drop over the small pressure wave and into the lower pool. Then it vanished, Robbie waited a long moment before lifting the tip of the rod and striking. He felt the power of the fish as his rod bowed and he retrieved line quickly as the fish paused to consider its situation. Then it ran downstream and the line sliced through the water towards the far bank with just enough drag on the reel to tire the fish. It turned when it reached the bank before fleeing further downstream towards the reeds and the safety of tangled limbs of a fallen willow.

Robbie turned the fish just before it reached the refuge. It was only then that he saw it. The fish threw itself from the water, fighting desperately to throw the hook—a gleaming, twisting brown trout—vibrantly alive and full of fight. He played the fish with care, using his line as if it were cotton and—slowly at first—retrieving line and releasing it, he forced the fish towards him.

At the end it was beaten. It came to him in a slow, reluctant sweep, fin above the surface of the water. Robbie saw its real dimensions and was delighted. "I knew we'd meet soon," he said affably.

Just for a moment he thought there was someone peering over his shoulder and he glanced quickly around but there was no one.

He unclipped the folded landing net from his belt and flicked it open. His eyes returned to the fish, now exhausted and moving very slowly through the long tendrils of water-weed almost within reach.

He watched it turn its side in the final surrender and, as it did so, the sunlight caught the rich sweep of red, brown and orange speckling that mottled its flanks like jewels and the deep, sombre grey-green of its back.

Robbie knew that he was not going to kill the fish. He knelt on the bank, placing his rod and landing net beside him. Pensive, the morning sun warming his back, he looked at the river flowing past. Shafts of sunlight through the trees lit the water and were, themselves, alive with whirling insects. He heard the magpies warbling in the eucalyptus branches above him and the 'plop' as a water rat dropped from a log down by the reeds. Before him, the water-grass waving gently around it, lay the great trout. He reached forward to draw the fish nearer so that he could release it from his line. "Ah!" he said. "How beautiful you are."

When Old Robbie withdrew his hand from Mavis's light grasp and reached both arms towards the forty-watt bulb hanging from the fly-spotted ceiling, Johnny Pell gasped and crossed himself and Con the Greek started, as if to rise, so that the legs of his chair squeaked on the linoleum. But Mavis held up her hand and he stilled.

Robbie's face was alight with pleasure. "How beautiful you are," he said. His eyes were open then, but he was looking at something beyond the walls of the Budawang Hotel. Smiling, his eyes closed and his life ended.

Mavis stood up stiffly, her eyes wet with tears, and she drew the sheet up over Robbie's face. Johnny and Con stood too, Johnny knocking over his chair.

"Well," said Mavis softly, not pretending to smile, "we've lost a friend." And because her two companions appeared stunned by events, she sought to ease their shock.

"He wouldn't want you to mourn over him, you know. You'd please him best, the pair of you, by going fishing tomorrow as usual—the rain will have passed and the fresh water will make them active."

Johnny appeared to notice her again. He shook his head and looked down at his hands. "I'm not going fishing. I'm going to church—that's where I'll be on Sundays from now on. I heard what Robbie said and I saw his face!"

"Me too," said Con the Greek, embarrassed and not meeting Mavis's eyes. "It mightn't be too late for me neither."

The Five O'Clock Cow

The upper reaches of a small tidal river marked the eastern boundary of our farm. On our side, between the river and the hills, there was a river flat on which my father grew the best lucerne in the district. On the far side of the creek, the hills came almost to the water and the cows that grazed there would stand for hours just gazing at our lucerne.

Driven into the side of one of the hills and facing our property was the entrance to an old gold mine. In its heyday, fifty years earlier, they had been taking out three ounces of gold to the ton, and the story was that more than seven hundred ounces had been won from the mine in its few short years of life. Now, the crushed rock straggled in a long untidy mound behind the remnants of the old steam-driven rock crusher that leaned drunkenly on a comparatively level piece of ground just below the mine entrance. The four great rust-covered iron stamps of the battery were stilled forever, and the slab timber hut that had housed the office and the safe was derelict and open to the sky. The whole area was covered in nettles and blackberries and provided a popular residential area for a great number of brown snakes who presumably enjoyed the view of the river and the lucerne.

The gold had petered out suddenly when the vein of quartz turned down into a twisted layer of granite and, although a number of attempts had been made to find its continuation, they had all come to nothing. The mine entrance had been fenced off and the post and rails that they had used were now silver-grey and partly covered in lichens.

About two years after the mine closed, there had been a minor gold rush on one of our paddocks. My cousin had picked up a rock to throw at a crow and, noticing its unusual weight, had taken another look before letting fly with it. When the piece of rock was found to contain three quarters of an ounce of gold, the people from the town descended on us like a rash; they spent three months digging up the paddock before giving up. My father reckoned that someone from the mine had been carrying ore home in their pockets on the quiet and had dropped the piece of rock getting through a fence. He had been very annoyed about the mess they had made of the paddock.

I was about fourteen and my brother was a year younger when the old Scot arrived. The story went that he had been prospecting up in the back blocks for twenty years—or it might have been seventy years—and he had come to stay in the town for a while until he got over a broken arm. He had been told about the old mine in town. Jim and I first saw him one day while we were fishing in the river for bream that came the fifteen kilometres upriver on the tide. We watched him fossick over the mullock heap and we laughed like mad when we saw him leap high into the air at one stage and then beat frantically at the ground with his walking stick. I did not see him for a while after that, but Jim said that he had been back every day and that he had gone into the mine with a lamp.

A week later he showed up at the house and asked my father for permission to look around the hills on our side of the river. My father told him that our place had been investigated by a great mob of mining experts and that they had found nothing. "You're wasting your time," he told the old Scot. "The lode just disappeared straight down and that's the end of it." When I was bringing in the cows next day, I saw the old Scot stumping around the slopes above the lucerne and chipping away here and there at exposed rock with a little hammer.

It was another two weeks before we saw him again, and then he reappeared with a vengeance. He came to the house to tell us that he had taken out a mining lease on our farm. My father was furious, but what he said when the old Scot told him that the lease was in the middle of the lucerne almost doubled my vocabulary of improper words. The old Scot started digging and he took the narrow shaft straight down for twelve metres. There was a ladder down the side and a windlass over the top for bringing up the clay and the rock.

The clay came up on the windlass and built up into an ugly yellow pile on the lucerne. My father put in a sprinkler system and deluged the mine every day, but the old Scot erected a galvanised iron roof and just kept digging. Jim and I sympathised with our father and undertook minor harassment of our own. We started chucking rocks down the shaft after the old Scot had gone home, then an old bicycle, and then a dead fox that we found; but he just took them out and kept digging.

Then, one day, we found it. We went down on the Saturday morning to fish the rising tide and discovered that we were unable to use our favourite pool. In the middle of the river floated a very dead cow which, I would estimate, must have passed away at least a week earlier. The temperatures had been over thirty for nearly a fortnight and the cow was so high that, even upwind, we could not get anywhere near it. We kept well back as the cow slowly made its stately way upstream on the tide, accompanied by a cloud of touring blowflies which were doubtless doing the round trip. After she passed, we baited our lines and took up our usual positions. Jimmy said, "The tide turns about four, so she should be back around five," and he looked at me suggestively. By four thirty we were back on the riverbank with Bessy, our old horse, and a rope. Sure enough, just on five o'clock the cow floated majestically around the bend just above our pool.

I wrapped my shirt around my face and managed to lasso one of the horns. With Bessy's assistance, we towed her, bobbing and swaying, back upstream to a shelving bank. There we adjusted the rope to separate the cow and us by as much distance as possible and led Bessy towards the mine shaft. We were accompanied on our trek by forty million blowflies.

I walked ahead to look at the shaft and I dropped a stone down to test its depth; there was water at the bottom. By careful manoeuvring, we got Bessy to deposit the cow on the lip of the shaft and then, with a gum sapling, we levered her in. Down she went, hitting the sides all the way, and there was a mighty splash when she hit bottom. Foolish Jimmy looked over the edge and nearly fell in when the odour hit him. We congratulated ourselves on a good day's work and took Bessy home. We were sure our father would be delighted with our efforts; nevertheless, there was no thought in our minds that we should tell him.

Just before lunch on the Monday, we saw the old Scot coming up the track with a policeman. My father answered the door and Jimmy and I hung around behind him wondering what was in the wind. We soon discovered that it was still the cow.

Accusations were made and denied by my father. "It was them bleddy boys," said the old Scot. After a certain amount of heated discussion, Jimmy and I agreed that we had been responsible.

"Well," said the policeman, looking apologetically at my father, "I'm sorry, Tom, but you'll have to get it out." He went on to point out that, should my father refuse to remove the cow from the mine, a contract would be let for what would doubtless prove to be a very expensive job. Should that happen, he said, costs would have to be recovered from my father in the local court.

I will never forget that day. My father put on his oldest clothes and, with a wet cloth around his face and a rope in one hand, went down the mine. Jimmy and I (following orders) attended with Bessy. He came up after five minutes and spent as long throwing up over the lucerne. When he recovered, he came walking slowly over to us with his head down. He waved a hand toward the rope tied around a log near the shaft. "I want the cow pulled up out of there and you two can get the pick and shovel and bury it." And then, over his shoulder as he walked away, "And tell Mum I'm down at the pub."

The trouble we had burying the cow on a rocky hillside in thirty degrees of heat should have turned our hair white.

The story would have a proper ending if I could say that the old Scot found the reef again but, to be honest, I don't remember. Ever since, though, if anyone mentions gold mines to me, I get this terrible queasy feeling in my stomach.

But I'm Not a Bloody Bee, Dad

"Hullo… Hullo… Is that you, Dad?"

"Yeah, it's me, Bill…"

I said, "It's Bill."

"Speak up, Dad, I can hardly hear you."

"How are things back there with all of you? And how are Mum and the kids?"

"No, of course there's nothing wrong, Dad. Why should there be? Shirley and me are both good-oh. I was just wondering how things were back in Conowombilly, that's all."

"Yeah, I know it's only been three days since we left. D'you think I can't count or something?"

"Yeah, it was a beaut wedding, all right. Me and Shirl had a great old time of it."

"Yes, Dad, I can still hear you."

"Sure, we're enjoying our honeymoon all right, but there's not much to do in Sydney, you know. It's a bit hard to fill in the time. Back in Conowombilly, I'd be down at Fred's tonight with the boys, having meself some fun. Wednesday nights are going to be a problem when we get back home, now that I'm married. I suppose that Shirl and me can go around and visit her old lady. It'll be nearly the same except Shirl will come home with me instead of staying there with her mother."

"Yeah, I know I don't have much news, Dad."

"You were enjoying yourself doing nothing? And I've interrupted you? Well, I'm sorry Dad."

"No, I'm not ringing up from the hotel. I got bored after tea so I came out for a bit of a walk around and I thought I'd just ring up to see how everyone was getting on back home."

"No, Dad, Shirl didn't want another walk. We've been on five walks to-day already and I think she's got sore feet. She stayed back in the room and she's going to start knitting me a pullover. She bought the wool this morning. You'd like it, Dad. The wool is a sort of greeny colour with a bit of yellery-blue in it and it's going to have a…"

"All right, Dad, all right. How was I to know that you weren't interested in my pullover? Shirl's only knitting it because she's bored stiff."

"What d'you mean, 'What else?' There's not much to do in Sydney, you know Dad."

"Today? Well, we slept in until after five o'clock this morning and we had to hang around until seven to get a bite of breakfast. Then we walked around the Opera House and up and down and around a few streets but there's nothing to see except shops. We soon got sick of that, so we came back to the

28

hotel; but it gave us the willies sitting around there doing nothing. So we've been going out on lots of walks."

"Why d'you say that, Dad? Of course we're not tired of each other."

"How d'you mean, we both sound a bit funny? We can't spend all bloody day kissin', can we? We got sick of that pretty bloody quick. I got sore lips."

"Eh? What was that again, Dad? You can get fined for swearing over the phone, you know. I didn't know you even knew some of those words."

"What do you mean, aren't we enjoying the rest of it all? What rest of it…? All right, Dad. I'll stop interrupting you. Go on then… Yeah… Yeah… Eh?… Yeah… Yeah… What? You've got to be joking… Tee hee hee hee. Tee hee hee hee. By gee, you're a card, Dad… you had me going there for a minute. That's pretty rude, though. Not like you, Dad."

"Sure, I know about the birds and the bees and all that stuff. What d'you take me for? I'm not a bloody bee, you know, Dad."

"Yeah… Yeah… And I know all about the cows and the bulls too. Gawd, I've been milkin' thirty of 'em for fifteen years. Anyone know about bloody cows, I bloody should."

"O.K. Dad, O.K., O.K. Don't get so excited. The post office will take your phone away if they hear you carrying on like that. But remember, Dad, that I'm not a cow so what you're saying would be silly."

"Shirley? What about her?"

"You mean Shirl? Hey, that's not very nice, Dad. That's not a nice thing to say at all about Shirl."

"No? Well, what did you mean?"

"What was that about the bull again?"

"Yeah… yeah… crikey… holy smoke, Dad. You mean to say that people… By heck, what will they think of next?"

"Eh, Dad? Did I hear you right? You mean me and Shirl?"

"Oh, crikey no, I couldn't. Tee hee hee, tee hee hee."

"I'm trying to stop, Dad. Tee hee hee, tee hee hee hee."

"Yes, Dad, I'm still here. I was just thinking. Shirley and me—gee whiz."

"Hell. Oh boy, us?"

"No, the phone is all right. You might be pulling my leg. You've always been one for a good joke, Dad."

"What's that again? You and Mum?"

"You're having me on this time for sure. Not Mum. No, never, Dad."

"Mum's not like that at all."

"Sure I know she's got nine kids. One of them was me, remember? That's got nothing to do with it."

"Yes, all right then. I'm certainly thinking about it all, Dad. I suppose I could give it a try. I don't know what Shirl will think, though. She doesn't mind me kissing her, but… Hell… I've seen her pick up a bag of wheat, no trouble, and if she fetched me a smack over the chops, I'd be spitting out bits of teeth for a week. And what's more, I reckon her mother'd half kill me if she ever found out. The old girl could tear out one of my legs by the roots without hardly trying if she decided to."

"Speaking about legs, Dad, reminds me that it's about time I was getting back to the hotel. Shirl might want to measure my chest for the pullover."

"Me breathing heavy? No. I might be getting a cold or something. I was just wondering if she was wondering where I was, that's all."

"Well, I certainly am thinking about what you've said, Dad. Hey, I nearly forgot to tell you about the great display of agricultural machinery we went to see last night. They had some real good stuff there—but I'll have to tell you about it some other time."

"Now? No. I can't tell you now. Shirl will be waiting for me. I've just re-membered that I was going to have an early night anyway."

"It's no good you yelling at me, Dad. I'll bloody tell you about it when I bloody get home. Got to run now, Dad. See you!"

Pawn to Bishop

"Rupert! I'm talking to you. Please have the courtesy to pay attention when I'm addressing you. A Church of England bishop is supposed to have more manners than you ever exhibit to me."

"I'm interrupting you preparing your sermon? Rubbish, you're just reading the newspaper. If I didn't interrupt you, we'd never exchange another word in this life. These days if your head isn't buried in the bible or a magazine, you've disappeared to heaven only knows where."

"You know full well that I have no intention of being quiet until I've had my say so you may as well listen to me and have done with it. And if you try to doze off, I'll wake you up. I'm determined you'll hear me out.

"I want a new coat. Yes, a new coat. I've seen one in Gander's window and I want it. It's priced at $114.99.

"I know perfectly well that you can hear me so it's no good you sniffing like that or banging your pipe out on the fireplace. Now, just look at that! You've spilled hot ash on the carpet. There, if it wasn't for me, you'd have the place on fire in no time and burned down too, more than likely.

"I've had my old coat for seven years this April. It's showing its age and it's quite out of fashion. It's high time I had a new one.

"You don't have to tell me that $114.99 is a lot of money. With the housekeeping allowance you give me, I should know better than most, I'm sure.

"I notice there's never a shortage of money when you need your tobacco though, is there? Or a new wheelbarrow for the garden? And you had no trouble finding the money for the trip to England for the wedding, did you? Yes, and when it suits you, you're pretty quick off the mark if there's an ecumenical conference on anywhere. Or, at least that's where you tell me you go. Oh yes, my word, yes. We can always afford it when you go off hobnobbing with your cronies at all those ecclesiastical councils… and goodness knows what goes on at some of those congresses you attend. Don't think I don't know what men are like when they all get together. Eating and drinking until all hours—and worse too, I wouldn't be surprised.

"Aha, yes, it's all very well for you. And don't bother to give me that old story that you only dress up because it's part of your job. If you've told me that once, you've told me a thousand times—and I don't believe a word of it. I'm quite aware that bishops have to look the part. But I've never seen one of you yet that wasn't done up like a Christmas turkey. Vain as peacocks the lot of you in your purple shirts.

"But as for me! You don't care how I look or that I don't have a decent coat to my back. I could run around stark naked and you wouldn't care. Not you. No, it never matters what wives look like does it? It's a great pity they aren't allowed to stand up in the pulpits alongside their husbands so that congregations can see that charity certainly doesn't begin at home. And you can stop that heavy sighing… it's wasted on me. Save it for the choir. Well, then. I've had my say. And what's your answer to that? Oh, so there's to be no answer, isn't there? You won't say anything, eh? Is that it? We shall just see about that, then. Oh yes, indeed we will. You've made your bed now and you shall lie on it. I'll raise the money for the coat myself. How do you like that? I'll soon show you, my lad.

"You may well snigger behind your paper. But I will. My mind is made up. I'll write a book. I'll write my memoirs.

"You find that highly amusing, do you? I can see the paper shaking so it's useless pretending that you're still reading it. You don't have to try to hide that you think your wife to be a fool. But we'll see who has the last laugh, mark my words.

"Now, let me see. About the book. I'm afraid my early life won't interest anyone. Perhaps I'll confine myself to my married life. After all, I am married to a bishop. Yes, that's what I'll do. And I suppose I'll need a title for it too, won't I? Mmm, what about 'Memoirs of a Bishop's Wife'?

"Yes, I think I like that.

"I'll begin my book with your posting to India when you tried out for the Central Missionary Service. I was only a young bride in those days, remember? On my way to face the unknown in the mysterious Orient. Yes, that sounds like a good start. No shortage of money for coats in those days, was there?

"Come to think of it, we weren't in India that long, were we? Five weeks if my memory serves me. Not that I believe it was entirely your fault, mind you. And I really do think it was a bit early for them to recall you. I'm sure you would have improved, given time. But that's life, isn't it?

"Remember when you got pushed into the river? Yes, I rather thought you might. We were lucky to get away that time. I did try to tell you but you wouldn't listen to me then either. Foreigners don't necessarily have to share your Anglo-Saxon views, you know.

"Ah, those were good times, weren't they? Fun-filled days. I'll never forget the address you gave at the Institute of Theology when you… oh, ha, ha, I'm sorry, truly. You weren't to know. I just can't help laughing when I think of it.

"Yes, I am aware that you were trying to put them at their ease, but oh dear, their faces when you finished talking…"

"Alright then, I'll say no more about it if that's to be your attitude. However, a book like mine must be true to life and I will simply have to tell it the way it happened.

"Then there was that service you gave in… um, what was the name of that town again? I'll have to look it up and get the spelling right. I think it was…"

"Oh, you don't want to hear about that either? No, I suppose I can sympathise with that view, but I do have obligations to my readers. I need to make my book interesting and, after all, I'm just a dull old housewife.

"And there's another thing. I'm sure everyone would like to hear about the Harvest Festival. Now that really was a riot. Certainly the sort of stuff to sell books. I believe your flock would be heartened to learn that any one of us can make mistakes and that even bishops are all too human. I know I don't mind them laughing at me in the least. Frankly, I think humility suits me. How much did I say was the price of the coat? Well, $114.99 actually. Yes, that is the full price.

"Oh I quite agree that writing my memoirs would be a hard grind. Though, as you know, I was never one to shirk hard work. But, as you so rightly say, if I had the money for the coat I wouldn't have to bother with all that tedious writing. Nevertheless, the more I think on it, the more tempted I am to press ahead. Who knows, it could be a best seller."

"What? You will? Oh, lovely. That's extremely kind of you, dear. Mind you though, the thought of being a published author is very attractive. Perhaps an article or two in the Parish Bugle?"

"Yes dear, now that is a thoughtful suggestion. I would like a nice pair of shoes to go with the coat as it happens. And, to be honest, I was thinking that perhaps a handbag would set the whole thing off…"

"The total? Oh, gracious, let me see now… Well, I expect that $170 would cover everything."

Mail Order Bride

The mail order, for one rubber female, life-size, bust large, hair black, came as no surprise to the management of R. Basoom Ltd. The supplying of "sex aids and appurtenances ancillary to the fulfillment of the true love function" was their business.

A red-headed and youthful assistant lifted her neatly folded form from the stack in pigeon-hole sixteen (rubber ladies are stored in a deflated condition) and dusted off some of the protective talcum powder with his sleeve. From pigeon-hole eighteen, he took a luxuriant black wig and a partly used tube of EAZYSTIK. He applied a thin coating of EAZYSTIK to the top of her rubber head and attached the wig. He then strolled languidly to the end of the shelves where stood a cylinder of compressed air. He shook his rubber companion out to her full length and inserted the air hose from the cylinder into a valve located in the area not normally visible to a casual acquaintance. He spun the wheel on top of the cylinder and watched the dial until it registered twenty-four pounds per square inch.

Pumped up, "Myrtle," as the red-headed youth called them all, was an impressive figure of a woman. By reason of her being as naked as the day she emerged from the moulding vat of 'fresh-pink' tinted liquid latex, her many charms were readily apparent.

Shapely rubber legs supported a voluptuous torso and, above that, magnificent breasts were capped by plum-coloured nipples. On her obverse side, a handsome chubby bottom positively glowed with a simulation of bucolic health.

Beneath the flowing ebon hair and noble forehead, a retrousse nose separated (but only just) two green eyes that stared off at approximately similar angles into the far distance. Cheeks were regulation pink, while lips—ruby red—were parted in perpetuity to show pearly white rubber teeth. A paint brush, dipped in some mystery mix, had been drawn along her bottom lip so that it appeared to have just been wiped with a wet and lascivious tongue. "Myrtle," despite her cost, was value for money.

Bert, the red-headed boy, patted her rotund rump. "Good luck old girl," he said. And to his superior, he called, "She's ready, Mr. Basoom."

From the front counter came the impatient reply, "Then pack her up boy and send her off."

Bert draped her in the cheese-cloth wrapper (supplied at no extra charge) and laid her in the long cardboard box. Before sealing it, he popped in the instruction book, the twelve month guarantee, the foot pump and the puncture outfit. He addressed the box to Mr. F. Reid, Railway Station, Olderbury, carried it to the station, dispatched it and went home.

In Olderbury (pop. 26,270), Frank Reid, owner of the city's new and only Emporium of Sexology, had been called up to Sydney to talk about his wife's alimony. He packed clothes for a few days, locked the shop and drove away. "Myrtle," then in a rattling goods train halfway between Mergun South and Lagamullah Lagoon, was unaware that there would be no one at Olderbury to meet her.

On the main street of Olderbury stood the weathered Church of St. Ignacia. The church had fallen on hard times. Its lawns were unkempt, its stonework discoloured and damaged and one of the stained glass windows had been boarded over. The pastor of St. Ignacia was eighty-two year old Father Riccotto. The stentorian voice of yesteryear had become a feeble piping and most of his congregation had left to join the new church near Riverview.

The only parishioners left were those who had aged with Father Riccotto and a few of their progeny. Most were from the old Italian families whose orchards were being engulfed by new housing estates. Their numbers decreased each year as had the church funds, and there was no longer any money for even minor repairs.

A month earlier, Father Riccotto had received a kindly letter from his bishop advising that St. Ignacia's was to be closed and that he was to be given honourable retirement as the reward for long and faithful service.

Father Riccotto had never dreamed of high office in the church, but he had hoped that, when he left St. Ignacia's, he would leave a church vibrant with the life of the parish and with a building fund sufficient to keep it in mint condition until Judgement Day. It irritated him that less worthy saints than Ignacia had become popular and trendy.

The bishop's letter brought Father Riccotto face to face with cold reality and with retirement a scant fortnight away, the end to the most modest of his hopes. He reached a decision. "Bugger the bishop," he thought (though in more ecclesiastical language). "St. Ignacia will at least have a procession before they close my church."

Cheered by his decision, he sought out Mrs. Connell, his housekeeper of forty years. "There will be a procession," he told her. "And, seeing it's to be the last time, I'll buy a new statue—I have a little bit put away. They'll be surprised at St. Brigid's, won't they?" and he gave a frail quavering chuckle.

"Humpf," said Mrs. Connell, and she returned to preparing the evening meal.

Father Riccotto telephoned Giororelli Bros. in Sydney. They dealt in religious articles and boasted they could furnish a church or dress an archbishop at a moment's notice. "Yes," they told him. "Yes" they could supply a plaster statue of a female saint, two-thirds life size and "Yes" they would send it immediately.

Three days later, the boxed statue arrived at Olderbury railway station and Mrs. Connell's nephew was sent with the presbytery wheelbarrow to collect it. At the station, he addressed the junior porter who was sluicing down the parcels' office steps.

"Is there a box for Father Riccotto?" The porter straightened up, looked contemptuously at Mrs. Connell's sister's child and spat in the bucket he was using. "Inside by the weighing machine," he said tersely, "'elp yourself."

There was a large box standing near the weighing machine. There was another box, just as large, over by the window but it remained unnoticed. Mrs. Connell's sister's child was pleased that the box was light. He loaded it onto the barrow, trundled it back to the presbytery and left it in the middle of Father Riccotto's study.

There was no reason for Father Riccotto to check the address on the box and he did not do so.

When he saw "Myrtle," Father Riccotto was stunned. He knew he was a little out of touch and he realised that it had been a long while since he had purchased any statues, but this! Still, Giororelli's was unquestionably a respectable firm. He pushed a large and errant rubber breast back behind the cheesecloth.

A lifetime of dealing with the problems of a flock had given Father Riccotto a certain resilience and it took only a few minutes before he adjusted to the situation. Times change and, to be honest, some of the plaster saints were a bit anaemic looking. St. Ignacia, after all, had been an Italian peasant girl, and unbidden into his mind swept a vision from his youth in Calabria where he and a girl not unlike the new arrival had once… Father Riccotto quickly busied himself. He lifted St. Ignacia, as he now thought of her, from the box and leaned her against the wall.

It was quite apparent to him that St. Ignacia had been some woman and that, as a garment, the cheesecloth was totally inadequate. He took a sheet from his bed and, with averted eyes, wrapped it toga-like about her body. He secured it with the cord from his dressing gown and, with a sigh of relief, stepped back. St. Ignacia watched him enigmatically.

Father Riccotto regretted that there was little time to publicise the procession, but time was running out, and if the entire population of Olderbury failed to attend, then that would be their misfortune. Intuitively he knew that those who were present would not forget her.

He tottered down to the kitchen where Mrs. Connell was shelling peas. "St. Ignacia has arrived," he told her.

"Humpf," said Mrs. Connell dourly. "My own sister's boy collected the box if you remember, Father." She spoke loudly so he would hear.

Father Riccotto continued. "I want her to be carried in procession after Mass on Sunday. Spread the tidings among the parishioners. Come and see what you think of her," he added, then turned and left the kitchen. Mrs. Connell stood up, a short, sturdy, grizzled figure, shook out her apron and, with a resigned sigh, followed.

Father Riccotto stood back so that Mrs. Connell could view the saint. Mrs. Connell pursed her lips. Her sharp eye did not miss the parted lips, the pearly teeth, the jutting breasts or the curve of a generous hip. She reached over and felt the inflated rubber arm. A puzzled look crept over her face.

Glancing at his watch, Father Riccotto excused himself and departed at a shuffling trot for the church just across the straggly lawn. When she heard the side door close, Mrs. Connell crossed to the empty box in which St. Ignacia had arrived. She was not surprised when she saw it had been addressed to Mr. Reid. She knew of the "Emporium of Sexology" and it was not difficult to see that a mistake had occurred. Despite her Catholic upbringing, or perhaps because of it, Mrs. Connell was a fatalist. She believed in the "will of heaven" and "the mills of God grinding exceedingly small." It was not up to her to attempt to deflect God's will. She carried the

box out to the incinerator and watched it burn. Then she returned to the kitchen and finished the peas.

On the Saturday, Mrs. Connell's nephew was detailed to drag the carrying litter from the garden shed. He was told to dust off the cobwebs preparatory to its being used in the procession on Sunday and to leave it in the clear space behind the pews in the church. Mumbling curses, he did as he was told.

The litter consisted of a wood platform, a metre square, secured to two long poles suitable for carrying on the shoulders of four or more of the devout. At the rear of the platform was a stout vertical pole to which whatever was being carried could be attached.

For reasons he had not analysed, Father Riccotto prepared St. Ignacia on the litter himself. Contrary to his expectations, the saint's apparel had not presented a major problem. With memories of his first encounter with her still fresh, he decided to leave well alone and the sheet continued as her sole garment. It covered her back, crossed above her breasts, and hung in folds to her ankles; her arms were bare.

He attached the saint firmly to the post on the litter by re-tying the cord of his dressing gown so that it circled the post as well as her waist; the post he artfully hid beneath the sheet. Then, in order that she would not prove a distraction during Mass, he covered her with an old cloth.

Mrs. Connell had spread the word and on Sunday, the congregation, though not large, comprised virtually all of his flock. They had heard that the church was to be closed and Father Riccotto's reading of the bishop's letter was met with murmurings of sympathy and sporadic boos for the bishop, which he quickly hushed. There was enthusiasm for a procession bearing their saint through the streets and, when the service was completed, Father Riccotto led them to the covered statue and whisked off the cloth.

Hands by her side, St. Ignacia stood gazing straight ahead, her parted lips lending her an air of slight surprise as though she had just been pinched by Mrs. Connell's nephew. The looks of admiration that the youth was now bestowing on her were directed at attributes quite irrelevant to her saintliness and it was readily conceivable that the thought of pinching her was not far from his mind.

The rest of the parishioners reacted too, with surprise and admiration predominating. There was no shortage of volunteers to man the poles supporting the litter, though there was a slight hiatus when it was first lifted. Diagonally across from Mrs. Connell's nephew (at right front) was Bernadette O'Riordan, captain of the Olderbury girls' basketball team and a good head and shoulders taller than the other three bearers. When the litter came up to shoulder level, it lurched to an acute angle and St. Ignacia gave a rubbery bow towards Francis Kilpatrick, at ninety-four the oldest church member. For one tremulous moment, Francis gazed down the front of St. Ignacia's toga into the biggest cleavage he had ever seen, and, for the first time in eighty years, blushed like a schoolboy. Bernadette O'Riordan was replaced and the litter bearing St. Ignacia was carried without further trouble through the front door of the church and down to the main road.

Led by Father Riccotto, the procession, such as it was, proceeded. Though every effort was directed at keeping out of the line of traffic, cars began to back up behind them. A group walking back from St. Brigid's at Riverview swelled the crowd and yet other citizens stopped to watch from the footpath. A stiff breeze which moulded the sheet against St. Ignacia's bosom secured their continued attention.

The process had not gone far when the police patrol car pulled up. "You're blocking the traffic, Father," said the driver. "You don't have a licence to march, do you?" Father Riccotto shook his head mutely. "Then I'm sorry, Father," said the policeman, "but you'll have to get off the road. Turn up Railway Lane and you can go home the back way."

The hooting of car horns by impatient drivers decided Father Riccotto. He turned and led the way up the narrow confines of Railway Lane, followed by the litter bearing St. Ignacia and a crowd of perhaps a hundred participants and spectators.

Railway Lane connected to a street which gave access to the rear of the church. It was bordered by small factories and old terrace houses.

A group cut through the grounds of the Masonic Hall to get a better view of the procession from ahead and, when the crowd moving up the lane with St. Ignacia met those moving down, the sudden crush of people brought the litter to a standstill. An old Italian woman touched the saint's feet for luck, another plucked her white robe. Bernadette O'Riordan, still surly at being replaced as a litter bearer, leaned across and, with her long bony arm, twitched at the tassel of Father Riccotto's dressing gown.

In dressing St. Ignacia, Father Riccotto had not noticed the stopper that kept the saint inflated at twenty-four pounds per square inch, nor had he noticed the short length of twine which the manufacturer had attached to the stopper to assist, when necessary, in its removal. He certainly had no idea that the end of the twine had been inextricably caught up in the sheet when he re-tied the dressing gown cord around the post on the litter.

When Bernadette twitched the tassel a lot of things happened very quickly. The dressing gown cord came loose and the sheet, no longer supported, slipped down around St. Ignacia's knees to reveal various attractions. There was a swell of sound from the crowd expressive of awe and admiration. Before they had time to absorb the wonder of it all, however, the weight of the sheet pulled out the stopper.

Like a child's balloon suddenly unleashed, St. Ignacia, stark naked, took off into the air like a rocket and disappeared at high speed over the roof of Murphy's Bakery alongside which they had stopped. The sudden hush was broken by Bernadette O'Riordan who shrieked and fell to her knees. "A blessed miracle!" she cried. Confusion reigned. A dozen voices took up the cry, then fifty, then a hundred.

"Humph," said Mrs. Connell to herself. She picked up the dressing gown cord from where it had fallen, opened her purse and took out a set of keys. The collective eyes of the growing and excited throng were on the dramatically empty litter and no one noticed Mrs. Connell open the wooden door of Murphy's Bakery. Once inside, she shut it behind her. Seeing that Mrs. Murphy was Mrs. Connell's own sister, it was, after all, all in the family. She moved quickly up the stairs and opened the door that led to the flat roof where Mrs. Murphy usually hung the washing. As she had expected, there was St. Ignacia, without a breath of air left in her, flat on her back, looking vacantly up at the sky.

Mrs. Connell gathered up the saint and took her back to the presbytery rolled up in an old laundry bag. With a large pair of scissors, she reduced her to small and unrecognisable pieces, and these were hidden in a wardrobe for future disposal. She had no sooner finished than her nephew appeared.

"There's another box for Father Riccotto," he told her. "They have just delivered it from the station."

"Humph," she said. "About time too. That must be the new coat rack I ordered for his going away present." (The lie tripped lightly from her tongue.) "Bring it in."

After the boy had brought the box and departed, she locked the door and took the plaster saint sent by Giororelli Bros. from its wrappings.

She wound the saint in a sheet and then, with the statue tucked under her arm, went out the side door and across the straggly grass to the empty church. It was the work of a moment to adjust the robe and tie the dressing gown cord she had recovered in Railway Lane around its waist. Mrs. Connell lifted St. Ignacia to a pedestal by the altar and departed.

After an exhausting afternoon, Father Riccotto had gathered his strength to conduct the evening service. A large crowd was waiting to get in when he went to open the church doors and the biggest congregation in thirty years surged in as he swung them back. Someone recognised the sheet and the dressing gown cord and then the saint herself. Bedlam ensued. The last of the congregation were removed by the police about midnight.

There was no way that the Church of Saint Ignacia was not going to be headline news, and it was probably going to be a centre for pilgrimages for years. On Monday, therefore, (after reading the papers) the bishop arrived to ask Father to reconsider his resignation and stay on. Father Riccotto agreed. He was never quite certain how it had all happened but he decided it was better not knowing. He had offered no comment on the changed physical appearance of St. Ignacia, nevertheless, when praying to her, it was difficult not to remember the parted coral lips, the white teeth and the jet black hair. He had a suspicion that Mrs. Connell's sister's child had similar problems.

Conversation With the Cat—and More!

I was sure our cat, Pew, was intelligent. I said to him, "One meow means yes, two meows mean no!"

"Meow!"

"Do you like milk?"

"Meow!"

"Do you like dogs?"

"Meow, meow!"

"Do you like warm beds?"

"Meow!"

"Do you like me?" Pew started licking his bottom. Could this be dumb insolence? Nah, no message there!

The cat held up one paw and nodded his head. "Meow!"

Then he nodded twice. "Meow, meow!"

This was extremely interesting. He could ask me questions if he could only find out how to enunciate them.

He held up his paw again. A breakthrough? Entranced, I watched him pull a paw along the ground. "Meow!"

He pulled his paw along the ground twice. "Meow, meow!"

Next time it was, "Meow, meow, meow!" He had counted up to three!

I stood up. "Two," I said… and, after another demonstration, "Three!"

"Eureka," I thought. Then, "But perhaps not," as I watched amazed as Pew's body began to shake. He was making a chuffing noise and then he fell over.

Suddenly I realised that Pew was laughing at me and that he had conned me into imitating a circus horse counting apples!

"I'm not here to play games, cat!" I told him. "Jerking me around, are you? Alright, get your own afternoon tea!"

Apparently annoyed, he sat down and began licking his paws. Then it happened: the cat suspended his cleaning activities and deliberately extended his middle claw towards the heavens.

I had just been 'given the claw'!

Before I could recover, Pew rose to his feet, walked casually past me and out the cat door.

Checkmate!

Well, we had communicated, and he did seem to be intelligent if misguided!

Pew seems to have realised that we are a little bit more than the amiable, pliable creatures he had supposed, decided to investigate us and simply got out of his depth.

He started sitting alongside my wife at the computer and she was pleased to have his affectionate company.

The first intimation of problems came a month later. We received a letter from our bank manager advising that a Pew C. Katt, presumably a 'Mr.' had taken over our bank accounts and sought to transfer ownership of our home to himself! The Bank Manager's reason for contacting us over a seemingly legitimate transaction, was that Mr. Katt had signed the document with what looked like the print of a cat's paw dipped in Vegemite spread. He thought he should check with us!

Well, we sorted that out—finally! But only after we discovered another paper under preparation which was to have taken care of us financially in our old age; so the cat was not all bad!

Pew did not panic when his plans came unstuck but reacted with aplomb and sagacity. He left an E-mail which my wife picked up in the morning take. It advised that he was sorry and, because of the shame he had brought upon himself, was about to depart our home, never to return. He said that, knowing we would still need a cat around the place, he had taken appropriate steps to make sure we were not left in the lurch by his departure. He informed us that he had read all about cloning on the Internet and, indeed, had cloned himself in order to leave for us a loving (but not too ambitious) cat like he should have been!

The new cat was everything Pew said it would be. It eats all its food without argument, it is tidy, obedient and affectionate, and it shows no interest in the computer.

Just one little problem. To believe that Pew was clever enough to clone himself was asking a lot but to accept that he was also able to clone his well-worn collar with his name-tag attached was a bit much.

So what we really had was Pew pretending to be his own clone!

Spouse and I made our decision. "Puss," we told him, "you seem to be a fine cat and we like you. We were really very fond of Pew, your predecessor, and we will miss him. So we would like to call you Pew Two or—to be really honest—Pew too!" That proved a satisfactory result for all of us!

Troutus Gigantus

"Frogs are top bait for trout," they both told me. That may well have been true but, while I was willing enough to use a grasshopper or a wood-grub, I could identify too readily with a frog to be able to fish with one.

At that time, with two companions, we were concentrating our fishing efforts on the waters below Burrinjuck Dam which lies to the west of Yass and some a hundred and thirty kilometres by road from where we all lived, in Canberra.

Marvellous fishing there was then: one of my companions never kept a fish under half a kilo—and he was always seeking to catch his bag limit with larger fish.

We would leave Canberra around 2.00 a.m. and arrive at the river just before dawn. The last thirty kilometres or so was over a dirt track which wound through bush country. We did the trip every weekend and it was interesting that over a couple of weekends during the season we would find, while driving in, that the road would be busy with frogs which presumably were migrating to or from somewhere or other.

My companions, both far better fisher persons than I, would always collect a few. "Top bait!" they'd say… and they would be expecting to catch fish weighing up to two and possibly three kilos.

A farmhouse marked the end of the track and there was a locked gate. Our routine was to park the car, collect our backpacks and rods and then be off up the track with just enough light to see where we were going. We would go our separate ways and meet back at the car in mid-afternoon after fishing, perhaps, three or four kilometres off magnificent Murrumbidgee.

I got back to the gate early one day. To pass the time until my friends returned, I decided to fish the big hole just below the farmhouse—an area with which we did not normally bother. A big rock shelf just above water level confined the 'Bidgee at the top of the pool. Deep water through the narrows extended well into the pool which was sheltered by willows and leaning casuarinas.

It had been a hot day and the walk back downstream from up near the dam had been hard work. So I was fishing so casually that I was standing on the rock ledge with my boots virtually overhanging the still, deep water of the channel. I was using a wood-grub which I cast out into the head of the pool before allowing it to sink slowly towards the bottom as it moved downstream and before I retrieved it. It was the hottest part of the day but, as I said, I was only passing the time.

I was winding in my tenth or so cast—waiting on a hail from up at the car when they found my pack—when there was a development. I watched as the wood-grub reappeared out of the depth and moved steadily towards my feet as I reeled in. Behind him, on this occasion, came something else. It was the biggest fish I'd ever seen. I can't really be sure it was a trout because it was so big. The fish had followed the grub up and, because I was so astonished, I kept on winding and the grub came out of the water. Behind it, and right at my feet, a fish of at least eight kilos. We shared a long look at each other before he faded back into the depths. Maybe it had been a big cod, but I don't think so and, besides, a seven kilo trout had been taken down river the previous month.

I told my companions when they eventually arrived. "Arr," they said. "You should've had a frog on. You'd have had him for sure. A frog kicks around— it's active!" they told me. "Not like a bloody wood-grub that just lolls around doing nothing."

It made sense. I thought about it. "Could I overcome my scruples and use a FROG?" I asked myself. "For the fish of a lifetime?" Despite my high moral stand, the answer was, "Yes, I could! I'd use the Dean of Canterbury or the Pope to catch that fish."

Next weekend, off we went again to fish the 'Bidgee below the dam. On our way in along the track, there were frogs migrating still—their little eyes gleaming like diamonds in the beam of the headlights. I got out, and, with my friends, caught a couple and put them in my lunch bag for safety.

By mutual consent my companions left me at the farm gate and I watched them trudge off into the dark before retiring to the car, my thermos of coffee and the radio. When it was almost light, I went down to the big pool. I edged down the bank, soundlessly and keeping low, so as not to be seen. I squatted in a little hollow behind the bank to 'bait up'. It was the moment of truth.

I took the cruel hook in one hand and the poor defenseless frog in the other. I found I couldn't do it to him. Nevertheless, he now owed me a favour, seeing as I was doing him one. The least that he could do, in appreciation, I reasoned, was to assist me in catching the monster fish. I thought I could read acquiescence on his little face.

I rummaged through my bag and found that which I sought—it was a rubber band. I adjusted it so that it went twice around the frog's waist (but not too tightly) then once, securely, around the hook. It seemed a fair and just compromise.

I tossed him in, well upstream and out towards the deepest water. I thought he'd sink but he didn't. He must have heard us talking in the car about the giant fish because he swam like mad, his little pop-eyes looking back at me over his shoulder. For all the world he reminded me of the belt-man of the Bondi Lifesavers swimming in shark-infested waters. I tried to look away but I couldn't. Any moment now the monster is going to swe-e-e-p up from the deep and, CHOMP—like in the film JAWS: the frog (and hook) would be engulfed.

The frog must have seen JAWS too. He wasn't doing that leisurely frog kick with the breaststroke. Oh, no—he was doing the crawl with an eight beat kick, and I was very glad that I hadn't learned to read frogs lips.

No, I couldn't do it. I wound him in, took his surf belt off and let him go. And I started fishing my way upriver.

I caught up with my friends a couple of hours later. They looked at me appraisingly, eyebrows raised, as I neared them.

"Did you get him?" they asked.

"Yeah," I told them. "Thirteen and a half kilos"—I allowed a pause—"gutted!"

They waited.

"No. I lied to you," I said. "I had him out on the bank but I tossed him back. Couldn't fit him into my bag."

Wrecked? Never

"The Wreck of the Edmund Fitzgerald" was the title of a ghastly folk song that once jammed the airways, and which was a personal embarrassment to me—partly because it described my state so exactly. It told the dolorous tale of a ship that sank in the Great Lakes of America with the loss of all the crew and it was sung by someone with a two-note range voice who accompanied himself on a guitar with one string. The song itself seemed to zip up and down the chart of the top two hundred pop songs and I was glad when it finally dropped out the bottom because, as I have intimated, it made me the subject of derisory comment.

The song led me to the discovery that I do not particularly like my name being featured in this crass way. While it seems quite reasonable for public figures like Messrs Clinton and Bush to be made the subject of unseemly doggerel, most of the rest of us are too unused to notoriety to accept it with aplomb. What, for instance, would be your reaction to your own name being used in a public, oft-repeated, dismal sounding threnody—accompanied perhaps on a nose flute—and which (for example) linked your name, say, with words like bibulous, saturnalia, satyriasis or even Pelagianist? Not so jolly to have that sort of fame thrust upon one, eh?

Thrust upon one or not, fame can, of course, be a matter of luck and so, equally, can be the lack of it. And what is more, there is fame and FAME. Fame, of a sort (and for example), was once achieved by that nursery rhyme character Chicken Little who scurried about the forest advising all and sundry that the sky was about to fall in. Chicken Little was held up to public ridicule and he achieved immortal fame for his chicken heartedness. I have long held a sneaking sympathy for Chicken Little because I have come to realise that the sky is quite likely to fall in. I now regard C.

Little as being a chicken before his time and as being a notable prophet rather than a figure of scorn. Were he alive today he would probably be recognized as an eminent guru—and possibly as the Maharishi Chicken.

While there are those among us who have missed out on fame, there are others who have had fame thrust upon them, usually by others who propose to benefit by so doing. Fame has become a political football to be manipulated by nations striving for pre-eminence in one field or another.

"We won more medals than you in the Olympics," say the Russians.

"Crapski," say the Americans. "We did".

"Harry Milquetoast invented the automatic articulated toadstool sorter in 1843," say the Americans.

"Bullship," reply the Russians in a Tass release. "Yuri Popoff invented it in 1841."

The classic international battle for hearts and minds featured one Pavlov, a Russian scientist. Pavlov's celebrated salivating dog (which had been taught that the sound of a bell meant food) achieved fame in the West because it evoked a pleasant image of some old hound dog dribbling all over the carpet whenever Pavlov's front doorbell rang. In a typical Pavlovian reaction, however, the Russians assumed that, if Pavlov was popular in America, he must in fact be an American and they leaped to denounce him.

"The American Pavlov is a fake," said the USSR. "The original experiments were carried out in Russia by the husband of a Soviet ballerina named Pavlova who leased the dog from the Kiev Kennel Klub."

"That last bit was a good touch," said the Commissar in charge of knocking Pavlov. "And see the Americans are all taken up with dogs and ringing bells at the moment, we may as well rubbish Alexander Graham Bell, who invented the telephone at the same time."

"The Pavlov of the American fabrication," fulminated the Russians, "taught his dog nothing. It used to drool when he got home because Pavlov was a butcher by trade and the dog knew on which side its bread was buttered. Furthermore," added the Russians, gilding the lily a trifle, "the chap who lived alongside the American Pavlov was part of the American deception too. His name was Alexander Graham Bell and, though the Americans claim he invented the telephone, he was really only the man who almost invented the telephone; he was, in fact, once bitten by the pseudo-Pavlov's dog. The real inventor of the telephone was Alexis Graham Bellovich who lived alongside the genuine Pavlova who later worked on the switchboard at the Kiev Exchange. Bellovich's invention occurred to him in a flash of inspiration. One day, while mowing the back lawn with his Victor lawnmower (named after Victor Korchnoi), he noticed that, when Pavlova kicked her salivating dog in the bum, the application of the ballerina shoe at one end corresponded almost exactly with the yelp at the other. At that instant, the concept of the transmission of messages was born. The message transmitted on that first occasion was, of course, one of discomfort and irritation for the dog. 'But what?' reasoned Bellovich. 'What if there had been another message entirely? Like 'Hello Babushka?' or 'So's your father?'"

It was obvious that such a message would have travelled at the same speed. Bellovich tried the same experiment with longer dogs and found that the speed of pain travelling at sea level from the bum to the vocal cords was a constant which could be expressed as $1+1=MC3$. As with all scientific experimentation, the next step was the dangerous transition to the use of a human volunteer. Bellovich's neighbour (on the other side to Pavlova), G.S.N. Stropotkin, whose name is now a household word and who is universally revered, was the choice. Despite his ideal length of 2.3 metres, his modesty led him to refuse to participate and it was only when Bellovich found him one morning, searching among the ranunculi for his copy of *Izvestia*, that he was able to complete the experiment. Bellovich confirmed that the message from the nerve ends in the human bum could be passed to the vocal cords in accordance with the equation 1+1=MC3.

It will be apparent then that my reluctance to bathe in the reflected glory of the song "The Wreck of the Edmund Fitzgerald" is soundly based on the premise that a little fame can be a dangerous thing. I have no desire to feature in an ideological war between the superpowers over who wrote the song or built the ship or who was responsible for the sinking. Fame, like Bombay belly, is something I can do without. And besides, someone told me that it gives you venereal warts.

The Good Life

I forget the name of the TV show, but I enjoyed it. It gave me the idea.

There was this couple in England who tired of the rat-race and turned their backyard into a farm. They had chooks and goats and a pig, and their electricity came from gas from the animal manure; self-sufficient, they were. I admired them.

I thought of them when my wife and I bought a house in the suburbs. The block was not quite big enough for what I had in mind, but I reckoned if someone could become self-sufficient in chilly old England, it should be a breeze in the antipodes. What's more, I was going to do it the Australian way.

To start with, I ploughed up the backyard from the laundry to the back fence and planted wheat. We had good rains and a warm spring and the wheat came up. I don't do things by halves, and I bought a reaper and binder and a header. I harvested two bags of wheat and carted them ninety kilometres to the nearest silo. My wife didn't like the mice that moved into the house once the wheat was gone. I did not make any money, but I was learning.

I decided not to waste the stubble, so I bought some sheep, a kelpie, and an Akubra hat with a wide brim. The sheep dealt with the stubble and, in October, I brought in a team of shearers. They stayed ten minutes and I got a quarter of a bale of wool; I took the sheep to the saleyards. My wife thought the sheep were messy and she was glad when they went.

Now that the backyard was bare, I decided on an open-cut mine. I sold the reaper and binder and the header together with the wool press and spent the money on mining equipment.

My neighbour had been following my activities and he begged me to let him help; I agreed reluctantly. He drove a hard bargain and I had to promise him two percent of the profits provided he worked an eighty hour week at the mine. We dug up the backyard to a depth of fifty metres without finding a mother lode. I used my truck and the front-end loader to get rid of the dirt and rock as fill for building sites and I almost covered expenses. My wife complained about the dust and mud and the cost of rescuing the cat when it fell into the hole.

I was getting the hang of self-sufficiency. I had a big hole and the Council had a big rubbish problem. We did a deal. My wife was not amused and claimed that the rubbish stank and attracted flies. But I liked the thirty thousand or so seagulls that lived on our roof, so it wasn't all gloom.

I dumped rubbish into the hole to within a metre of the brim. I left the hose running for two months to fill it and then put in yabbies. They ate through the rubbish within three months, lowering its level a further metre—and proliferated. My wife got nipped by a yabbie and discovered that they disagreed with her. I went close to making ends meet that time.

I added topsoil and put in a market garden. Even the dwarf beans were ten metres tall, and they had us on the news one night. My wife said the rhubarb stopped the sunlight from reaching the loungeroom window and that she couldn't watch the neighbours.

That was the year I blew it. I had been thinking of a small space station for rocket launches—the house *is* right at a bus stop. But my wife's doctor announced that she was pregnant with twins. By the time the kids were born, we had a little lawn in the backyard with a garden gnome and edged with bricks. We had a patio and a pergola, a rotary clothesline and a flower bed with daffodils, and she wants a swings and slide set and an above-ground pool. Furthermore, she's become allergic to me.

I look at the garden. It's not the same.

The Bushwalker

We assembled at 8 a.m. It was freezing cold, but bushwalker groups do not believe in wasting good daylight by lolling about on Sunday mornings in warm beds. Nervously, I looked at my companions-to-be on my first organised walk but there was little opportunity to meet anyone. We were whisked off without ceremony to the starting point in vehicles owned by some of the twenty-odd walkers who had turned up and off-loaded. The bush track wound away between the trees and, like all walking tracks, it sloped up-hill at a steep angle.

The group tended to walk in twos and threes and, where the path narrowed, in single file. Somewhere up front, armed with map and whistle, walked our leader. I started out near the front but as almost everyone was more energetic than I, they gradually worked their way past; it gave me an opportunity to sort out who was what. Most of them matched steps with me for long enough to exchange the odd word and then, as they forged ahead, I could eavesdrop until they passed beyond earshot.

Some of the bushwalkers were obviously seasoned and serious hikers and they plodded purposefully past in huge boots with enormous packs on their backs, occasionally grunting at each other. There were the usual young lovers out for a frolic, and there were those who were trying to take off weight or put it on or shift it back to the right places; there were others who were in no category that I could detect.

First to pass were two men who nodded at me in unison without slowing. They were discussing the fiscal policy of the pre-war Romanian Government and I listened in until an active old lady in a red tracksuit and sandshoes joined me.

She nodded at the two ahead without ceremony. "Treasury and Foreign Affairs I call them," she said. "Foreign Affairs always wears cavalry twill trousers and a hunting jacket, and Treasury carries a pocket calculator in his rucksack. Treasury used to be a scoutmaster and, if you give him half a chance, he'll bore you stiff with bushcraft and campfire lore. Watch out for him." She winked and scampered on ahead.

After we crossed a creek (where I nearly fell in), I was joined by two girls. One was large and hearty and the other one was not. Large-and-hearty addressed me in robust tones. "Hullo there. My name is Roberta and this is my friend Leslie." She thrust out her hand and gazed unflinchingly into my eyes. "Call me Bobby. I think we're going to get on fine. Right, Leslie?"

I introduced myself. She looked me over carefully and said, "I can see that the bush is new to you. A real tenderfoot, eh? Breathe deeply, Edmund, and take God's good air deep down into your lungs. Gets rid of the cobwebs, doesn't it, Leslie?" To demonstrate she sucked in a cubic metre of air and her woolly-covered bosom surged like a tethered zeppelin.

Unerringly, she had picked me as a novice, and she proceeded to give me the benefit of her accumulated wisdom. "Soup is better in a Thermos than coffee—coffee goes a bit peculiar. Wear thick socks like Leslie's. She knitted them herself, didn't you, Leslie?"

Bobby nodded towards Leslie shuffling along between us. "Been a bit off colour lately. Time of the year probably. The sap goes down in the autumn and all that." After ruminating briefly over the state of Leslie's sap, she was back to business. "Take matches, compass, chocolate, and a mirror. Remember to carry toilet paper—we bushwalkers call a spade a spade. The outback is no place for the squeamish. Right, Leslie?"

We passed Foreign Affairs and Treasury, who had stopped to work out a balance of payments problem for the Seychelles. Bobby gave them a scathing look. "Fancy dressing up like that," she said. "No sense of occasion. Jeans suit us fine, don't they, Leslie?" We trudged up a steep rise.

"Sometimes I bring my Labrador," said Bobby (puff puff). "She's pedigreed, of course." The track widened and we slowed. Foreign Affairs and the scoutmaster were close behind us. "I didn't bring her this time because she's on heat." I looked back uncomfortably, hoping not to be overheard in such a delicate conversation. Bobby looked carelessly around and continued in her robust voice, "I didn't bring her this time because I get sick of being followed around by a mob of randy mongrels."

I had time to see Treasury and Foreign Affairs, mouths agape, transfixed in horror and embarrassment before I turned and hurried on down the hill. Bobby chattered on obliviously and unheeded, except perhaps by Leslie.

When the girls eventually moved ahead of me in a single file to traverse some rocks, I found that every time I raised my eyes to find a new handhold, the horizon would be completely filled by Bobby's large jean-encased backside writhing salaciously/obscenely/delightfully. So I sat down and let most of the walkers get ahead of me. There seemed to be another chap on his own. They said his name was Muffy or something like that. He wore army boots at one end and a khaki-coloured knitted helmet at the other and I was under the impression that he was covering up some fearful deformity on his face. I found out that the odd lump at the side of his head was a transistor radio that he left wedged under the headware so that he would have both hands free to deal with the cans of Pilsener with which his capacious rucksack seemed to be filled.

Our walk leader fell back to him at one stage and (they told me later) gave him a good talking to about defiling the environment because he was discarding an empty can about every ten minutes. The walk leader told me on his way back to the lead position that I should ignore Muffy's example and that he was by no means typical. He added that, in view of Muffy's attitudes and habits, he would not be permitted to take part in any

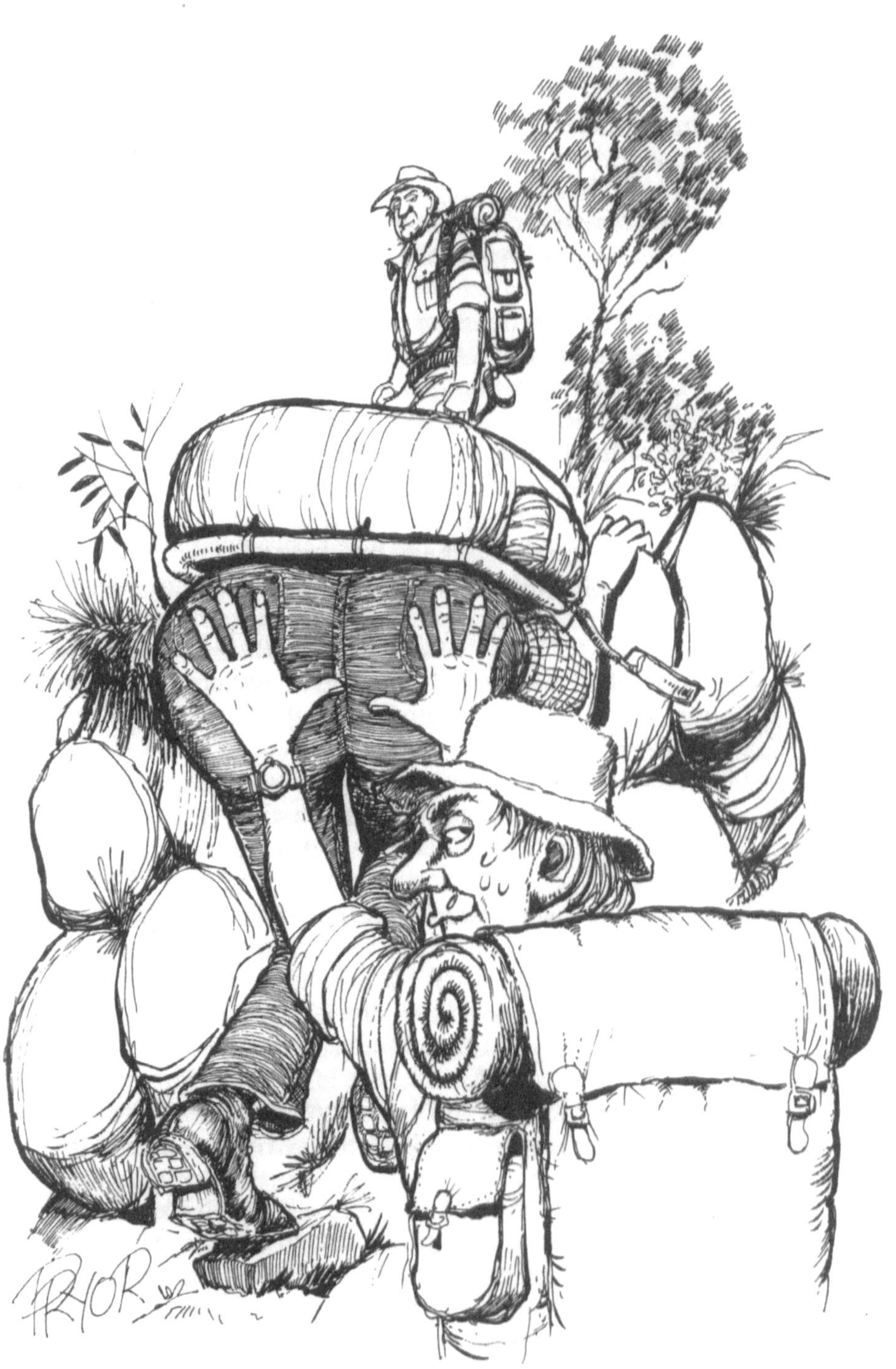

more club walks. I had my own doubts that he would even get home, far less go again. With each mile, he had been getting further and further behind and his gait more and more erratic. He seemed to disappear entirely after about two hours walking.

When we stopped for lunch, Treasury beckoned me aside while Foreign Affairs was building a fire. "That frightful girl had no right to say the things she did, you know. Her accusations have no basis in fact," he added. I nodded silent acquiescence. "As man to man," he continued, "I'd like to know if she mentioned the name Gladys?" I told him no and he pondered a moment. "When I was a scoutmaster," he confided, "there was a bit of malicious gossip in the pack at one time. You know what the lads are like at that age." I tried to look as if I knew what lads were like. He spoke sadly, "Brown Owl and I were checking the gymnasium mats and she tripped on a dumb-bell and…"

Foreign Affairs had got the fire going with his gold Ronson lighter and he came over to where we were talking. As I moved away to get coffee to put into my mug, I heard him raise the matter of Brown Owl with Treasury, a note of aggrieved interrogation in his voice. I listened in turn, as Treasury, temporising and evasive, launched into an oration on the ornithological peculiarities of owls in general.

They had not quite finished with me, and Treasury gave me a lecture on tracking by means of bent grass and scuff marks and how to tell the difference between the spoors of kangaroos and lyrebirds. He was jammed chock-a-block with bushcraft and, by scouting around our lunch area, found a goanna, half a lady's brassiere, and a dead field mouse. He called us all over and showed us the spot where "a very rare spotted bandicoot" had "defecated within the last six hours." Bobby, when her turn came, said, "That's bloody dog poop!"

Actually, she and Treasury got on quite well. He had stopped to cut a switch with his knife. She saw the knife and expressed interest. It seemed that it had some fifty-seven blades, not counting bottle openers and things for horses' hoofs. They had only looked at about nine blades before he cut himself. From Leslie's pack, Bobby produced a first aid kit which was equipped with enough medical supplies to handle a medium war situation. After she bound the wound, the four of them walked together. About 4 p.m., and many weary miles later, one of the women was thought to be overdue from a gully to which she had repaired for unknown purposes. Bobby's traditional bush calls of "cooee" were a joy to the earhole. I was reminded of poor Muffy, now probably two hours back along the track, and I wondered if he was also yodelling at that very moment and perhaps in a very different fashion.

The missing lady reappeared blushing modestly and talking about getting a photograph of a robin. Like a horse with the smell of home in its nostrils, our pace quickened as dusk began to fall and we descended towards the cars, fresh, cheerful, and full of energy.

Some concern was now being expressed for the absent Muffy and there was relief and laughter when we noticed the four empty cans lying on the grass and the pair of boots poking out of the opened window of a car. It was Muffy all right, and he was fast asleep in the back. The pleasure of having found him evaporated when it was discovered that he had first taken time to be sick on the front seat.

A Matter of Priorities

Jeremy Fellows believed that, before marriage, a potential wife should be made aware of any peculiarities or odd quirks that her future husband might possess. She would not then be in a position later to offer comments like "If I had only known," or "I would never have married you had I dreamed for a moment that you…"

Two weeks after Jeremy announced his engagement, he said to his fiancée, "Lucinda, beloved, I am a trout fisherman and, through the trout season, it is my intention—on perhaps one day of each weekend—to go fishing for that crafty and resourceful adversary."

Lucinda had been aware of Jeremy's hobby and she had intended to wean him of the ridiculous habit when they got home from the honeymoon. She was somewhat taken aback, therefore, by his unexpected frontal attack but, being a quick-witted girl, she replied, "Yes, dear," which committed her to nothing.

Jeremy was not so easily satisfied. "I am going fishing tomorrow, my dearest," he said. "You must come with me, and it may be that you too will become enchanted by the delights of being on a riverbank at dawn's first light." Lucinda repressed a shudder and, assuming an air of girlish outdoor-ishness, smilingly agreed.

They got away early next morning. Jeremy turned his little car off the bitumen and onto the potholed track that led to his favourite river. With Lucinda alongside him, he felt himself telling his loved one just what fishing meant to him. He spoke of the still pools where the trout rested and of the deep runs beneath the ti-tree where they foraged. He told her of the white water in the rapids where the trout wait to pounce on anything the river might bring down to them.

Carried away by transports of love, Jeremy told her his ultimate secret about the huge brown trout that lived in what he called the 'Willows Pool' to which he was taking her. He emphasised that no other living soul knew of the great trout's existence and that, if word leaked out, there would be anglers twenty deep along the banks.

Jeremy confessed that he had been trying to catch the monster for two years and claimed that, should he ever be fortunate enough to land it, he would be prepared to join his maker without further ado.

Lucinda pursed her lips but forbore to comment. Nevertheless, while accepting what Jeremy had told her with a grain of salt, she realised that his affliction was not of minor proportions as she had thought but was a deeper malaise for which major surgery would be necessary.

Eventually, Jeremy turned in through a farm gate and parked the car. Then they walked. Lucinda followed where Jeremy led and, in time, they reached the Willows Pool.

"There it is," said Jeremy proudly. Water reached the pool over a rock shelf before flowing gently to filter through reeds and water lilies at the bottom end of the pool. Willows overhung the opposite bank while, on the side on which they stood, a level stretch of cropped grass reached the water's edge. Behind them, eucalypts crowded up the slope.

Jeremy shrugged off his pack. "Usually I sneak up here on hands and knees and try to catch the big brown," he told Lucinda. "After the noise we have made he'll know we are here, so I will forget him and we can have a picnic."

Jeremy got out the thermos and spread the rug while Lucinda un-packed the sandwiches. Jeremy stood looking across the dappled water. "I might as well set my rod up," he said. "I might fluke something."

He put on a yellow dry fly and flicked it up to the head of the pool where it lay almost unmoving on the still surface. He laid the rod down near the rug.

"Coffee's ready, darling," Lucinda said. She was sitting on the rug, fluttering her eyelashes, showing her white teeth, keeping her shoulders well back. "Have a sandwich sweetheart," and she reached over for them, at the same time managing to display, to its best advantage, a tanned and shapely knee. Jeremy gulped, sat down, and ate a sandwich. Lucinda saw that she had the situation in hand.

They finished lunch and, recollecting that major surgery was required for Jeremy's ailment, Lucinda sank languorously back on the rug. Jeremy's throat was dry, but he read the message in her eyes. "Well, we are engaged to be married, my love, and there is no one for miles…"

Jeremy, making love to Lucinda on the riverbank beside his favourite pool with the sunshine filtering through the branches overhead, forgot about fishing. Lucinda was halfway through smiling contentedly to herself in the certainty that, in future, Jeremy would regard fishing as a very minor pursuit, when the tip of the fishing rod was jerked vigorously towards the water. There was no doubt that a fish had snapped up Jeremy's little yellow fly.

Any fisherman could sympathise with the predicament in which Jeremy found himself. There he was, making love to Lucinda, while, a foot away from his hand, line was being wrenched from his reel by what could be the monster trout which he had sought for so long.

Lips glued to Lucinda's, he cocked an eye and cautiously reached out one hand. Grasping the rod and oscillating his lips even more ardently to keep Lucinda from knowing what he was up to, he gave the rod a firm jerk. The cruel hook did its work. Up from the depth surged the trout and Jeremy's right eye goggled as the giant fish soared above the surface of the water in a gleaming, twisting arc. It landed with a splash which would have secured the immediate attention of Captain Ahab himself.

When she heard the splash, Lucinda realised that all was not well. She opened her eyes to find that Jeremy, who was making love to her, was, at the same time, holding a fishing rod in one hand and playing a fish.

A really considerate woman, at that point, would have appreciated the niceties of the situation and would, at least, have given her intended some encouragement with, "Let him have his head for a while, dear," or perhaps, "Give him some slack line to play with, darling." But no! Lucinda, in that moment, revealed that she was not the holder of such liberal views. Her eyes flashed fire but her voice was icy. "I do not wish to compete for your interest with a fish," she said.

Jeremy looked into her eyes and then he looked at his rod which was bent almost double by the weight of the great trout. He held the view that it was reasonable to expect one's future wife to appreciate the importance of a fish of this nature. For one fleeting moment he thought of abandoning the fish, but sanity prevailed. Gently, he withdrew the arm that had clutched Lucinda to him, and, with the newly released hand, tightened the tension on his reel to prevent the great 'brown' from escaping down into the reeds.

Lucinda did not speak on the trek back to the car. Jeremy, revelling in the thought of the six pound fish in his pack, did not notice. He could have sworn it would have weighed twice as much.

When they reached the car, Jeremy laid the trout reverently on the back seat. Whistling happily, he flung his pack into the boot, handed Lucinda the keys and opened the gate for her to drive out onto the track. She drove out and Jeremy, about to close the gate behind her, realised that she was not going to stop. He watched open-mouthed and aghast at the thought of the long walk ahead with dusk about to fall, and it was with considerable relief that he saw her stop further down the track by the old bridge over the gorge. "She was only fooling," he thought. "Thank the lord for that."

Then he watched as she got out of the car and opened the rear door. As he started running to catch up, she reappeared and, in her hands, was the great trout. She held it up so he could see it and then, with a casual gesture, tossed it off the bridge and into the gorge. Jeremy stopped, paralysed with shock. Lucinda got back into the car and slammed the door. Then she leaned out the open window, looked back at Jeremy and gave him a two-fingered salute before driving off.

As he watched his car carry his fiancée out of his life, Jeremy realised how foolish he had been and what a terrible mistake he had made. In his anguish he spoke aloud. "To think," he said, "that I never thought to use that yellow dry fly before."

Wetting the Baby's Head

Raylene backed the car past the side gates and stopped it halfway down the drive. The two children had settled down in the back, already preoccupied with comics, and the ten-year-old Ford was set to go. Yet, she hesitated. A sixth sense, perhaps.

Raylene looked at her husband, Norm. He was standing by the car waiting to wave goodbye and, at the same time, being careful not to appear too eager at the prospect of his wife's departure. She scanned Norm's deceptively guileless face, seeking in it a recognition of moral obligation or responsibility. Seeing nothing, she sighed and shook her head.

"I'll be home about six on Sunday," she said. "I'll pick up something on the way so don't bother to cook anything. And I'll send mother your regards! Now—you've got the rest of today on your own, and most of tomorrow…" Her voice tailed off as she noticed Norm's attention wandering and it crossed her mind that he had probably not heard a word she had said.

Coming to a decision, Raylene's voice became strident. "So, you know bloody well what I'm getting at, Norm! There's to be NO PARTY! NO PARTY! Right?"

As if regretting her outburst, her next words were placatory, full of sweetness and commonsense—as if addressing a child. "No one has parties without a reason, Norm. No one. And YOU don't have a reason! Surely you've learned your lesson by now?"

Norm, rubbing a hand over thinning ginger hair, accepted the admonition with sang-froid. "O.K., dear. I wasn't going to have a party. I'm going to clean up the garage and mow the lawn. I'll be busy," he said virtuously. He moved forward to peck Raylene's cheek and, as she backed the car down the drive, called after her, "Have a good time, love. My best wishes to your mother."

On his way inside, Norm held the door open for the dog, which was normally barred from inside because of certain offensive personal habits.

"Come in, Audrey," he told it. "I might be able to find you something to nibble on."

There had always been in the back of Norm's mind an image of a handsome and faithful spaniel seated at his master's feet and gazing up at him with adoring eyes. So, although Audrey did not look like the dog of his dreams, he let the animal inside whenever he was alone. In fact, the dog was a decidedly unattractive beast. It was squat, pug-faced and of mixed breed.

It once had claims to being a long-haired dog, but the passage of years had left sections of its back and haunches almost bald—revealing large areas of grey and vaguely leprous skin. Notwithstanding those minor shortcomings, the family watchdog's unique feature was its shape. It was, intrinsically, a greedy and gluttonous animal and its insatiable demands were usually and unwisely met so that, not only was it overweight, but it bulged and protruded in the most unlikely places.

Norm collected two cans of beer from the fridge and, at the dog's yammering, gave it a slice of fruit cake and a leftover dim sim.

"Get that inter ya, Audrey," he said.

While disposing of the first can, his faithful hound at his feet (belching intermittently), Norm told himself righteously that a party was the last thing he had in mind. It was time he cleaned up the garage—he could not even get the car inside it—and, furthermore, as far as the lawn was concerned, Raylene was quite likely to get lost in it searching for the clothesline.

"What would I want a party for?" he told himself. "Noise, drunks, mess… and the guests never go home. No, a quiet weekend will do me good."

By the time Norm finished tidying the garage, it looked great and he had made room for almost a third of the car. The lawn proved the bigger problem. By dusk, it was down to around knee-height, and that was only after vast labour with a scythe borrowed from the old Italian over the back fence.

Norm, exhausted and resting from his chores, was moistening his throat with a cool ale when Big Lennie arrived. Big Lennie accepted a beer.

"Raylene's gone off and left you, eh? You're lucky, mate. Great chance for a party."

"Nah," Norm said. "Raylene would do for me. She still hasn't recovered from Wacker McGurk's party tricks at the last one."

Norm and Big Lennie sat in amicable silence. Big Lennie got up to replace his emptied can. His eyes fell for the first time on the recumbent dog.

"My god," he said in awed tones. "She's going to drop a litter any minute!"

Norm, while he was always aware of the animal, never really saw it. Now he leaned forward to make an inspection.

"She always carries a bit of condition," he opined, not really convinced. But, after a moment's reflection, added: "Yeah, I admit she looks ready to go. I hadn't noticed."

"Bloody oath she's ready to go," affirmed Big Lennie emphatically. "I've got four racing greyhounds. I know about bloody dogs whelping, you know. She's going to drop a litter any minute. You're going to be a father again," and Big Lennie shook with high-pitched laughter.

"Maybe you're right," Norm said thoughtfully. "She is like a bloody balloon, isn't she? What'll I do? I don't want pups."

Lennie sauntered over to inspect the wheezing Audrey more closely.

"By crikey, she's a bit on the bugle, old mate. I wouldn't like to be downwind of her for too long—take the lining off your lungs, I reckon… and she wouldn't pass a compression test if she was a car, either. Anyway," Lennie resumed his seat, "my expert opinion is that she'll drop her pups tomorrow. You can bet on it."

"D'you want a pup, Lennie?" enquired Norm hopefully, suddenly conscious of problems likely to be encountered in disposing of half a dozen bald-backed pups with short, hairy legs. "Take a pair? Their breeding is immaculate you know. Related to the Queen's corgis, they are."

Lennie was unimpressed. "Tell you what," he said. "With a mother like her you're going to have trouble getting rid of any of them. D'you want a suggestion?" His question was rhetorical. "She'll be dropping them tomorrow, so you COULD get rid of the whole litter in one go if you wanted."

"How?"

"Well, hold a celebration. The miracle of birth, you know. A coming-out party. Doesn't matter what you call it. How about a nativity barbecue? Just invite the mob along to wet the babies' heads and give the pups away as presents."

Norm, full of admiration at being presented with a solution to what had the hallmarks of a major problem, did not hesitate.

"Righto," he said. "Tomorrow at eleven. I'll get hold of Slasher Johnson and Ackie Dummett and Fred and you can organise Wowser Tyrell and Arnie. Don't think we'll ask Tacky O'Rourke this time—the lemon tree died after his last visit. I'll get the meat from Mick, and the bread rolls and the salad and stuff—Mick'll have to be asked, and you're in charge of the grog. Right?"

Sunday morning was fine and sunny. Norm, weary from his labours on Saturday, was awakened at eight by someone hammering on the back door. He staggered out, bleary-eyed, to hold the door open for Mick who dropped a load of steak, chops and sausages on the kitchen bench.

"Jesus," Mick said, gaping at Audrey who had followed the meat inside. "You'd better get the show on the road before it happens."

About nine, Norm was presented with a minor problem. Mrs. Embury from next door poked her vinegary face over the fence.

"I see you mowed the lawn at last."

"Yes," agreed Norm affably.

"Are you having a party? Lucky for some! I haven't seen Raylene for weeks. Grass too high probably. Don't suppose she could get out the back door!"

"No," said Norm, who had waited patiently to answer the original question, "we're not having a party. Just a few friends to celebrate a blessed event, as it happens." Then, feeling that he had met the requirements of basic politeness, he scurried off round the end of the garage and joined Ackie Dummett who was preparing the barbecue.

"Nosy old bag," Norm told his friend. "Luckily she'll be out of the way at church in another hour."

By eleven, most of the celebrants had arrived to do honour and rejoice at the miracle of birth. The guests were laden with gifts—not, however, as offerings to either the mother-to-be or the progeny thereof, but instead, were for the purpose of quenching the thirsts of those present.

All marvelled at Audrey's condition and Wowser Tyrell (who was not really a wowser at all) arranged a sweep: a dollar a guess and the prize for the nearest guess to the time of birth. There was fifty-seven dollars in the pot by eleven-thirty.

Tomatoes and onions sizzled on the hot plate and the air was redolent with the smell of grilling steak. The sounds of fat from sausages and chops spitting as it dripped on glowing embers helped provide an atmosphere conducive to the drinking of cold beer and the enjoyment of the friendly and smiling faces of one's friends gathered together.

The celebration was proceeding admirably. The beer was flowing freely, all were enjoying the barbecue and the corpulent Audrey was ensuring that there were no leftovers to leave the place untidy. To such an extent did that noisome animal stuff itself that it was at last forced to retire to the kitchen to rest. There it lay on its back, breathing stertorously, skin stretched to seeming bursting point over its distended paunch. Big Lennie was making frequent checks on its condition on behalf of the sweep committee.

It was about one-thirty when the squeaky side gate opened and slammed shut again.

"Ahoy there, anyone home?" It was a slightly fruity voice, full and round, florid even.

Norm emerged from behind the garage, can in hand. "Hullo, Reverend," he said, surprised. "We didn't expect you."

"Oh, I knocked on the front door but could get no response so here I am at the back door"—jovial laugh—"Mrs. Embury told me you had a celebration going for a special event. How very nice. The best of reasons, and friends with whom to celebrate. Delightful!" The Reverend Whicker gazed around him smiling benevolently.

Together, Norm and the Reverend gravitated towards the barbecue. Slasher Johnson handed him a paper plate largely covered by a sizeable steak, tomatoes and scorched onions, together with a thick slice of buttered bread.

Wowser Tyrell shoved a can into the Reverend's other hand, thus completing his barbecue equipment.

The Reverend Whicker saw himself as a man of the world and it was well known that he would take a glass of alcoholic refreshment on appropriate occasions. He could, therefore, hardly reject the friendly overtures of guests in the home of one of the more active lady members of the church.

"Cheers," he offered, making the best of things. And, after a few sips, "Well, where is she?"

"Arr," said Norm, "she's having a lay-down at the moment. Got stuck into the sausages. Wolfed them down and they gave her wind."

"Just as well she took off, Reverend," said Johno, grinning. "Otherwise, *we'd* have had to! Fair dinkum, wind wasn't the word for it. What with the bangers and the chocolate biscuits she had this morning, she's in no fit condition for civilised company. Gawd alone knows what her milk'll be like. Probably poison a brown dog."

Reverend Whicker choked on his steak and, if Arnie Brewer had not thumped him vigorously on the back, may well never have recovered. Arnie, who had desisted when the Reverend Whicker revived, took a swig from his can and wiped froth from his lips with a hairy forearm.

"We've got a sweep going, Rev," he said. "A dollar in, winner take all. The nearest guess to the old girl's time. If she hasn't had 'em within twenty minutes, I've done nine dollars in cold blood. You want a couple of bucks worth?"

"It can't be too long now, Reverend." Ackie Dummett was all encouragement. "Lennie's in there now watching her so as to let us know. We should have another sweep on how many there'll be."

Reverend Whicker's face blanched. His hand shook.

"Them?" he said. "You mean you're expecting a multiple birth? Here? In this place?" The jovial fruitiness had gone.

Norm felt vaguely offended at the implied suggestion that his home was not a suitable place for a dog to have pups.

"Of course it'll be a multiple birth. What else? And, what's more, I'M going to get rid of the whole bloody lot of them. D'you want me to put one or two aside for you, Reverend? I'll give you a black one if you like. She's sure to have at least one black'n." Norm opened another can. "She hasn't always been on the straight and narrow, you know!" He winked to show that he and the Reverend Whicker knew something about the morals of lesser creatures.

Reverend Whicker put down his drink, placed his plate and unfinished lunch on the grass, and looked about him to see to whom he could appeal for sanity. He saw no one among the guests likely to meet the criteria.

At that moment, Audrey, woken by the smell of barbecuing meat, staggered out of the back door to see what was on offer.

"Here she comes now, Reverend," said Fred.

There were a few cheers and the Reverend Whicker watched, hypnotised, as Audrey, collecting a chop bone on her way, lurched towards him, eyes bulging and making a snorting sound.

"I… I… I…" he started.

The side gate squeaked again and clanged shut. Around the side of the garage, eyes blazing, came Raylene.

"The street's full of bloody cars… I knew the moment I saw them… you weren't going to have a party, were you? Oh, NO! Remember?

"And you here too, Reverend. You should be ashamed of yourself, encouraging them. A man of the cloth. It's a disgrace!"

"It wasn't a party," implored Big Lennie. "It was a 'coming out' for Audrey's pups. She's due any minute. We've got eighty-three dollars in the sweep!"

Raylene was nonplussed for a moment. She looked at the dog gagging on a piece of steak.

"What do you mean, 'she's having pups?' Are you all mad? You just never listen to me, Norm? The dog's name isn't Audrey—it's Aubrey! It's not a her, it's a him! I knew I shouldn't have gone out."

"I hope your mother was well, dear," said Norm hopefully.

The Love Nest

It is widely recognised that homo sapiens has an affinity with the dog to the extent that hound and master, after years of mutual admiration, are even said to acquire a resemblance to each other. Cats, too, develop characteristics which can readily be seen to have marked similarities to the behaviour of human beings. It is said also that the pig has much in common with man and the reverse is inarguably true. Nowhere though have I read that the ways of birds can, in any way, be likened to the ways of mankind. I had accepted this apparent fact without question until a prolonged spell preparing a vegetable bed provided the opportunity for me to form my own opinions.

A pair of blackbirds began to build a nest in a plum tree in one corner of the garden and we became quite friendly. They were young birds and they built their nest to last. No sooner was it finished than the young bride began to put on weight and next time I checked there were four eggs in the nest. She sat hatching the eggs whilst the prospective father rushed about getting worms and grubs to feed her, and, a week or two later, there were four little blackbirds clamouring for attention. "How idyllic," I thought in my ignorance.

Both parents began the never-ending search for food for the children and I helped with the odd worm that I turned up in the garden. With both parents working, I noticed that discipline fell away and that the children were rapidly becoming a problem. The mother blackbird became harassed and short tempered. She obviously let herself go and her feathers became untidy. I never saw her, but she was vaguely bedraggled. She began to scold her hard-working mate and berate him when the supply of worms was not up to scratch. The brats never stopped complaining and their greed was insatiable. "There," I thought, "there is a marriage heading for the rocks."

Sure enough—a couple of days later I saw the male bird pause while grubbing for beetles in the compost to eye a young female blackbird perched on the fence. Her feathers were smooth and shiny and her eyes were bright. She made no secret of her interest in the beetle-grubber. I tried to assess her attractiveness from a blackbird's viewpoint and gave her a high rating. Her tail stuck up at a jaunty angle, and although her bosom was nothing to write home about, her long, yellow, pipe-stem legs were attractively scaly and her knees were delightfully knobby. As I put the spade away that evening, I heard him getting the rounds of the nest from the wife and kids.

Next morning, yellow-legs appeared again and my friend the blackbird devoted most of the morning to her; I dug a few worms for him to take home for lunch. Later in the day he surreptitiously began to build a new nest. This time the nest was not in a severe and upright prunus but in a magnolia up near the back fence. When I peered in there was no mistaking that this was a love nest. It was well hidden, of racy construction, and there was a back exit. Magnolia blossom overhung it so the heavy scent of the flowers would waft through it with every breeze.

From then on, life for my friend grew hectic. He would work frantically in the mornings, gathering worms (with assistance from me), take them home to his nagging wife and squalling brats, head off again after lunch and circle back to the magnolia bush where yellow-legs would be waiting. There was no carping from her and they got on famously. He spent most afternoons on the nest and I have seen him at dusk with a bemused smile on his beak hardly able to fly from the magnolia to the lawn. One evening, I watched him give the end of a worm a twitch to draw it from its burrow. The worm pulled back and brought him to his knees with his beak jammed down the worm-hole.

I kept busy providing his afternoon take-home provender and I was therefore privy to the tragic aftermath of the affair.

The love nest had only been established a week when yellow-legs laid four eggs and they all hatched soon after that. She became harassed and short-tempered and the four little blackbirds set up a never-ending clamour for attention. Yellow-legs was obviously letting herself go and her feathers became untidy. I never saw her, but she was vaguely bedraggled.

The poor blackbird was at his wits end with two disgruntled wives and eight wretched children, so I abandoned the vegetable bed and concentrated on worm gathering; he was pathetically grateful.

Three days of that routine and I noticed a young female blackbird alight on the side fence. She cocked an interested eye at my friend as he searched the rhubarb for snails. Without a moment's hesitation I hurled a ripe tomato at her and she flew off twittering. The blackbird's eye met mine in a long, understanding look before he returned dejectedly to the rhubarb.

A Little Knowledge Need Not...

Knee-deep stood William and the cold, cold sea swirled about his bare legs. Further up the beach, behind him, his fishing gear: hooks, bait, knife, sinkers. A plastic jacket. A rucksack. A hessian bag for any fish that might fall to his inexpertise. In his hands a rod, and the nylon line it carried reached out into the white water that marked the channel he was fishing. Black and brown seaweed washed across his feet and receding waves dragged each time from under him the sand on which he stood.

When William lost his bait—perhaps to a ravenous crab—he trudged up the beach and prepared to bait his hook with what, to his dismay, he found to be his last prawn.

Along the beach, the odd fisherman; in the far distance, a pre-breakfast jogger and, walking towards him—heads together and deep in conversation—two women. He ignored them all and, having affixed his bait, walked back down to the sea. William allowed the end of the long beach rod to almost touch the sand behind him before giving it a wristy flick that was intended to cast the prawn out and into the channel.

There was a piercing shriek behind him and he turned to see that his hook, with the prawn still attached, had buried itself in the septum of the older woman's nose. He wound some of the line back onto the reel as he walked up the sand towards them. The younger one, William noticed, was decidedly attractive. She was trying to get a glimpse of her companion's face but that lady was holding one hand tightly over her nose and was making muffled noises suggestive of displeasure. "Let me see, Mother," the younger woman implored and, in so doing, established for William the relationship.

"I say," William said, "I would be obliged if you would do your shrieking elsewhere. You will frighten the fish."

The mumbling noise that 'Mother' had been making went up an octave and increased in volume. She removed her hand from her nose for a moment. "Get this dreadful hook out of my nose and your disgusting bait with it," she said furiously. And to her daughter, "Don't just stand there, Elizabeth. Do something, girl!"

"May I," said William, addressing Elizabeth. "May I present myself?" He bowed from the waist. "My name is William. I heard your mother call you Elizabeth. A delightful name."

Elizabeth smiled at him. "Thank you," she said, "This is my mother, Mrs. Weatherstone."

Mrs. Weatherstone's eyes bulged above her hand. "I have no desire to meet socially with this barbarous nincompoop. I just want medical attention for my nose. Immediately!"

Elizabeth recollected herself. To William she said, "Your fish-hook has caught in my mother's nose. What will I do?"

William was concerned. "Tell her to take it easy," he said. "It is my last prawn and she will squash it the way she's carrying on! If she is not more careful, she will knock it right off the hook. I certainly do not wish to lose it."

William lowered his voice and spoke in a confidential and more mollifying manner. "Look, Elizabeth. I do not want us to get off on the wrong foot. I sympathise with your mother. I really do. To be frank, however, I do not suppose that the prawn is enjoying her company any more than she is enjoying his. I cannot say, furthermore, that I find your mother a particularly likeable person. She took my hook, bait and all, and really I think that the least she could have done was to put up a bit of a fight. I obtained no sporting enjoyment at all from her performance."

He had been keeping a concerned eye out for the prawn's well-being and on Mrs. Weatherstone's activity and, at last, was unable to refrain from expostulating any longer. "Hold on there, I say. Ease up. Ease up. You'll bend my hook doing that, Madam." His natural reserve of patience and sympathy had at last run out. "Stop that at once," he said firmly. "You've had your fun. Be kind enough now to return my bait and hook."

Mrs. Weatherstone spoke, as though through thick soup. "You unfeeling wretch. You polygamous mountebank. I'll sue you within an inch of your life unless this hook is removed immediately."

William rolled his eyes at Elizabeth, a picture of stoic endurance. "I will be only too happy to I do as you ask," he said. He rummaged in his rucksack. "See? I have this Swiss army knife which has a trillion blades and implements to handle any conceivable emergency. With this knife I could perform a vasectomy on a gnat or winch a three-tonne truck out of a bog. I am sure there will be a tool for getting fish hooks out of noses. Perhaps a little slit a few centimetres long?"

Once again Mrs. Weatherstone removed her hand from her nose. "You so much as lay a hand on me." Elizabeth wrapped a protective arm across her mother's broad shoulders.

"I cannot see why you are carrying on in this fashion," William remarked in aggrieved tones. "The simple fact of the matter is that I want my bait and fish-hook back. You will find that the law is on my side. You have taken a fish-hook that belongs to me, illegally affixed it to your nose and you refuse to return it. That, Madam, is larceny."

William took a breath and continued. "I have offered you the solution of having me effect a tiny and hygienic gash in your nose. You must realise that the hook has to come out some time. You do not wish to look like an Ubangi from Africa for the rest of your life, do you? Why not let me do it now before the prawn dies of old age or wastes away?"

William's flight of rhetoric was interrupted by Elizabeth. "I really am appalled at your callous attitude, William," she said reprovingly. "My mother should not have to suffer the attachment of a crustacean to her nostrils."

"You wrong me, Elizabeth," William replied. "I am deeply concerned with your mother, just as I am for the poor unfortunate prawn, and, indeed, as I am for the rest of God's creatures. I have shown her the hook-remover on my knife, which has been endorsed by the United Nations. A small incision, a quick twist—perhaps a twinge or two of agony—and Bob's your uncle. No more hook, no more pain."

Mrs. Weatherstone opened her handbag, and before William could divine her intentions, she had withdrawn a small pair of scissors and had cut the line.

"Come, Elizabeth," Mrs. Weatherstone said icily. "It is clear that we are to get neither help nor consideration from this reptile," and she turned to go.

Elizabeth, her arm held firmly by her parent and about to be whisked away from William, probably never to see him again, gave him an imploring look. William too had just realised that their ways were about to part but, in the immediacy of the situation, could think of no way to prevent it. He turned his face despairingly towards the heavens and shrugged his shoulders expressively. "*Comme ci, comme ça*," he said.

Mrs Weatherstone stopped and turned. The suggestion of a smile hovered behind the prawn's antennae. "That's French, isn't it?" she said. "Oh, la la… I do so like an educated man."

"So do I," William agreed. "So do I," and then tentatively, "*Mes amis disent que je suis très belle. Je cherche une petite femme avec une grande poitrine.*" It was a smile on Mrs Weatherstone's face, and William, having miraculously found the secret of success, was not one to do things by halves. "*Mata saya hitam, kulit saya kuning langsat,*" he opined.

"What was that?" asked Mrs. Weatherstone, eyes shining. She had let go of Elizabeth's arm.

"Just a bit of Malay," said William modestly. "*Sono una buona cuoca ma un'innamora migliore*," William said. "That's Italian. *Sie braucht nicht sehr schoen sein, so lange sie reich ist.* That's German."

Mrs Weatherstone was almost incoherent. "Oh, you are a naughty boy," she said. "You must be a university professor at least and I've been so rude to you. Just a varsity prank, I'm sure. You simply must come home for lunch. We won't take no for an answer, will we, Elizabeth?"

Expertly, she herded Elizabeth and William ahead of her and William had just time to pick up his gear as they struck off towards the road behind the beach. "There is a garage just up here," said Mrs Weatherstone cheerfully. "They'll get this hook out for me in no time. The whole thing really does have its funny side without a doubt. You educated people are all like that though, aren't you—avant garde, flamboyant, rococo." She did not expect an answer.

"Are you really a mad 'perfessor'?" Elizabeth asked. "Where did you learn the languages?"

"Well, we won't tell your mother," said William, "but I work as a type-setter on a lonely hearts magazine for migrants and, all things considered, I don't have a bad memory."

Defrocked!

Newly defrocked evangelist Jimmy P. Toogood straightened his tie before tripping nimbly down the carpeted staircase and onto the brightly-lit stage.

He stopped, centre-front, at the microphone and adjusted its height.

He was relieved to see there were no empty seats in the huge auditorium and he judged, by the swell of noise at his appearance, that his audience might not be as angry with him as it might have been.

Smiling widely to reveal unbelievably snow-white teeth, he raised his hands to quell the hubbub and then, as the tumult lessened, opened his arms as if to take them all to his heart. He, Jimmy P., was, if nothing else, a master showman.

He waited until they stilled and quietened before he spoke. He got straight to the point—not that he had much choice!

"God bless y'all, brothers and sisters," he said in the deep rich voice they knew so well. "Y'all know thet ah hev been wrongfully defrocked! They made a turrible mistake!"

Before the audience could offer an opinion, he continued, "Deah brethren, y'all know that ah'm the first to admit that ah hev sinned. But ah hev wrestled with mahself and ah'm proud to say that ah hev emerged victorious from mah battle with the devil. Halleluiah!

"Never again will ah be tempted by the sins of the flesh! Why, when ah was comin' heah today, I walked right past all those hordes of women in the street—all wearin' low-cut dresses, ogglin' their eyes at me and er, um, a'swayin' their hips and er, um, a-jogglin' of their um, er, anatomical parts. Ah took no notice of them. Didn't see them at all! Mah eyes were directed up at heaven where I expect to be called the very second the Lord needs mah help and advice!

"Ah hev to tell y'all thet mah real reason for goin' down to that sleazy motel area, where the devil tempted me, was to help mah fellow brothers and sisters who work long hours in the hotel and nightclub industry for very little pay at all! Why, many of those hotel employees are red-headed barmaids with hardly any clothes on and with shapely calves which are constantly exposed to the clientele who always order their drinks off the top shelf! And"—he is warming to his evangelical oratory—"And there are all those blond chamber-maids with curvaceous legs and trim ankles and big er, um, er big families a'waitin' at home for their supper!

"Ah, where was I, brothers and sisters? Oh yeah, ah was a'thinkin' thet ah hev heard the Lord a'talkin' to me, askin' me to maybe give a helpin' hand to some of our less fortunate friends in some tropic Third World country where the Lord has work for someone like me. The work'll be hard, and it will be hot. Yeah! In those places there are steamy languorous nights too… and sisters a'wearin' grass skirts and bare er, um, er, bare feet and…"

The audience erupts and Jimmy P. raises his voice in order to be heard. "Quiet! quiet! Ah'll hev ya'all thrown out! Ah'm heah on the Lord's business to tell y'all about my return from the brink of eternal hellfire and about the good works I plan to do to make up for my little slip. So you lot shut up, y'heah? Or y'all are out on your wretched butts!"

The noise is deafening. "What's that? What for? What hev ah done? Oh, y'all want me to stay defrocked? That's rubbish, mah deah brothers and sisters… and , speakin, of frocks."

The Terrorist Threat

Constable Murphy answered the telephone on its fourth ring. "Hullo, hullo, hullo, First Constable Murphy here. And what can I do for you?"

He listened, then reached to draw a notebook towards him. He took a pen from his pocket and commenced writing. "What do you mean, you're a terrorist?"

He paused, ear pressed to the telephone. "Oh, I see. You're only an urban terrorist then, are you? That's a relief." He listened again. "Righto then. You're about to launch an attack on the state, eh?" He shook his head, bemused. "Yeah… yeah… well, we'll see about that, me bucko!"

He turned over a page in his notebook. "And you're at the post office, are you? That's just down the street from here so I'll be there directly. You stay put, me lad."

The post office clock chimed 9 p.m. as Murphy arrived. A cold autumn wind was stirring the dead leaves along the gutter and Murphy shivered. The only person in sight was a small man of around forty years wearing a tweed jacket, a tie and immaculate slacks. He appeared to be in sole charge of a wheelbarrow.

"You with the wheelbarrow!" said Murphy. "Did you ring the police station a minute ago? Are you the urban terrorist I've been talking to?"

"I am he," answered the small man; he had a very precise voice. "My name is Bernard—with the accent on the last syllable, if you please. I have decided," he added, "that terrorism is the only way to get the ear of the government and I am prepared to oppose the capitalist running dogs and their lackeys and die for my beliefs if necessary."

Murphy relaxed. It struck him that no one seemed to be mentioning running dogs these days. "You don't look much like a terrorist to me," he said.

"I am so! You don't look like much of a policeman to me!"

"Well, what have you done? Have you perpetrated a crime?"

"No, I'm still getting myself psyched up. I've stamped my foot a lot!" He demonstrated.

"Dear me! Oh my! Tut tut! I don't see that achieving much!"

"And I've kicked the post office! The building is a symbol of government oppression of the masses. And to show what I think of those pigs, I'll do it again! Watch this! Ow, ouch ahh, my foot!"

"Goodness gracious," said Murphy. "Tsk, tsk. We are a naughty boy, aren't we? Assaulting the post office. And now you've gone and split your shoe, haven't you?"

"I wish I had not worn my Raoul Mertons," said Bernard, examining his shoe. "They don't make footwear to last these days. But my suedes are too soft!"

"Well then, may I assume that your terrorist attack is over and that the populace can rest easy in their beds."

Bernard was not mollified. "No, you may not assume any such thing." He lowered the handles of the wheelbarrow so they rested on the ground and then lifted a piece of sacking to reveal its contents. "Voila! I throw bricks too. That's why I brought the barrow."

"Yes, I see," said Murphy agreeably. "Three house bricks and a pink thermos. And what's in the thermos? Not nitro-glycerine, I hope?"

"No, it's only cocoa for when I get tired, or in case I get into a siege situation and have to fight off the SAS. See! I hold the brick thus and… oof—there, I've thrown it at the post office window."

Murphy stifled a laugh with difficulty. He was thinking of the story he would have for the troops on the morrow. "Now that's enough of that. Consider yourself lucky that the brick only went two metres. Where did you learn to throw? At a girls' school?"

Murphy picked up the brick. "This is how you throw! Grasp it firmly and throw overarm, not sideways!" Murphy, carried away with educating Bernard, forgot to hold on to the brick. There was a crash of breaking glass.

Murphy: "My God."

Bernard: "Oh, dear."

There came the sound of two pairs of feet running and another sound which might have been made by a wheelbarrow.

Fowl Play

It was Wilf who built the fowl house in the backyard. It was relatively commodious and well-appointed (chook-wise). While its construction had not exactly been a labour of love, Wilf believed in what he called 'free range' eggs and, besides, he liked chooks for themselves. He had eight in all and, seeing they were friends, they were all given names. There were the three Parker sisters, Germaine, Di, Maggie, Golda and, lastly, Veronica. She, Veronica, he had nostalgically named after a film star of the fifties who had worn her hair alluringly over one eye and after whom he had lusted as a callow youth. Veronica's red comb, hanging saucily to one side, reminded Wilf of that long ago siren. There was also the rooster whom Wilf, in a private joke, called Richard.

Wilf's liking for chooks stemmed from a period when, after a broken leg, he spent a week—virtually immobilised—in bed. Daytime television had palled quickly and he had spent an increasing period each day observing his neighbour's bantams as they went about their daily activities.

He observed that they woke early and rose without complaint. Thereafter they toiled through the day, tilling the soil with feet and beak, and did not cease until dusk. They worked cheerfully and appeared to share an ordered and, indeed, civilised existence.

"Up with the lark, rain hail or shine," Wilf told himself. And, with sudden respect engendered by the implications of his idle thought, toiling the long day through, the burden shared. Even the rooster, Wilf observed, master of all he surveyed, did not shirk from his obligations and performed them with seeming enthusiasm, no matter how inclement the weather or the state of his personal inclinations.

Wilf liked the fecundity of it all, and on his recovery built his own fowl house which he populated with the eight girls and Richard.

He came to see that they were just like people, just like the neighbours in fact. All had their little likes and dislikes and their particular friends and interests. Some, he thought—like people—would be Presbyterians, others fundamentalists, Roman Catholic, agnostic. One would be the president of the golf club or a process worker at the canning factory while another might work for twenty years—unpaid and unthanked—in the school tuckshop or an orphanage.

The rooster, of course, was in a different category. By definition a rooster is a rooster—confident, vain, obsessed with his profession—but even he had his neighbourhood counterpart.

All in all, the small world of the fowl yard represented an ordered, disciplined and caring society. None of the chooks, he noted, sought personal wealth through the accumulation of the grain he gave them, there were no fashions to keep abreast of, no need for a loan from the bank to build a nest—and therefore no lifetime mortgage—and no rates or taxes.

After Wilf fed the chooks each morning, he would usually remain for a chat. He would remove the cover from an old wooden chair that he left in the sunniest corner and sit down. Thereafter he might give them a brief talk on the Middle East situation, the share market or the country's prospects in the next Olympic Games. Once he spoke on the economics of the cost of chook food versus productivity which he illustrated by means of a graph with one red line and one green line. Later, when reviewing his chat, he decided that the subject matter had not been in the best of taste and he resolved to keep future talks non-controversial. The event left him with a feeling of disloyalty which may well have led to the over-reaction that was a consequence of the incident with Veronica.

That incident took place soon after his unfortunate talk and occurred while Wilf—as he did each week—was 'mucking out' the pen.

For no particular reason, he had been vaguely irritated and, in a bout involving the overly vigorous use of the rake, Veronica had been struck on the head and rendered unconscious.

Wilf was overcome by guilt at his carelessness and lack of consideration for a friend. From the house he obtained warm water and a cloth and began to bathe her forehead. He thought about chafing her wrists, but found them even harder to find than her forehead.

When she showed no signs of regaining consciousness, he again repaired to the house, returning quickly with a bottle of French brandy and an eye-dropper. After a dozen or so applications of the eye-dropper, she showed signs of recovery but seemed unable to awaken; she was snoring lightly.

A concerned Wilf fetched a blanket and a thermos of black coffee. He settled himself on the chair beside Veronica who, lying on an old pillow, gave every appearance of being asleep; she was breathing stertorously. He left her when the light woke him at dawn and, though she was asleep, she appeared to be out of danger.

Wilf, after a disturbed night, did not surface again until ten, when he went down to check on Veronica. She was scratching through the straw, obviously fully recovered. When she saw Wilf, she abandoned her labours and came over to the wire mesh. He was pleased that she had recovered and flattered by her attentions. He thought no more about it until he discovered that he could not appear in the backyard without her leaving whatever she was doing and walking up and down alongside the wire mesh looking at him appealingly and smacking her beak.

"It's the brandy she's after," said his wife. "Not you!"

After a day or two, Wilf accepted that Veronica had become an alcoholic and he blamed himself.

He spoke guardedly to a few close friends and eventually was given the name of a veterinarian who had something of a reputation as an animal psychologist. Wilf took Veronica along in a cat box and the vet listened to Wilf's story, gazing pensively upon Veronica as he did so.

"It's you that's been traumatised," the vet told Wilf at the completion of his recital. "The chook is not a problem." He leaned forward earnestly, holding eye contact. He spoke with authority. PI recommended she be given some hot spa therapy—in a broiler—and subsequently that she be introduced to some thick gravy, stuffing and snow peas.

Wilf took Veronica home and told his wife what the vet had said. "I am not satisfied with his advice, or rather the lack of it. I was responsible for her condition and I must attempt to rectify the harm I have done her. I'll try her with alcoholism withdrawal—see if she can go 'cold turkey' as they call it. Keep her fully occupied with other concerns."

He gave the matter some thought that night and next morning re-moved the Parker sisters, Germaine, Di, Maggie and Golda to a 'holding pen.' Veronica he isolated with Richard the rooster for company.

Richard left her no time to dream of the delights of brandy and, within a week, the longing she had felt for it had passed entirely from her mind.

Wilf's affection for chooks had also passed. He returned the other girls to the yard with Richard and Veronica and resolved to leave them to run their own lives henceforth. "I could breed canaries," he told himself, "or I could put in a pond. Fish are said to be intelligent, and some may well live organised and communal lives…" His spirits lifted.

To Catch a Fisherman

Tully Robinson's relationship with the female sex left room for a lot of improvement. While he was quite at ease with older, motherly-type women and could talk to them by the hour about young Malcolm's spots or how to live with varicose veins, his relationship with young and nubile women of around his own age could best be described as calamitous.

In their presence his legs would turn to spaghetti, his eyes would goggle, and his normal eloquence would desert him so that he was rendered virtually inarticulate. Nubile young females would give him a wide berth after one meeting, which was a pity because they could not but be impressed were they ever to see him as the trout fisherman of surpassing skill that he was; in that environment grizzled old veterans sought him out for advice and hung upon his every word.

Tully's only problem, really, was that he was shy. Apart from that, he was entirely normal so that the sight of attractive females with legs and hips and long hair and big eyes made his pulse soar and his heart race as it did other young fellows of his age. Being shy, however, he was unable to proceed from that point and there lay the trouble.

Unfortunately, Tully was in love, and although he had been in that state for some twelve months and although he saw the paragon every day, he was no nearer speaking to her than he had been on the day he first laid eyes on her.

Tully actually met her every day—after a fashion. It was his custom to alight from his train each morning at 8.03 and, after leaving the railway station, proceed north along City Road following the footpath that bordered the municipal gardens. Most users of City Road were not pedestrians and the users of the footpath were few.

Twelve months earlier, Tully, walking along City Road under the spreading trees enjoying the dappled sunshine and thinking about fishing, espied in the distance an approaching female. As the interval between them decreased, she appeared to Tully more and more attractive until, as they passed, he saw that she was entirely divine. He fell immediately in love.

It seemed that she strolled from somewhere beyond the park to employment in the city. Thereafter, then, Tully saw her every day, falling on each occasion more deeply under her spell.

He prepared a four-word speech which he practiced each morning but by the time their paths crossed he would be quite unable to open his mouth. After two months she began to smile at him. Most mornings Tully managed to wiggle his eyebrows but the flood of things he wanted to ask her, tell her, and talk about never saw the light of day.

This situation might have continued on until Tully eventually retired on his sixty-fifth birthday or until someone less inhibited carried her away—had Tully not got an invitation to fish a stretch of private water on the famous Goodradigbee River.

Tully's invitation included a sketch map and it requested that he meet the property owner at the homestead for early breakfast before the two of them would proceed to the fishing. Tully, holding the map upside down, managed to find the right gate and, after passing through it, traverse the mapped two miles of dirt track to the river's edge. The road continued on the other side of a rocky ford and swung off behind scrub to the south.

It was then that Tully made his error. He decided that the ford was a trifle deep for his car and chose to walk. He set off, garbed in waders and safari jacket and carrying his rod. He turned south, not realising that the track swung north just out of sight.

He expected to come across the homestead at any moment but the fact that he had not reached it in an hour did not concern him in the slightest—the fishing was too absorbing.

Tully was enjoying himself. It was a glorious day and he was fishing new and exciting water. Already he had caught, and released, three fish, including the largest rainbow trout he had seen all season. Each pool was a new delight, a new challenge.

It was around midday when he arrived at **THE** pool. He decided, as he approached, that he would fish from under a willow tree where he could cast into a deepwater channel which formed where water from rapids was diverted towards the bank by a rock ridge; it was a stretch that would provide safe, deep water for fish facing upstream waiting to dine on whatever the rapids channelled towards them.

He approached the pool carefully, in a half-crouch, through a screen of high brown grass. He straightened slowly when he reached the steep shelving bank; below him dark water ran swiftly.

It was only then, as he prepared to cast, that he became conscious of not being alone.

Someone further along the pool was fishing from a large rock that encroached a short distance into the water. Tully's movements attracted attention and eyes met. With stunned disbelief, Tully recognised the girl from City Road with whom he was in love; he also noticed that she wore nothing but a pair of waist-high waders and a hat. Tully did the only thing possible—he fell in.

It is inadvisable to fall into a river while wearing waders because one cannot get them off quickly and they immediately fill with water. Naturally, if the river is deep, one drowns.

Tully's instincts were good. He managed—as he toppled—to clutch a slender hanging willow branch that at least kept him upright as his head disappeared beneath the surface.

His thoughts fluctuated between the prospect of imminent death by drowning and his appreciative recollections of those of What's-Her-

Name's charms that had been only newly revealed to him. He also spared a moment to mentally berate himself for not having spoken to her when he had the chance.

His feet struck a sand bottom. He was still clutching the willow branch which also served to prevent his being swept downstream. He was lucky—the water was just chin deep and he kept his head back and sucked in air with vast appreciation. He could hear What's-Her-Name fighting her way up towards him through the brush.

Preparatory to attempting to get himself back on dry land by pulling himself along the slender willow branch, he carefully felt around with one foot, seeking a shelving approach to the bank. To his horror, he discovered that he seemed to be standing on a small eminence for he could not touch bottom a foot away on any side. He opted to remain exactly where he was. What's-Her-Name, carrying her rod and looking exceedingly attractive in the green waders, arrived at the point from which Tully had fallen. Her breathless state and heaving bosom did nothing to lessen Tully's admiration.

"Hullo," she said. "Fancy seeing you here. Are you alright?"

Tully was about to wiggle his eyebrows at her, as usual, but he recollected that he had all but drowned. So he gulped. "Hi there," he said. "Do you come here often?"

"Yes, I do." What's-Her-Name gave him a dazzling smile. "I live here except when I stay in town through the week."

Tully smiled back—which was a good effort seeing that he was standing on tiptoe in a two-knot current. "I hope I see you tomorrow in City Road." The willow branch almost slipped from his hand and he threw caution to the wind. "Seeing you is the highlight of my day!"

What's-Her-Name beamed. "Mine too," she said.

They looked bemusedly at each other and Tully, whose jaw had dropped at the wonder of it all, accidentally took in a large amount of river water.

What's-Her-Name suddenly became conscious of and embarrassed at her revealing attire in which she had expected to privately enhance her suntan. Furthermore, she felt at a loss carrying on a conversation with a head sticking out of a stretch of turbulent water.

"Do you think it'll rain?" she asked. "It was a nice day yesterday, wasn't it?"

Tully was alarmed at the thought of rain. He coughed up a pint or two of river and, when he could speak, said, "I bloody hope not. If the water level goes up another inch, I'll drown."

What's-Her-Name had placed her rod tidily on the ground and the grasshopper-pattern fly she had been using before Tully arrived—and which had been circling lazily in an eddy—suddenly swung out into the current. Just as suddenly it disappeared and the line commenced to race from the spool.

"Heavens, it's a fish," said an excited What's-Her-Name, picking up the rod. "What do I do?"

Tully's instincts triumphed over his present adversity. "Keep the tip of your rod up, ease the tension. No, don't jerk it. Steady, play the fish. Easy, easy—keep him out of the reeds. Yes, that good—left a bit more. Let him run—rod up, more, more. Now wind in, steady does it. O.K., O.K., let him run again. Get the line in—in, in, in…"

Five minutes later, What's-Her-Name, puffing and blowing from her exertions, was admiring a two-pound brown trout and that, taken on a light line in rapids, is a good fish.

"Now I know who you really are," said What's-Her-Name. "You're the fisherman my father was waiting for. I guessed when you supervised my catching that fish."

Tully sought to change the subject to something more immediate. "I'm going numb. You're going to have to get me out of here."

All contrite she was then. "Oh, I'm sorry. I was forgetting. Look, here's a long branch. You hold it and walk back to the bank and I'll pull slowly. When you reach it, there's a shelving bit just here to climb out!"

Getting Tully out took another five minutes and, because neither of them had made allowance for the deeper water that surrounded the little knoll on which he had been standing, Tully had to walk some eight feet under water. In so doing he again nearly drowned.

He lay on his back, eyes closed. What's-Her-Name gazed possessively down on him and smiled—she knelt and began to give him the Kiss of Life. After a moment or two, Tully opened his eyes. "I haven't drowned," he said, looking into deep green eyes.

She pushed black hair out of her way and bent over him again. "I know," she said.

There is a Tide in the Affairs of Men...

It was not as if anyone thought Arthur to be stupid; he was not that. But he *was* different: strange. But hardly a murderer.

Arthur lived just out of town in one of those rickety old places up near the cemetery. And he lived, so everyone said, on the smallish profits of his inventions like the improvement he made to truck refrigeration systems and a new type of water pump and a fireproof building panel. Yeah, he was smart in his own way.

Arthur always seemed so innocent, so young, and not at all like the man of mature years that he was. He was agonisingly shy and avoided talking to people, even to those of us who made it obvious that we thought well of him.

He had a love for animals and he forgot to be shy if ever he found anyone mistreating them. He was not popular with the vet because he collected sick and injured creatures and dropped them off at that gentleman's premises. The token payment he would leave was probably a composite of what he could afford and what he thought that a professional animal lover like a vet could expect for a labour of love.

We, the younger element of Goonda, used to pull Arthur's leg and, when he fell in love with Mrs. Scrimshaw, I guess we gave him a hard time. She was the wife of Buzzy Scrimshaw, a hard case who had a run-down property an hour's run up the river road. It was no secret that Buzzy gave her a rough time and I knew that Ken Brewster, the police sergeant, had called a couple of times to warn him about his behaviour, but she would never sign a complaint so the sergeant never got far.

She, Mrs. Scrimshaw that is, used to come into town on Fridays to do the week's shopping and, when Arthur started following her around with a dazed look on his face, he gave us all the ammunition we could want.

Not that Arthur would have spoken to her. He'd be too shy. No, he just followed her into the supermarket and the fruit shop, down to the bakery and wherever. Poor Arthur, poor silly Arthur, we thought. But I guess she knew what he was doing so he may not have been so silly.

And when Buzzy Scrimshaw came to town to complain to the police, and I heard the story, I must admit that Arthur's name was the first to spring to my mind.

Sergeant Brewster was talking to my father who was ringing up the cost of the oil and grease I had just completed on the Sergeant's utility.

"A bit of a joke to have him complain to me!" Brewster pocketed his change without bothering to count it, and said dismissively, "I'd have liked to have told the old bastard that it served him right."

"What happened exactly, Ken?" my father asked, coming around from behind the counter to walk with him to the door. "I hear that someone tried to electrocute him."

Brewster laughed. "Nah," he said, "it was not that serious. Someone connected Buzzy's front gate, down by his letterbox, to an electrified cattle fence. Used a long lead—in fact a very long lead." Brewster was still smiling. "Old Buzzy has to open the gate every morning to get his newspaper from the box. Gave him a bit of a charge and put the wind up him—especially when he read the message wrapped around the paper. Letters cut from a magazine to read, 'WARNING. KEEP YOUR FISTS TO YOURSELF.' Buzzy wasn't too happy."

"Who…" my father began, but Brewster anticipated him.

"Well," he said, and he was at the door of the ute by then with his key in the lock. "Well, I'd suspect anyone that might have been a bit fond of his wife," and he gave me a wink. "But I'd have to say that I've had a word with one particular suspect who I know takes the side of all mistreated creatures."

"And?" I asked.

"And nothing," said Brewster, "I don't have an official suspect and I'm not looking very hard for one." He was in the car ready to go when my father asked the big question.

"What about the flood, Ken? Any news? When is the peak due?"

Brewster's smile faded and he shook his head, despairingly. "It's still on its way. There's been more rain on the Bogan and it's raining out west. The peak went through Yallaba yesterday, so we'll get it Sunday. It was two metres above the '83 level at Yallaba, so it's bad."

We watched Brewster drive off. My father spoke thoughtfully, "We can handle two metres—just—but if it goes much above that we'll lose half the town." I turned away to attend a customer at the pumps.

The river: like a lot of towns in inland New South Wales, Goonda was born of the river. It was grazing country and the river represented permanent water. As the district developed, the river served to transport wool down into the Darling. That ended when they built the railway but the links with the river had been forged by then and it remained a living and vital part of the town.

In the driest years, the river sometimes broke up into long, isolated, willow-fringed pools where the catfish would lie, hardly moving. When the rains came in the spring, the river would become deep and swift and dangerous. There were minor floods most years but every now and again it would rain for days up in the headwaters and there would be a real flood.

The water would run down the hillsides in the catchment area, funnelling into the creeks and the river. From a gentle and tranquil stream, it would become a raging brown torrent full of debris and the carcasses of drowned sheep and cattle—caught when the river broke through the levees to surge over the river flats. It would gnaw at the edges of our town and threaten its very existence. At such times, the river brought down silt from the hills and, when it eventually retreated to its bed, the long stretches of river flat would be the richer for its visit.

Brewster's news that the flood peak would come through around midday Sunday galvanised the town. We were ready for it and, in truth, those whose homes or businesses were not at risk were looking forward to events.

They say, "It's an ill wind," and it's true. There was an air of excitement and lots of activity. Oh yes, a good few of us were out early that day. In fact, the whole episode proved decidedly educational. Not only were those of us who took part in events invited to accept that we were thieves, but we were given the opportunity to make judgements concerning the moral values of several townspeople. And then, of course, there was the question of murder.

The centre of attraction that day was the white bridge which provided a single lane of traffic across the river. I think it carried the name of some eminent councillor but everybody called it 'the white bridge' because it was painted white.

When I arrived, the river was brown and sullen beneath grey skies. Debris had collected around the piers of the bridge, but the water level was still well below the roadway. There were thirty or forty people gathered, many with nets or wire and rope nooses on long poles.

They were waiting for the rising waters to break through the levee banks upstream. There were market gardens on the river flats and pumpkins and paddy melons not only grew well there but floated admirably too. They would be the first things to appear and after that there could be anything. People erected sheds in flood-prone areas and built pig pens and chicken runs and there would be sheep and cattle that would be caught between the rising waters and wire fences.

We watched the water level creep up past the post on the bank—still marked off in feet and inches. More people arrived, most of them just curious.

The town's leading religious crank, Mrs. Barden, started it off. To attract our attention, she banged her walking stick on the tin sign that said NO DIVING OR FISHING FROM THIS BRIDGE. Then her shrill voice rose above the rumble of the water: "Ghouls! You're all ghouls! Preying on the misfortunes of your neighbours!"

Her companion, Mary Chivers—whom we all liked—took up the message in her deep, husky voice. "Was not what we were doing stealing? And did not that make us no more than robbers?" she asked.

We did not like being called thieves, even by Mary, and we looked around for someone to speak up for us. Then, when Catsy Garrett, the mayor, answered the charge, we had the opportunity to decide just where we stood on the subject of property ownership and on our honesty or otherwise.

Mr. Garrett finished ringing the neck of a hen he had caught. Then he said, as if reading it straight from a book: "The first person singular, hereinafter referred as the party of the second part, has vestigial rights to flotsam and jetsam found above the high water mark by those about their lawful pursuits." He put the wet and bedraggled hen down beside his canvas bag, ignoring everyone else on the bridge, and busied himself resetting the running loop on the long pole which he had used to effect its capture.

That stopped the nonsense about dishonesty and allowed us to feel almost righteous. He might have only been the local saddler with no legal training, but all of us appreciated His Worship's official ruling. We looked at him respectfully before getting back to the nefarious activities in which we had been engaged. After that, nobody took any notice of Mrs. Barden, or of Mary Chivers either.

Arthur arrived about then. He smiled shyly, not meeting anyone's eyes, and positioned himself alongside the rail where he could lean over and watch the water.

That must have been about the time the river broke through the levee. As we all expected, the first stuff to come down were the melons and the pumpkins and people busied themselves gathering the harvest with nets on long sticks. Later, we began to see the real debris from the breakup of the sheds and sties. Four or five sheep swept past us on their way downstream, buoyed up by their wool, and then the wreckage of a shed. Catsy Garrett added to his collection of hens.

When I saw the horse come down, I wished I could help it. I'll always remember the way it looked up at us. I gave my net away. Mrs. Barden and Mary Chivers hadn't got it quite right but there was something to what they said.

Anyway, the people on the bridge were enjoying themselves and keeping busy with what the river was bringing to them. I knew that this would be a flood to talk about in the pub for years.

Then someone pointed upriver. And someone screamed. People stopped what they were doing and eyes strained to see. A terrible sort of moan went up that went on and on. There, clinging to what looked like a large branch from a dead tree, was a woman. The branch came bobbing and twisting towards us, born swiftly by the current. We could see the woman shift her grasp on one of its limbs as the branch rolled.

Garrett tried to manoeuvre his pole to help her, but it was hopeless.

She was looking up at us now, black hair plastered across her face, eyes wide, mouth open in a soundless scream. It was Mrs. Scrimshaw. A man threw a rope but it landed short and its end was lost in a swirl of foam.

With horror we watched, helpless. And then Arthur came to life. He pulled off his jacket, dropped it in the mud, and kicked off his shoes. He climbed onto the rail and, as the bobbing branch reached the bridge, jumped. I saw him vanish under the brown water and then reappear, one hand reaching out, and I saw another hand extended to his, and meet. Then they were gone—down through the narrows and around the drowning willows at the bend.

No one moved on the white bridge. We were numb. Then a woman sobbed and the frozen moment ended. People started leaving—just going, not bothering to take their trophies or equipment.

I saw the police car advance swiftly down the road and slew to a muddy, gravel-spraying stop on the shoulder of the road at the bridge approach. Ken Brewster got out and I watched him as he spoke to the straggle of people as they came off the bridge. I knew he was getting the story on what had just happened.

When he finished talking to them—and it took a while—I waited as he trudged slowly towards me along the bridge. The wintry sun shone just as it had before, and the brown waters still buffeted the piles, but the excitement had gone with the sound of cheerful voices.

I knew that Ken Brewster was on official business and I found myself thinking of him as Sergeant Brewster and not, for once, as my father's best friend and a man I had known and liked all my seventeen years. He was tired too, I could see. His shoulders drooped and his usual purposeful stride was not in evidence. His face was slack with weariness and his normally ruddy cheeks were drawn and fuzzed with a grey stubble that suggested to me that he had been busy all night with concerns about the flood.

I shifted a little so he could sit beside me on the bench. He let out a long sigh of relief, leaned back and stretched his legs.

"G'day, Ron," he said. "I heard all about Arthur and Mrs. Scrimshaw. It's a shocking, shocking thing—a tragedy." He sat, lost in thought, and I did not interrupt him. Then he gathered himself and pushed his shoulders back and I knew it was back to business.

"You had a lot of time for Arthur," he said. It was not a question but a statement. And it was true. Arthur was the champion of the sick and injured and the weak and I admired him for that. I admit that I laughed at him sometimes, but you can do that about someone you like and, besides, I always gave him a few of the fish I caught in the summer, and he always got a rabbit or two when I went hunting up in Emu Hills. We didn't say anything to each other, Arthur and me, but we had a sort of understanding.

"So?" I said.

The sergeant closed teeth over his bottom lip, considering what he was going to say. "I'm a mate of your father's and I'm talking to you now as a family friend. You knew about Arthur and Mrs. Scrimshaw?"

"Yeah," and I nodded.

"And you knew about Buzzy beating her up?"

"Yeah."

"O.K. then. I think it was Arthur who wired up Buzzy's front gate. It had all the hallmarks of a backyard inventor."

I laughed. "The thought did cross my mind."

"Then, if he *did* do that, *he* wrote the warning that was wrapped around the newspaper. What I do not know is whether he meant it and, if he did, what he might have done if Buzzy hurt her again."

I thought about that, but the sergeant had not finished. "I'm trusting you, Ron, and this is in confidence. But you probably saw Mrs. Scrimshaw on Friday when she came in to do the shopping. She had the biggest black eye you'd ever wish to see… and Buzzy did it, of course. Drunk, I'd expect."

"Yes, I saw it. And so did Arthur!"

The sergeant nodded acceptance and drew a breath that hissed through his teeth. "I thought that was probably the case. I went out to see Buzzy. I was going to threaten to knock his block off, unofficially of course, if he ever laid a hand on her again. But I was flat out warning farmers to move stock and here, back in town, telling people to get their carpets up and the power off and to unchain the dog; it kept me busy.

"I was up all night and I did not get out to the Scrimshaw place until eight this morning. I knocked on the door—no answer—so I looked around. I found Buzzy, eventually, down behind the cowshed. He was dead. He had fallen forward into the horse trough and I thought he might have had a heart attack and just dropped or, maybe, even drowned. He stank of whisky so he could have fallen in."

The sergeant scratched at the stubble on his jaw. "That's what I thought at first! It had started raining, lightly, and it crossed my mind that I should move him to somewhere dry—silly, really. And then I noticed a clear set of boot prints leading up from the paddock gate to the horse trough where there was a jumble of tracks and then the boot prints going away. Buzzy was wearing rubber yard boots that would not have left those prints and, I'd have to say that, while he just might have drowned while drunk, it looks mighty like he had a helping hand. And that's murder! You'd have to agree that Arthur had motive and opportunity and it would not be too hard to prove that he made the threat."

I tried to take that in. Murder! Arthur a murderer? But why should I be surprised, I thought. I could see him exterminating Buzzy for hurting a defenceless woman like Mrs. Scrimshaw whom Arthur loved. And, knowing what a miserable old sod Buzzy had been, I could not really see that he would be any great loss, accident or not. I would not have dreamed of telling a police sergeant that, but I could tell Ken Brewster what I thought and Ken Brewster—not the sergeant—sounded as if he might have had some sympathy with my view.

"To finish the story," said the sergeant, "whatever I've told you does not mean much because a heavy shower swept across the cow yard while I was thinking about it and, in minutes, those clear, deep prints had become just a few depressions in the mud. There's not a mark on Buzzy, I checked… and he stank of whisky so there is no case against Arthur unless he was seen or confesses. And that's not likely now.

"So I called an ambulance and waited until they took Buzzy away. Then I searched for Mrs. Scrimshaw. Not a sign of her anywhere. I called at Arthur's place, out by the cemetery, just in case, you know, but the place was deserted. I came down here hoping for a word with him to find I'm too late."

The sergeant looked downstream beyond the sullen waters, there was a break in the clouds and just a hint of pale sunshine. "It wasn't suicide, anyway. He didn't jump to end his life but to save one. I can't help admiring that crazy Arthur," and he shook his head, unable to put words to the thoughts that were in his mind.

While he was talking, I was listening, but I was also wondering where Mrs. Scrimshaw had been. Not with Arthur, for sure! Where else would she be but home? And if she was there, why was the sergeant unable to find her? One good reason would be that she did not want to be found. And why not? Well, I expect that if I had just killed my husband, I would not want to be found either!

I thought of Arthur. I had never seen him wear boots, ever. In fact, discarded on the bridge a dozen paces away, was his jacket and the sandshoes he had kicked off when he jumped into the river. And, now I thought about it, I had seen Mrs. Scrimshaw in boots… jeans and boots when she came into town in the utility, jeans and boots at the supermarket and the baker's. And why not her, anyway? Maybe she was not totally helpless, totally cowed. It was she who had held Buzzy's head under the horse trough and then… afterwards… well, she'd be afraid, terrified. She would hide but she would know that, sooner or later, Buzzy would be found and then the police would come and that there would be gaol and a trial and a judge and then more gaol.

All these things would pass through her mind and she would wonder. She must have heard the sergeant calling her and she had hidden. But she knew he would be back, with others. She would look for escape and there was the river, just below the cowshed on the river flat. The river was loud and frightening further down, in the channel, but it would be creeping up only gently over the green grass of the paddock… a way to lose yourself, perhaps? A way to pay for what you had done?

Whatever had gone through her mind, she *had* come down the river and I could not see how she could have fallen in by accident. So, she had made her decision and then, not long after, so had Arthur. And for better or for worse, they had been together.

Of course, a search was made but everyone agreed that no one could have lived through that torrent and the police surmised that the bodies might never be found. Some people remembered that Arthur used to follow Mrs. Scrimshaw around and that, after all, Buzzy Scrimshaw himself had never appreciated her. And someone wondered aloud if, perhaps, the two of them had not drowned after all. The money in Arthur's bank account was never claimed and Buzzy's farm went to some distant relative eventually. And that, they said, proved that both of them were dead.

The inquest ended the speculation. There was no water in Buzzy's lungs, so he had died before falling forward into the horse trough. A big heart attack, they said, and proof enough that Mrs. Scrimshaw had not killed him. So, what had sent her into the river—shock? Despair? No one knew, of course, and people soon found something else to talk about.

But I remember coming home from fishing the narrows about a year later. Just at dusk. I had stopped walking just short of the white bridge to fix a twisted shoulder strap on my rucksack and, when I saw the car coming down the road to the bridge from the other side, I waited to allow it to come through. A big, black car it was, moving very slowly. I might not have thought of Arthur and Mrs. Scrimshaw but it stopped on the bridge just where Arthur had jumped. Someone turned the engine off and I saw a window wound down. No one got out. I watched for two or three minutes and then the car started up again. I waited on the approach to the bridge but by the time it reached me the window had been wound up. The glass was dark and I could not see the occupants.

I believe—but I'm not sure—that someone inside the car waved and that I heard feminine laughter. I like to think that Arthur and Mrs. Scrimshaw made a new life for themselves from the flood at Goonda and that they had come back to view the unlikely place where, together, they found happiness.

Ban Obligatory Sex

While I enjoy reading fiction, I am hugely irritated by the sex scenes which, nowadays, seem to be obligatory and as much a part of the book as the cover.

I did not have this problem when I was young and reading Enid Blyton, or later when I followed the adventures of Biggles and Billy Bunter. I doubt that Biggles knew there was an opposite sex and I would be surprised if Billy Bunter ever had a mother.

There is only so much that can be written about a sex scene. Like everything else, there's a beginning, a middle and an end. But, not satisfied with that, the authors strive to outdo each other by deluging the reader with details and adjectives: they try to turn the whole thing into an Olympic event. To maintain the Olympics analogy, one could liken sex to the high jump where one runs up, soars for a moment and then, thump! You're back on land.

The hero in these stories always carries a torch for some long-lost love and purports to have no interest in females while 'she,' for one reason or another, has eschewed men forever.

So when eyes finally meet, or they accidentally brush against one another, there is a surge of electricity between them. This, however, only strengthens their resolve to remain celibate. The hero manfully fights his desires while she busies herself with her job or with looking after mother and the cat. Eventually though, the author has to get on with it.

But, just as Pythagoras could not begin writing about geometry without a triangle or a parallelogram, the authors of those enactments cannot proceed until they have prepared their readers with supposedly sensual references to "parted ruby lips," "sidelong glances" and the like. "She smiled softly" always gets a mention.

Another sign that things are moving along is that she begins to whisper and to move languorously. There is none of that 'whizz-bang, thankyou ma'am' stuff. Oh no! The writer would have to fill all those extra pages with the real story.

The scene builds slowly to the first gentle kiss which is always "fresh and sweet": no alternative is ever on offer.

Then follows a serious bit which involves a lot of twitching and writhing. After that, there are breathing difficulties as pulses quicken and those half-closed eyes finally shut behind hanks of hair—usually blond.

Next their mouths open and they "move together." Her back arches and that seems to be a crucial element of the whole event. I always thought that back-arching was a gymnastic performance linked to double handsprings and the like with a 4.7 degree of difficulty. In the last book I read, the author—speaking of the heroine (whose name, as a gentleman, I cannot divulge)—claimed "her back arched dramatically!" How about that!

Preliminary skirmishing over, we move to the absolute pinnacle of the whole drama where planets collide, angels sing and bands play. This is followed by a period of hyper-ventilating while "everything seems to float."

Then, for some unknown reason, they call out each other's names! Are they checking that they have the right partner? Or is there satisfaction in having someone trill, "Oh, Raylene," or, "Oh, Jason!"? It would make infinitely more sense to call out, "The footy starts in three minutes," or, "Remind me to get some rat poison." Dear me, nothing so practical.

One solution to this growing problem could be a publisher's notice in all novels and biographies: "If you do not enjoy the mandatory sex scene required by the Literature Board, do not read chapters 3-6 (or whatever)." Alternatively, a new category could be added to specialised book categories like 'Big Print Books' and 'Talking Books.' I favour 'Intercourse-less Books' and I reckon they'd sweep the world.

It is not that I mind these fictitious characters having their fictitious but boring fun. I just don't like them doing it on my time!

The Spectators' View of Fine Leg

The second test between England and Australia was in progress at Lord's; the stands were full and the day glorious.

Rowley watched the bowler walk back to his mark with measured and ferocious strides.

"'Chucker' Clough was pleased with that last ball," he said into the microphone. "He seems to have settled on a good length and he is worrying the Australians with his inswingers." Rowley chatted until the bowler turned at the top of his run to deliver the next ball.

"Chucker runs in again." Rowley watched the Australian, Taylor, step down the wicket to meet the ball. "Oh, well struck!" he said enthusiastically, and then, more loudly, "He's pulled it and it's going through to the boundary. Lower is running but he won't get there in time."

The rest of the players, the crowd, and the national and international viewers waited while Lower collected the ball and returned it to the keeper.

While such lulls in the game are inevitable and usually brief, there are occasions—especially when a four has been struck or a ball hoisted over the fence for six—when the delay may be longer.

On these occasions a lull may occur because the ball is returned to the bowler often through several pairs of hands. Or, as is sometimes the case, when a six has been scored, the ball first has to be 'found' and the 'finder' divested of that which he has surreptitiously secreted in his pocket or satchel. If, perchance, the finder is a lady, a great amount of time may be taken recovering the ball because of the ability of members of that gender to disguise the ball as part of their anatomy.

The cricketers themselves, and particularly the batsmen, do not mind a lull because it allows them time to regain their breath. And while the bowler appreciates the chance to stretch his muscles, rotate his patellas or scratch his bottom, he is also using the time cogitating and planning just how to bowl the next ball so it will hit the batsman in some vulnerable part and, hopefully, incapacitate him!

There are others to whom the 'lull' is an affront! An anathema! Principal among them is the television commentator. He is responsible for keeping his world-wide audience of cricket devotees entertained, awake and glued to their TV sets so they will not miss the advertisements.

Rowley Withers, sixty-two, is an 'old hand' and a skilled practitioner of his craft with a number of options and artifices open to him to negate the dreaded 'lull.'

While lunch, tea breaks and drinks breaks constitute lulls, they are accepted as part of the proceedings and do not inconvenience the spectators. But all other lulls must be filled with chit-chat so that viewers do not become bored.

There is the weather to be discussed: "There is hardly a cloud in the sky," or, "Any rain will come from the south, but none is expected for a month!" Then there are the seagulls, always to be found foraging at long on. They can be described, their health assessed, and they can provide an excuse for recalling stories of various birds which have been smitten in mid-flight over the past thirty years.

Another good fill-in is the sight board and its placement. Weighty consideration as to whether it should be moved to the left or the right, and how far, can easily take ten or fifteen minutes over a session.

Then there are the spectators and the environs. Fortunately, in this respect, Rowley has at his disposal the cameraman, whose duty it is to record the flight of every ball, its disposal or otherwise, wickets captured or forfeited, catches, collisions, streakers, cloudburst and any other incident that might titillate viewers.

The cameraman also listens to the commentator with whom he has a symbiotic relationship. A good, empathetic cameraman can react appropriately when the commentator wants a shot of the seagulls, the distant city skyline or a scan of the spectators.

This particular cameraman is only nineteen. His name is Joseph, but he is likely to strike anyone who calls him that, and he answers only to 'Joe.'

Without knowing it, Joe has been waiting all his adult life for the happening that is about to overtake him and answer his wildest fantasy.

It appeared that Rowley's expectation that Chucker Clough was about to decimate the Australian batting was premature. Taylor and Watson were taking to the bowling and scoring freely, having struck between them several fours and a towering six.

With the surge in the run rate, the 'lull' became more frequent and, as the fieldsmen wearied, longer.

Rowley was coping with his usual aplomb. An aeroplane had flown over the ground and he had managed a well-turned, little exposition on the subject of flight and what happens to a ball when an unscrupulous bowler (and, believe it or not, there are such) surreptitiously adds a modicum of saliva to one side of the ball before bowling it. Rowley managed to stretch that over two overs.

Joe, bored by Rowley's discourse, opted for a brief independent foray, albeit low-key. He filmed a sequence involving a little boy who had just dropped a very messy ice cream into his father's lap, and the flustered mother trying to stem the boy's tears and, at the same time, placate her husband. Then, in front of the public stand there was a brief fight between two feckless, reckless youths doubtless under the influence of that volatile mix of beer and testosterone.

Rowley slotted in these events seamlessly and without missing a ball bowled, fielded or hit.

Still vaguely restless—perhaps a premonition—Joe ignored Rowley's mention of a cloudless sky. Instead, he panned the camera to the melange of buildings surrounding the ground. Shops, offices, hotels and flats. Bricks, mortar, cement, marble! There must be more than just that!

He panned swiftly across a series of featureless windows in a ten-storey building—something caught his eye. He backtracked and used the zoom lens. The large window was open, and behind, a spacious room. Curtains moved idly in the breeze.

At that moment, a Junoesque and unmistakably female figure passed in front of the open window looking neither to left nor right. She walked casually and gracefully and carried in her hand what appeared to be a towel. Joe could not see her feet so he did not know if she was wearing socks: she certainly was not wearing anything else. He stopped moving, stopped breathing—paralysed with shock.

When she vanished from sight, perhaps on her way to the laundry or shower, Joe regained some of his senses. Through a fog, he heard Rowley analysing the placement of the slips fieldsmen.

While Rowley, preoccupied with the cricket, had not seen the incident, some of the spectators had not missed what had been displayed on the big screen. At her appearance there was a burst of applause and then sporadic cheering—none of which had anything to do with the cricket.

However, the loud and untoward noise had been such that the bowler, unsure of what had occurred, stopped halfway through his run-up.

Rowley was aware that the spectators had been distracted and was concerned. He tried to get the game back on the rails. "The seagulls at long on…"

But the time for seagulls had passed and Joe found himself between a rock and a hard place. Could he tear himself away from a window where the vision might reappear at any moment? Or should he get back to the cricket?

He knew that behind that window a beautiful lady was wandering hither and yon in the altogether and that such visions might never recur.

He swung the camera back to the window. Nothing! And again. Nothing!

With an unvoiced cry of anguish at the thought he would never see her again, he returned to the cricket.

"That will be a six!" (Rowley's voice.) Joe managed to catch the flight of the ball against the afternoon sky.

And a six it was—which meant that there would be a lull and more fill-in chatter about wear on the ball or the problem of borers chewing holes in the stumps.

Joe tracked the camera back to the window. And there she was—minus the towel—and Joe got a fleeting impression of pink and white and cascading black hair.

It lasted but a moment, but on this occasion, the spectators were ready. A roar of approbation swelled from 23,483 throats (all seats had been sold). That was followed swiftly by another, and another.

A Mexican wave erupted and swept around Lord's cricket ground like a tsunami. And again. There was a great roar like surf thundering onto a tropic beach.

As Rowley watched in disbelief, the cricket match, in an instant, was no more. The umpires stood together watching the big screen, their backs to the pitch. All but one of the cricketers—Taylor, seated on the grass smoking a cigarette—were at the boundary, faces uplifted as rarely they had been on more appropriate occasions.

The noise must have alerted her to the fact that something unusual was happening. She approached the window and looked out.

Joe quailed. It must be apparent to her that she had been appearing, naked, on a silver screen the size of a tennis court. But no! Her gaze was casual, and brief. She shut the window and gently closed the curtains.

"We were nearly discovered!" Joe told himself. "All two hundred million of us!"

The crowd had swarmed over the fence in large numbers and some were kicking a soccer ball around. All the cricketers had disappeared and the groundsmen were trying to cover the wicket. It was apparent that order was not likely to be restored before day's end.

Joe packed up his camera and returned to the broadcast box where Rowley was sitting gazing into space.

Rowley still had not come to terms with events and he had not been able to sort out quite what had happened. He thought sunspots to be the most likely answer but was not at all sure.

"I don't know what went wrong today," he said.

Joe had no answer, so he remained silent.

"This wasn't the week for Halley's Comet, was it?" Rowley added hopefully.

Joe did not reply to that question either. What he did say was, in part, an admission of involvement, of responsibility.

"She was an angel," he said, considering. "Her first appearance was alright. Hardly any of them saw her. It was her second appearance that caused the problem."

Rowley looked at him strangely, "You did well today, my boy," he said. "Thank you! I think you should have an early night, Joseph." (There was one exception to Joe's rule about the use of his name.)

Joe trudged off, camera over his shoulder. He was thinking of 'her' and he knew he would never forget.

Rowley looked at Joe's retreating back and made up his mind. He turned on the microphone and spoke into it: "Owing to severe turbulence in the lower stratosphere, caused by sunspots, we regret to announce that the match has been abandoned. Play will resume tomorrow. Thank you."

Meanwhile, at a meeting in the dressing room, the England captain was addressing his team. "Look," he said reflectively, "we were doing better than they were when the wheels fell off. And, yes, I know the Australians like to win, but they couldn't possibly have organised that... *could* they?"

Beyond the Call

Inspector Pugh stared fixedly at the unopened cable that had just been placed on his desk by a young constable. He did not acknowledge its arrival and made no move to open it. The postmark, he saw, was Florence. His face was suffused with rage.

"I'll kill that bastard when he gets back," he announced to the room in general. "Please God, send him back to me soon." And he smashed a clenched fist down onto the desktop.

The three young detective constables, seated at their desks on the other side of the shoulder-high partition that separated Pugh's "room" from the main office of the detection unit, kept their heads down and pretended total absorption in their work. Pugh, when upset on such occasions—and he was upset—was to be left quite alone; events surrounding the McMullen affair at Bagot's Crossing provided the best of reasons for the Inspector's fury.

One of the key figures in the McMullen affair was, of course, McMullen. As described by Watty (and leaving out the colourful adjectives which Watty habitually used to illustrate the English language), McMullen was a hard man. It was a fair description.

McMullen worked from dawn to dusk, six (if not seven) days a week. He also ensured that Watty, who was employed as a general hand to help him on the property and who lived in the sleepout at the back of the farmhouse, worked just as diligently.

It was reasonable, therefore, that occasionally—and usually on a Saturday night while in his cups at the Drover's Dog Hotel—Watty was known to express the wish that McMullen was not so single-minded.

McMullen was the manager of Kurumbutt Station at Yellow Box Flat, half an hour in the utility from Bagot's Crossing (pop. 2713), which served as commercial centre for the region. Kurumbutt was a mixed property of sheep and a few cattle. It extended over fifteen hundred hectares and was a smallish holding for an area which rates only one sheep to the acre in good seasons.

Despite McMullen's zeal, it was tough going at Kurumbutt. The drought had lasted a long time. The creek had dried up and there was so little grass that even grasshoppers had starved. From three thousand sheep and ninety breeding cows, McMullen was down to six hundred sheep and twenty cows, and he was hand-feeding all of them. Furthermore, the hay shed was emptying fast.

Fortunately, there was still water in a big, deep dam in a gully just below the house. Access to it was difficult, however, and McMullen and Watty had been carting water for the stock since the creek failed.

McMullen's battle with adversity was relieved by two interests. The first was his passion for fishing. On becoming manager at Kurumbutt, he had purchased two hundred fingerling trout from a Snowy Mountains hatchery and released them in the dam. It was his pleasure, each evening, to stroll down and feed the trout with stale bread from the Bagot's Crossing Bakery. Occasionally he augmented the bread with mince from whatever was left of the odd sheep he slaughtered for household use.

The fish thrived, and when they reached the size at which it was legally permissible to catch them, McMullen did so. Several times a week, usually at dawn, he would repair to the dam with an old cane fly-rod and there he would fish for his and Watty's breakfast or dinner, as dictated by the state of the larder.

McMullen's second interest was Mrs. Beale. Maddie Beale was a widow, of middle years, pleasant looks and a loving disposition. Her husband, dead for eight or nine years, had been regional agent for Boswell's Farm and Agricultural Advisory Service. Maddie had always known more about the business that Clive ever had and Boswell's did not hesitate to offer her the agency after he died.

Maddie lived alone in a cottage in Bagot's Crossing, and although there was a bit of travelling with the job, she was seldom away for more than a week or so. She and McMullen had known each other ever since they were kids at the fourteen-pupil Yellow Box school, and their friendship benefited them both. Maddie's garden was looked after while she was away; McMullen benefited from Maddie's loving disposition and considerable skills as a cook. McMullen might not see her for a week or two if he was busy and then he'd be off to visit her twice in the week. And if Watty noticed that McMullen sometimes did not get back to Kurumbutt before dawn, he felt nothing but envy that the manager was able to get a break from the place occasionally.

There was one distinctly irregular feature about Kurumbutt. It was owned by a consortium of twenty ladies, all of them the wives of the district's most prominent landowners. The consortium had its beginnings when half-a-dozen ladies adjourned for lunch at the Bohemian Restaurant in Bagot's Crossing after a fundraising drive by the Hospital Auxiliary. Lunch at the Bohemian became a regular social occasion and the number of participants increased. Eventually the group formally constituted itself as the Bagot's Crossing Ladies Club (BCLC). No husband of any of the BCLC's twenty members owned less than twelve thousand hectares, and it was common knowledge among the ordinary rabble of Bagot's Crossing that no lady whose husband owned less than ten thousand hectares would ever be proposed for membership. BCLC's president, Mrs. Standish, and its secretary, Mrs. Pomfrey, were referred to by the hoi polloi as Mrs. Nineteen-Thousand-Hectares and Mrs. Fifteen-Thousand-Hectares, respectively.

When Kurumbutt came on the market, the BCLC bought it. The number of shares in the property held by each member varied according to personal resources or husbandly indulgence. In two cases, a reluctant bank manager had to be persuaded to advance sufficient funds to purchase an equity. It was rumoured in Bagot's Crossing that the property had only been procured to thwart the social aspirations of one of the district's lesser social lights whose husband—a mere seven thousand hectares—might have been induced to spend a lottery win acquiring Kurumbutt.

Meetings of the BCLC were held on the last Thursday of each month. At the Bohemian, over chicken and moselle from the supermarket next door (most of you will be aware that the Bohemian has no liquor licence), the ladies discussed important subjects like the Picnic Race Club Ball, the Show Society Dinner and, of course, as the district's social leaders, the various charitable and other good works with which they were concerned.

The BCLC had become exceedingly fretful over the worsening Kurumbutt situation. Despite advice from wiser heads, the property had been bought at the top of the market. Because of the drought, the investment had never shown a profit and there was every indication that it would be years before it might. Though the grazier husbands of the members of the BCLC were also finding times hard, the ladies were only human, and they wanted someone on whom to lay the blame for the failure of their venture. Naturally they laid it on McMullen.

"He is incompetent," they told each other, and anyone else who would listen. "Inefficient, a drunkard, lazy."

"He'd be a wife-beater if he was married," said Mrs. Pomfrey.

McMullen withstood their calumny for months before he quit. He just up and left and did not say goodbye, even to Watty, who suddenly found himself manager of Kurumbutt Station.

When they heard of McMullen's departure, the ladies of BCLC agreed to sell Kurumbutt as quickly as possible, before they lost more money. They were furious at McMullen.

"He left us in the lurch," they told each other.

"Disloyal," they said. "He betrayed us."

They used words like "opportunist," "unreliable," "slippery" and "perfidious."

Though the BCLC held Watty in small regard, they needed him to keep Kurumbutt going until they found a buyer. Their attitude to Watty, therefore, was one of friendliness combined with a dash of regal superiority; Mrs. Standish gave him a yellow cardigan that Mr. Standish no longer wanted.

Watty heard (in the pub) that Kurumbutt was to be sold and he knew full well what the BCLC was about, but he held the view that a job is a job, and he stayed on.

To Watty's surprise, he found he was missing McMullen. He went into Bagot's Crossing to see if Maddie Beale knew where he was. She was not there, and a neighbour said that Maddie had taken off for the north-east to push a new fertiliser spreader.

While he knew that the BCLC had been getting McMullen down and that his departure should not be a surprise, Watty remained uneasy. Though the utility had gone, there were still clothes lying around as well as an old photo album McMullen had valued.

He phoned the police in Adelaide. "Just to let 'em know," he told the dog.

Watty's concern over McMullen was noted by the police. Inspector Pugh of the Criminal Investigation Branch drummed fingers on his desk when he read the incident report—and made up his mind. "Probably nothing in it, but I'll send someone up to take a look," he told the desk sergeant. "Ask Perkins to come in if he's there."

"This McMullen fellow probably just up and left," Pugh told Detective Perkins. "Seems the owners of the property may have been making life difficult for him. But we'll check it out, just in case. You're free, I know, so take a couple of days and see what you can turn up."

Perkins, a suave and confident thirty-five, sitting at ease in the visitor's chair opposite Pugh's desk, nodded.

"And I want you to go today." Pugh was apologetic. He consulted his watch. "The train leaves in an hour, in fact. Tell the guard to stop at Bagot's Crossing." Then, in answer to Perkins' unspoken query, he added, "There's accommodation at the pub."

With the essentials communicated, Pugh relaxed. "Sorry about the short notice, but McMullen has been missing for five days already and… well, you never know!" Then Pugh was back to business. "Now, expenses for a couple of days. Unfortunately, the petty cash is down to sixty dollars and we can't get any more until accounts open up again at 4 p.m. You'll be long gone by then."

Pugh took the cashbox from the safe, opened it and took out three twenty dollar notes which he handed to Perkins. "And you'll need this as well for accommodation and meals—whatever." From the cashbox Pugh took a plastic credit card and passed it to Perkins, who looked at it with interest.

"It's a police force credit card," said Pugh. He passed Perkins a pen. "You'll have to sign." He watched as the signature was added beneath that of the commissioner.

"I'll want the credit card back Tuesday morning with your report. Good luck!"

Perkins rose and turned to go. "Thanks, inspector," he said. "I just may have an interesting couple of days."

When Perkins arrived at Bagot's Crossing, he hired the only available car in town and went out to Kurumbutt Station. Watty finished yarding some sheep while Perkins sat under a peppercorn tree smoking a cigarette.

Watty told Perkins what he knew, showed him McMullen's room and the tin shed where McMullen kept the utility. "He took his fishing gear," said Wally, "so at least he didn't go off his rocker."

Perkins was noncommittal and left soon after, the dust hanging in a cloud to mark his passing.

It was Friday night and Watty went into town after dusk for a few beers at the Drover's Dog. He found a space at the bar and, with a brimming schooner of Foster's before him, relaxed. Behind the bar he could see through to the bistro bar where they served meals from a carvery. He noticed Perkins seated at a table in animated discussion with Tom Rowan from the Bagot's Crossing travel agency. Perkins, at least, was making inroads into a plate of salad. Watty promptly forgot them. He never laid eyes on Perkins again.

Inspector Pugh was not concerned when Perkins failed to make an appearance on Tuesday. He asked for news of Perkins on Wednesday, but it was a busy day. He asked again on Thursday and was about to phone Bagot's Crossing when the young constable placed a cable on his desk:

CABLE: IMMEDIATE

TO: INSPECTOR PUGH, POLICE H.Q., ADELAIDE, SOUTH AUSTRALIA.

FROM: LONDON, UNITED KINGDOM. DATE: WEDNESDAY 8 MARCH.

REFERENCE: BAGOT'S CROSSING INVESTIGATION. SUDDEN DEVELOPMENT NECESSITATED MY URGENT DEPARTURE FOR UNITED KINGDOM IN PURSUIT OF SUSPECT. REGRET INABILITY TO ADVISE PRIOR MY DEPARTURE. OFFICIAL POLICE CREDIT CARD WILL SUFFICE FEW DAY'S EXPENSES. ARREST OF SUSPECT ANTICIPATED. WILL INFORM YOU EARLIEST.

PERKINS (DETECTIVE SERGEANT).

Pugh was incoherent with fury. He managed (after he regained the power of speech) to confirm that J.N.R. Perkins had indeed been a passenger on a flight to London on Saturday. He phoned the Drover's Dog Hotel to be told that J. Perkins had booked for two nights but had stayed only one and had left at dawn the next morning to catch the milk train to Adelaide. Pugh had done what he could and could now only wait. He received the next cable on Monday.

CABLE: IMMEDIATE.

TO: INSPECTOR PUGH, POLICE H.Q., ADELAIDE, SOUTH AUSTRALIA.

FROM: PARIS, FRANCE. DATE: SUNDAY 12 MARCH.

REFERENCE: BAGOT'S CROSSING INVESTIGATION. REGRET INABILITY TO CONTACT YOU DUE TO AROUND-CLOCK SURVEILLANCE. ORIGINAL SUSPECT CLEARED BUT NEW LEAD NECESSITATED IMMEDIATE DEPARTURE SATURDAY FOR PARIS. DUE PRESSURE OF WORK (AND ON YOUR AUTHORITY) I REQUESTED INTERPOL ASSISTANCE. FRENCH JUNIOR DETECTIVE (FIRST CLASS) DUBOIS SUBSEQUENTLY ALLOCATED TO ASSIST. MLLE DUBOIS AND SELF DEPART FOR ROME TONIGHT PURSUIT NEW SUSPECT. EARLY APPREHENSION OF MISCREANT ASSURED. WILL CONTACT SOONEST.

PERKINS (D/S).

When he finished reading it, Pugh frothed at the mouth and fell back in his chair, his heels drumming on the linoleum. One of the young constables called in a doctor but, by the time he arrived, Pugh had recovered sufficiently.

Back in Bagot's Crossing events were moving—not with the haste and bustle of the city, but steadily nevertheless. A buyer had been found for Kurumbutt and negotiations, which included the social vetting of the prospective buyer's wife, were in train.

Pugh was in total control of himself when the third cable arrived, apart from a facial tic and the dribbling.

CABLE: IMMEDIATE.

TO: INSPECTOR PUGH, POLICE H.Q., ADELAIDE, SOUTH AUSTRALIA.

FROM: FLORENCE, ITALY. DATE: WEDNESDAY 15 MARCH.

REFERENCE: BAGOT'S CROSSING INVESTIGATION. ROME SUSPECT IDENTIFIED AS CATHOLIC PRIEST FROM PERU VISITING VATICAN ON FIRST OVERSEAS VISIT. UNFORTUNATELY CLEARED OF SUSPICION. DUBOIS IS PROVING AN ABLE AND CO-OPERATIVE ASSISTANT. COLLETTE DUBOIS AND I DEPART TOMORROW EN ROUTE VENICE, COTE D'AZUR, TO INVESTIGATE POSSIBLE MAFIA AND TRIAD LINKS WITH BAGOT'S CROSSING UNDERWORLD. REGRET OUR DEPARTURE ROME TWO HOURS BEFORE ARRIVAL YOUR MOST-URGENT CABLE AND LOCAL TECHNICAL PROBLEMS WHICH PREVENTED MY TELEPHONING YOU FROM PARIS, ROME AND FLORENCE. AM CONFIDENT YOUR CABLE CONVEYED YOUR FULL APPROVAL MY ACTIVITIES (YOUR SUPPORT ENCOURAGES ME TO PERSEVERE DESPITE GROWING EXHAUSTION). YOU WILL ALSO BE PLEASED THAT POLICE CREDIT CARD IS PROVING INVALUABLE AND GRATIFIED AT ITS READY INTERNATIONAL ACCEPTANCE. SHOULD HAVE FORWARDING ADDRESS SOON BUT AM CONFIDENT OF EARLY BREAKTHROUGH ON CASE.

PERKINS (D/S).

"Dubois," Pugh said to the sergeant, his eyes not focusing. "Sounds as if she's French, right enough. And they're off to Venice, eh?" Mopping at his chin, he lapsed into silence.

Five days later, Pugh passed cable number four to the sergeant without comment.

CABLE: IMMEDIATE.

TO: INSPECTOR PUGH, POLICE H.Q., ADELAIDE, SOUTH AUSTRALIA.

FROM: RIO DE JANIERO, BRAZIL. DATE: TUESDAY 21 MARCH.

REFERENCE: BAGOT'S CROSSING INVESTIGATION. AT DUBOIS' SUGGESTION AM FOLLOWING UP POSSIBILITY OF RED BRIGADE INVOLVEMENT IN EVENTS AT KURUMBUTT STATION. COLLETTE NOW WORKING UNDERCOVER AS SPOUSE (NOTE SAVINGS ON HOTEL BILL). OUR IMAGE AS WEALTHY GRAZIER/ GRINGO TOURIST COUPLE NECESSITATED SUBSTANTIAL OUTLAY ON APPROPRIATE APPAREL PLUS HIRE OF PORSCHE. THESE EXPENSES BILLED TO EMBASSY, YOUR AUTHORITY. ADDRESS MAIL TO HILTON RIO, BUT DURATION OF STAY LIKELY TO BE BRIEF. APPREHENDED PICKPOCKET IN BUENOS AIRES (ARGENTINA) EN ROUTE FOR RIO AND FEEL CONFIDENT THAT WHOLE TRIP PROVES JUSTIFIED. MAY NEED FEW WEEKS OFF ON RETURN TO RECUPERATE.

PERKINS (D/S).

The sergeant read the cable and, apart from raised eyebrows at one or two points, kept his face expressionless. On balance, he thought, Pugh was looking better and seemed to have accepted the situation. "Goodnight, sir," he said, and left Pugh gazing out the window, cracking his knuckles.

In Bagot's Crossing, the BCLC had discovered that the uncle of the wife of the prospective buyer of Kurumbutt had been an Anglican bishop, so there was no further question as to her suitability and the sale was agreed.

It was Mrs. Fourteen-Thousand-Three-Hundred-Hectares who had the brilliant idea.

"What about all the fish?" she said. "All those lovely trout. Why should they go to someone else when we sell? They're ours!" She was supported by the others, and at the club's next meeting, they agreed they would partake of grilled trout which "should go very nicely with the moselle." They made appropriate arrangements with the management of the Bohemian and told Watty to catch twenty or so fish and bring them into town for storage in the Bohemian's freezer until required.

Pugh opened the fifth (and, as it transpired, the last) cable himself. He was indeed much better. The string of curses and obscenities that he uttered when he saw the familiar envelope were as music to the aural orifices of the young detective constables. He read it while at the same time making a sound with his teeth like a cement mixer filled with heavy gravel.

CABLE: IMMEDIATE.

TO: INSPECTOR PUGH, POLICE H.Q., ADELAIDE, SOUTH AUSTRALIA.

FROM: QUEBEC, CANADA. DATE: SUNDAY 26 MARCH.

REFERENCE: BAGOT'S CROSSING INVESTIGATION. EXHAUSTION OF DUBOIS AND SELF NECESSITATED THREE-DAY BREAK INCOMMUNICADO TO AVOID FURTHER STRESS. NOW BACK FROM NEW YORK. HAVE MARRIED DUBOIS AND AM RESEARCHING POSSIBLE FRENCH CONNECTION, CANADA. PENDING YOUR APPROVAL HAVE SWORN DUBOIS (MRS. PERKINS) INTO SOUTH AUSTRALIAN POLICE FORCE AT INTERPOL SALARY EQUIVALENT. PAYMENT BEING EFFECTED MEANS OF POLICE CREDIT CARD. OVERTIME CLAIM EN ROUTE TO YOU CONSEQUENCE CONSIDERABLE OUT-OF-HOURS ACTIVITY DUBOIS AND SELF. NOTE: WHILE SHADOWING PROBABLE CRIMINAL WITH POSSIBLE SOUTH AUSTRALIAN CONNECTIONS (IN GUISE OF TROUT-FISHING TOURIST) I FELL IN LAKE. SAVED ONLY BY

KISS OF LIFE FROM PERKINS-DUBOIS (CITATION RECOMMEND-
ED). IN VIEW OF UNEXPECTED DIFFICULTY AVOIDING DROWN-
ING, EARNESTLY SUGGEST DRAGGING DAM AT KURUMBUTT
STATION, YELLOW BOX FLAT, FOR MISSING PERSON.

PERKINS (D/S).

Pugh finished reading. He leaned back, linking hands over a large stomach and gazed ceilingwards. He was remembering a day when, as a child, he had fallen into a river wearing gumboots.

He called the sergeant. "That McMullen business up Bagot's Crossing way. The missing person. We didn't drag the dam, did we? Get someone up there, will you?" The sergeant nodded and disappeared. Pugh remained deep in thought. Drowned? Could be! Could be!

Watty was very busy out at Kurumbutt and he left his fishing until the day of the monthly luncheon, knowing full well that he could easily net the trout in an hour or so.

He awoke early that morning. Walking from the sleepout to the kitchen he saw the dawn. The ground was heavy with frost and the air was still. The arc of red-gold sun was visible though the layer of mist at the foot of the hills and the sky was grey and clear. He was thinking of McMullen as he walked down to catch the fish.

At mid-morning he delivered twenty-four freshly caught trout to the Bohemian.

The luncheon was an outstanding success. The trout were greatly enjoyed by all. The ladies decided to break the news of the sale to Watty immediately and it was agreed that, with bad news, he would be given a little something extra to soften the blow. Mrs. Pomfrey telephoned Watty and asked him to present himself at the Bohemian at 3 p.m.

It was a merry group that Watty beheld on his arrival. What with the trout and the moselle and the sale of Kurumbutt, everything was as it should be with the BCLC. The ladies told him the news and presented him with a cheque for two weeks' salary at award rates.

Now that she no longer needed him, Mrs. Standish was able to speak her mind to Watty.

"That lazy wretch, McMullen, ran the property down," she said. "Had he done a fair day's work for a fair day's pay, the place would have prospered. We're well rid of him." There was a chorus of agreement from the BCLC.

Watty looked about him at the cream of Bagot's Crossing and District society. There was a glint in his eye.

"I reckon you're wrong there, missus," he said, quietly. The members of the BCLC gasped at his temerity.

"McMullen was a bloody hard worker," Watty addressed his remarks to them all. "He couldn't have done more for you lot than he did. You all enjoyed the trout? Well, you've got McMullen to thank for them, too. And you're well rid of him, are you?" Watty smiled grimly at them. "Well, it happens that he didn't quit, after all. I've just finished fishing what those trout left of him out of the dam. So you're not quite rid of McMullen yet, are you?"

Pugh was happy. The pall of depression that had enveloped him since the McMullen case had come up had lifted. McMullen's body, still in the utility, had been found in the dam. Marks on the track down the gully indicated failure to take a steep bend. Admittedly, it had been the handyman on Kurumbutt who had discovered the body, but only half an hour ahead of the arrival of the police diving team. Besides, the handyman wasn't concerned if the police took the credit.

And credit was another matter: he (Pugh, that is) would now be able to attribute the resolution of the case to an overseas lead given to a junior detective despatched—for that very purpose—by the astute and intelligent

Pugh. Fortunately, and coincidentally, Perkins was due home tomorrow! The police credit card had an effective life of one month only and Perkins had come to the end of his leash with a jerk.

Pugh was looking forward to seeing Perkins. He hoped that Perkins would seek leave to get over his wearisome activities so that he (Pugh) could say no. He fervently hoped that Perkins would try for sick leave so that Pugh could have him examined by the police medical officer. But more than anything, he was looking forward to assigning Perkins to new duties. There was the murder at the abattoir, a missing person at the sewage farm and a host of very unpleasant "domestics." Furthermore, if there was anything to Perkins' suggestion that Bagot's Crossing might be a centre for mafia or triad activities, it seemed appropriate that a sergeant was appointed to the town—and he rather thought he knew just the man to fill such a position.

Sometimes Pugh thought he was a lucky man to be in charge of the CIB.

There's Fishing and There's Fishin'

I had been celebrating Zac's birthday with him at the little palm-thatched beach hut he had rented in a village just south of Vigan and way north of Manila. It was a great spot.

For some inexplicable reason (in retrospect), I had agreed to stay over and go fishing with Zac next morning. He's an old friend—and he's persuasive. We had once been junior bankers together, back down south: he had quit, to come up here and live, and I, on my holidays, had come to visit. I envied him—well, I had envied him until that fishing trip.

Around dawn, Zac had harried me off the grotty sofa on which I had slept and into my shorts and thongs. After a night's partying, I did not feel well but he ignored my complaints and my assertion that I had changed my mind about the fishing.

It was at that point that the Major would have settled the matter emphatically and, had I followed his example, I would have been saved a best-forgotten experience.

I have to tell you about the Major. He featured in *The Boy's Own Weekly*, a comic that I used to devour as a beardless (and possibly witless) youth. Major D'Arcy Bloodstone MC., MM., of the Seventh Hussars, spent most of his time performing impossibly daring feats in the world's trouble spots on behalf of Queen and country. In so doing, he displayed a complete disregard for his own safety, a total lack of fear, and the useful ability of being able to emerge from all these imbroglios with his moustache unruffled.

In those days it did not take me long to realise that the Major was a man who met life's problems head-on. "How would the Major handle this situation?" I would ask myself, and I would remember the MC and the MM and steel myself to be fearless and scornful of adversity. Despite my built-in handicap of not having an MC or an MM, the Major became my role model.

Zac's plan to go fishing reminded me that the Major had another string to his bow as a noted trout fisherman who, in his rare spare moments, would be off to Scotland with his faithful ghillie in search of the most inaccessible Highland streams to pit his skills against that noblest of piscatorial adversaries.

The only fishing line for him had the thickness of gossamer and he would often fight all day to land a monster that the ghillie (man and boy) had never seen the like of (sorry about the preposition). What's more, the ghillie—whose name you will be amazed to hear was Old Jock—would periodically pass to the Major his chased silver hip flask (bearing a representation of the family crest) from which that gentleman would imbibe cheering draughts of Scotch whisky of impeccable brand. The whisky was used solely to give him the strength to continue his Homeric battles with huge denizens of those Scottish streams and lochs.

So, what would he have thought of Zac dragging *him* out of bed and ordering *him* about when he did not wish to go? I hate to think! But then, Zac *was* my friend!

When we emerged from the shack it was pleasantly cool; the air was awash with light and the sky shading already from grey to blue. I could hear the voices of the village kids and I was breathing in the earthy smells of the market, all of which were a constant reminder of where I was.

Zac and I shared a paw-paw with Esmeralda on the front step. She was an attractive bar-girl that Zac had brought back from a hotel the previous evening. When we finished, the three of us left for the beach—Zac carrying a box full of San Miguel beer which, I presumed, was lunch.

Zac had arranged for Old Topo from the village to take us out to the edge of the Luzon Trench where the big fish are supposed to lurk. The old man was waiting at his boat and he showed no surprise that Esmeralda was to accompany us.

I looked with concern at the craft in which we were supposed to embark and was not impressed. It was a hollowed-out log, big enough to seat about six people and there was no sign of an outrigger or, for that matter, of life jackets. A small outboard motor was fixed to the tiny stern and two metal arrangements like toilet-roll holders were bolted to the port and starboard gunwales. I recognised them as handline holders.

While I had not expected a two-hundred-tonne yacht, this was ridiculous, and I said firmly that I was not going to sea in a hollow bloody log. "Ah," said Zac, waving a dismissive hand, "it's quite safe. The trench is not far out and we could easily get back if the weather blows up." Reluctantly, I allowed myself to be persuaded.

As he talked, he off-loaded a cardboard box from the space in the bows and replaced it with the beer. Because the box that Zac discarded held all the bait, it was unfortunate that Old Topo had not seen him do it. In any case, Old Topo would not have said anything. The only sound I ever heard him utter was, "Ha, ha, ha, ha." This verbal riposte entailed his closing both eyes and manipulating his face into a grimace which revealed toothless gums stained a depressing shade of orange. I thought the old man compared most unfavourably with the ghillie who accompanied the Major on his fishing trips.

To be brief, we disposed ourselves along the narrow dugout, Old Topo in the stern, in charge of the outboard and navigation, me amidships facing aft, and Zac and Esmeralda towards the bows. The old man pushed off, started the motor and set our course for the open sea. We proceeded towards the horizon through calm sunlit waters.

I had recovered somewhat from my initial trepidation and was almost enjoying myself despite a certain queasiness which I recognised as a hangover. "We'll probably stop quite soon," I thought, "then throw in the lines and have a beer or two."

An hour later we were making steady progress—now through long, oily swells—which occasionally slapped water into the canoe. I had become concerned that, for the most part, there was only half a handspan of freeboard between the sea and the top of the gunwale and that the mainland was lost to view in the haze.

Despite my entreaties to be returned to land, Zac only scoffed at my fears and, after a brief moment to deal with my complaints, returned his attentions to Esmeralda whose ear he had been nibbling.

Light, warm rain fell for a while, after which—with hand signals—I tried to direct Old Topo to turn his wretched cockle shell about before a typhoon or a hurricane overtook *us*. "Ha, ha, ha, ha," he said.

If the Major ever learned of this ridiculous fishing exploit, he would take me for a fool, and I wondered what would have been his view were he to discover that I was about to wet my pants from sheer terror! He would have looked at me askance and his aristocratic lip would have curled. Old Jock would have given me a serve too.

I was actually delighted, therefore, when the engine failed—reasoning that, at least we could go no further.

Old Topo fiddled with the motor for a while before deciding that he may as well be fishing as he worked. He sidled carefully past me and then past Zac and Esmeralda only to find that the bait was missing and that Zac's beer occupied the space where once it had lain. He did not speak but appeared to be gritting his gums. When he returned to the stern, he withdrew from under a thwart two short lengths of thick bamboo, around which great lengths of heavy line had been wound. At the end of each line was tied the sort of hook one would use to catch a white pointer.

"What the bloody hell's he fishing for? Sharks? Whales?" I called back to Zac (I could hear my voice becoming squeaky). "If we hook anything that size it'll pull us straight under!" I looked back at him but he was gnawing on Esmeralda's ear in earnest and I surmised that he was probably too well-mannered to speak with his mouth full!

Old Topo had not given up on the bait and I watched him slice a large sliver of skin from a callous on the side of his foot; it looked like a piece of frayed buffalo hide. This enticing morsel he attached to a small fishing line that he apparently kept for catching bait. He fished for a while until the skin either fell off or was eaten by something. He then rummaged in vain for more bait before finally giving me a long, searching look through screwed up eyes. I knew he was wondering if I had been circumcised.

I bared my teeth at him, shook my head vigorously and immediately regretted it. That action, together with my queasy stomach and the disconcerting way that the horizon was moving up and down, plus the smell of petrol and dead fish, suddenly became too much for me. I threw up over the side.

"Ha, ha, ha, ha." Old Topo was pleased. He cut the top off a wart on his leg and put it on the hook. He cast into the middle of my donation and in no time had his first fish, and then a second.

The big lines went out with live bait on and ten fathoms down. He set the handlines into the holders on the gunwales so they could run freely should a fish strike, and settled himself to fiddle with the motor while chewing ceaselessly on imaginary gum.

I turned to check on Zac only to find that he had stopped drinking beer and biting ears and was busily fornicating with Esmeralda under very difficult conditions in the bottom of the dugout.

I faced Old Topo again. "Love is a many-splendoured thing!" I told him.

"Ha, ha, ha, ha," he replied.

The old man busied himself with the motor while I watched, casting an occasional and casual eye at the fishing lines. When it happened, I was surprised—paralysed even—for a moment. The heavy line spun off the bamboo drum at an incredible rate and I watched as fifty or sixty metres of it disappeared beneath the water in seconds.

One's life is supposed to pass before one's eyes during these 'near death' experiences (and I was sure this was one). However, all I could think of was that, had the Major been in my place, he would not have been sitting miserably praying to God that what was about to happen would not happen, and how infuriating it was that Zac and Esmeralda were busy behind me with not a care in the world.

Perhaps the Major would have fixed Zac with a gimlet eye and tried, "I say there, Zac old lad, that's hardly cricket!" or, "Zac, my dear fellow, I think a fish has taken your bait. You will wish to attend to it."

"I must be mad," I told myself. The likelihood of Zac stopping what he was doing for a mackerel or whatever was minuscule. And, besides, the Major never spoke like that. No! A steely look was more likely—and probably followed by a straight left to the jaw as well. That was more his style.

I could see that, in a very short time, there would be no more line on the bamboo and that whatever had taken the bait was going to be pulling directly on our frail vessel.

Without a moment's pause I whipped out the little sheath-knife I kept at my belt and slashed the line as it spun over the gunwale. And not a second too soon. There was about enough left on the bamboo to make a pair of shoelaces.

Old Topo looked at me in disbelief. But I was suddenly glad! I had been put upon—a situation I knew the Major would not have acceded to for an instant—so, why should I? I swung the knife again and cut the other line; I knew we were now fresh out of bait and hooks too! I felt much better. I looked Old Topo right in the eye. "Ha, ha, ha, ha," I told him triumphantly.

It was almost dusk when I heard the chug-chug of an inboard motor. Old Topo rose stiffly on his rickety old legs and waved some tattered garment or other. The small launch turned towards us, the setting sun behind it, and there was a quick burst of cheerful voices speaking Tagalog. Next minute, Old Topo caught the line they threw over to us, looped it over the peg in the bows and we were underway.

I was delighted that someone seemed to be in charge at last and that we were heading for land again. It was dark when we hit the beach and Zac wanted me to come home with him and said that Esmeralda had a friend who…

I thanked him for his hospitality, retrieved my hired motor-cycle from alongside the pig-pen, and departed for my temporary lodgings back in Vigan. While starting the bike I resolved (a) never to go fishing in the Philippines again, (b) never to go fishing with Zac again and (c) to review my relationship with the Major.

As I drove along the narrow dirt road—slowly, because there were still plenty of villagers wandering around—it came to me that, in the last episode of the Major's adventures, he had gone north again to fish some hidden loch famed, of course, for the size of its fish.

In hiring a small rowboat, the Major had overridden Old Jock's advice that it was unsound and that there was no way that he (Jock) would take passage in it. The Major said that he had come to fish and that fish he would! With that he bade Old Jock make himself comfortable ashore and had set out for the deepest water.

The story brought back by Old Jock was that a big trout had taken the Major's tiny artificial dun and battle had been joined. The Major, still wearing his waders, had risen to his feet to play the fish and it was Old Jock's opinion that the Major's weight, suddenly concentrated in the one place, had sprung one of the vessel's seams.

Old Jock claimed to have called out, "For God's sake, mon, let the bleddy fish go and come back to shore."

The old Scot stated that the Major had then given a careless laugh and had responded with, "Would you have me leave a hooked fish to die ignobly?" He did not speak again and Old Jock, with tears in his rheumy old eyes, related how the boat had sunk under the Major as he reeled in his catch, and how that gentleman had gloriously held the fish up before the boat, the Major, and the fish disappeared beneath the dank, dark waters of the loch!

"His cap floated a wee while." Thoughtfully, Old Jock wiped his nose on his sleeve and added (with admiration in his voice), "That fish must have weighed the best part of half-a-pound!"

I thought of the gallant Major heroically playing that miserable little fish while the boat sank under him and with only a potty old ghillie to see him give up his life because he could not be the cause of a fish dying in an unsporting manner. It made me realise that both the Major and I had shared fishing experiences which, in one sense, were not so very different. He died for a fish weighing ounces and in keeping with his stupid code of honour while I saved myself from a watery grave by cutting a monster fish off on the very sensible principle of my survival.

"No. I was not wrong in what I did," I told myself. "It was the only thing to do! The Major was a bloody idiot who threw his life away for nothing and I'm pleased that I have, at last, outgrown him! "And yet… and yet… I think I might just go to Scotland when my holidays come around again. I'll see if I can find Old Jock and ask him if he'll take me fishing on that loch."

The Thin Green Line

My fishing companion and I had walked in along the river at first light, and we were a couple of kilometres upstream of the bridge where we had left our car. By mid-morning, the fish had stopped responding to our earnest endeavours to catch them and we had agreed to rest for an hour in the hope that they would become active again, as often they do.

We ensconced ourselves comfortably at the river's edge below a bracken-covered bank. The still waters of a pool lay before us, tranquil in the morning light and, if you can call just sitting and enjoying the view with a baited hook in the water fishing, we were fishing.

We were not even talking, just soaking in the sun, the river, the delicate touch of the breeze and, of course, the silence. After the constant undercurrent of noise back in town, the complete silence out in the bush is sometimes almost palpable. So, when we did hear the sound, we looked at each other enquiringly.

Far, far away and ever so faintly, the sound. It was a sort of a humming, a muted murmur that hung trembling in the air. It did not abate, and, for some reason, it made us restless and uneasy. It spoiled our mood.

Half an hour later it had increased in volume, and it had become more of a buzzing than a humming, like a distant swarm of bees. Another half hour and we knew. It was the sound of people.

They, whoever they were, obviously were following the same path along which we had come. Back near the bridge, at which we had parked, there had been a steep, heavily timbered hill to climb and then descend to the river; it saved a tortuous scramble through a rocky gorge. After that, the going became much easier and a sheep-track ran along a narrow and lightly-wooded river flat and afforded pleasant views of the river for most of its course. There was no doubt that 'they' had reached the track.

As the hubbub increased, we became able to distinguish individual sounds. Through the babble came the occasional raised voice, a shriek of laughter, and once the sound made by a rock crashing down a hillside. It was inevitable, therefore, that 'they' would pass within a few scant paces of us, and we huddled down below the bank, hoping that the bracken would hide us.

Over a little rise they came, eventually, led by a stalwart lady of middle years wearing a safari jacket of camouflage material and a slouch hat; on her back was a small green rucksack. Behind her, in ones and twoes and threes, and spread out over two hundred metres or so, came a crocodile of miscellaneous bushwalkers. All shapes and sizes, they appeared to range in age from, perhaps sixteen, to eighty and more. Some carried huge back-packs that could have held rations sufficient for a decade while others car-ried nothing. Apparel varied from shorts, blue jeans, bright T-shirts and sneakers, to tweeds, deer-stalker hats, and heavy work boots.

The explanation of what had earlier been a buzzing sound immedi-ately became apparent. Not only were they all talking at once, but some-one in the vanguard seemed as likely to be talking to someone in the rearguard as to his or her immediate neighbour. It was understandable, therefore, that many of them found it convenient to speak at the top of their voices.

Although the track followed the gradual curves of the river—and it was therefore impossible to get lost—the walk leader paused at regular intervals to check a small compass against a large map. She seemed also to be constantly monitoring the whereabouts of her flock.

No-one saw my companion and me and we watched in amazement as they passed—trudging, sauntering, dawdling, scuttling, tottering; chatter-ing, bellowing, ranting, gabbling, mumbling; snuffling, whiffling, burp-ing, grunting.

To my companion's undoubted surprise, I rose to my feet after the last of them had shuffled past and, like a frog hypnotised by a snake, fell in behind them, abandoning my fishing rod in the process.

Differing abilities and energies among those participating in the walk had brought about the elongation of the procession. The old and the gnarled were naturally slow and were last and I passed them quickly. Another group had gathered around a wombat hole into which some ancient had apparently tumbled. Yet others were busy prosecuting the rescue of one of their number who had fallen into the river. In no time, I caught up with the leader.

That lady was proceeding at a moderate pace surrounded by a small group whose members seemingly viewed her with some veneration. Initially, I walked beside a voluble and plump lady of middle-European extraction who told me that her name was Magda. I was told by Magda that her leader's name was Mrs. Rattray. "She's marvellous," I was informed. "An inspiration to us all."

The other members of the small coterie that surrounded Mrs. Rattray appeared to have the hallmarks of a junta and, because of my proximity to them, I was able to listen as they furnished her with a constant stream of intelligence on just what was occupying the various other sections of her motley company. Soon after, I managed to insinuate myself alongside Mrs. Rattray herself.

"I was fishing in the river when you all passed by," I explained. "I thought I'd walk as far as the waterfall." I like to think that my open and ingenuous face won her confidence. She gave me a steely glance and accepted my explanation without further comment.

"Well," she said. "You cannot but be impressed by my little band. From nothing I've forged them into a team of madcaps and adventurers—most of them are now trained athletes, mountaineers, bushmen. Any of them would face death with a laugh on their lips."

"I… er… um…" I started saying but she did not require comment.

"Ha," she continued in a ringing voice. It was an exclamation of bold defiance that encapsulated an entire philosophy. "I can assure you that the untamed Australian bush holds no terrors for us!"

With some difficulty, I made what I hoped were appropriate noises. She had not finished with me yet. She looked at me levelly. "It is not all for pleasure, you know. There is a far greater purpose behind all this."

I lifted my eyebrows the barest fraction. It was enough. A confidential note crept into her voice and she nodded back in the direction of the unserried ranks of her troop (I noted that another of them had fallen into the river). "To be truthful," she continued, "it has been in my mind that, when this fair and sunburned land of ours is overrun by the Asian hordes—and I do not doubt that such an event is inevitable—my group will become a guerilla force." She ruminated momentarily. "I've a mind to call them Rattray's Raiders. We would retreat to the bush on the outbreak of war and live off the land. Then, at appropriate times, we would sweep down from the hills mounted on wild brumbies, wreak havoc in the midst of the enemy and then back to our mountain fastness. Unexpected raids and forays by a force trained in *blitzkreig* tactics and hand-to-hand combat would strike terror into the enemy, you know." Her eyes glazed as she strode forward, lost in her vision. I let her forge ahead to be alone with her thoughts.

Not long after, we reached the waterfall. It marked a change in the nature of the river, descending as it did over a series of rock shelves that were the beginnings of the more mountainous and rougher terrain further upstream. There was a pleasant pool at the foot of the falls and Rattray's Raiders prepared themselves for lunch.

At this point, a check by Mrs. Rattray and two senior members of the junta revealed that some nineteen members of Rattray's Raiders were lost en route. How this was possible I could not explain but a search party was dispatched. The remaining madcaps and adventurers opened sandwiches and poured hot water from thermoses into containers and over tea bags and powdered coffee.

Eventually, several of the younger and more venturesome Raiders climbed the slope that bordered the pool in order to see if their missing companions could be sighted from a higher elevation.

Emboldened, Magda essayed a minor climb of her own and, for some unaccountable reason, became paralysed with fright on a ledge at about eye level for those of us who had stood up at her cries of alarm. Like a flash, Mrs. Rattray's qualities were displayed to the rest of us. She was alongside Magda in trice, firmly grasping one elbow to assist her the two or three steps back to level ground. Mission accomplished, Mrs. Rattray mounted the slope again and turned to address us as if from a podium.

"It was a mere trifle," she told us. "Heights mean nothing to me. I'm like a mountain goat among the crags—absolutely fearless and never happier than when I'm face-to-face with danger." Modestly, she raised a hand to still the burst of cheering from two or three admirers. Then, stepping down, she fell over a rock and sprained her ankle.

Eventually, those Raiders who had been lost were recovered. A stretcher was produced ("We always carry one," Magda told me) and the intrepid Mrs. Rattray loaded onto it. I helped carry her for a bit, relinquishing my end of the litter only when I saw my fishing companion, still at the pool, hold up a handsome rainbow trout for my supposed edification.

I joined him and we watched as Rattray's Raiders, spread out over two hundred metres or so, lurching and tottering, gabbling and bellowing, snuffling and grunting, wended their way over a little rise. We waited as the sun began to set, not talking, just enjoying the river. And the hubbub became a drone and then a buzzing and then, finally, a muted murmur that hung trembling on the evening air. Then there was silence.

Where Will I Put My Legs?

I rather think that a catchy title like that makes for a good start. It has focused your attention. There would be those who, having attended thus far, remain interested only because their heartstrings have been twanged by that title.

It has doubtless evoked in their minds an image of some unfortunate butcher lamenting at finding that there is no more room in the freezer for the latest delivery of legs from the meatworks.

I have come to the subject of butchers by a circuitous route. It so happens that, in those long-past and halcyon days of my youth—rendered forty times as idyllic by the passage of time—I worked for a butcher on Saturday mornings. Then a whey-faced sprig of twelve, my job was to help Old Fred, the boss, with the deliveries while his brother looked after the shop.

Early on those occasions I would call at Old Fred's place to begin work. He lived in one of Melbourne's outermost eastern suburbs, and he kept the horse and cart in a stable in his backyard. Old Fred lived in Railway Terrace in a house with an Aboriginal name and a front garden full of flowers. I have thought since, that it would have been more appropriate for a butcher with a nice garden, had he lived at an address like Lavender Cottage, Slaughterhouse Lane.

I would help Old Fred harness Chester, the horse, and attach him (Chester, that is) to the cart. This vehicle was really a two-wheel chariot with a wood floor and an open back with a sort of waist-high front to separate us from the horse. When the chariot was in motion, we would both stand, Old Fred with the reins in one hand and me beside him hanging on and keeping an eye on the order boxes to see that they did not fall off the back.

Up front, of course, was Chester—fat and frisky in the early morning—
and, if you have not travelled behind a horse fed recently on new mown
hay (or whatever it was he ate for breakfast), you haven't lived. Reconsti-
tuted whatever it was can be heady stuff.

Although Old Fred claimed to have graduated summa cum laude from
the abattoir and to have gained honours in the laying out of tripes and
arranging sweetbreads, he was not what you would call an educated man.
For that matter, the ranks of educated men were thin in those days. Anyone who had got as far as high school was regarded as an intellectual.
Indeed, if you had spent a couple of years there, you could become a professor at the university or better.

Whatever, old Fred treated me as an equal, and when the occasion
arose, he would give me the benefit of his accrued wisdom in his gnarled
old voice. "Ahhhh," he would say, "there's a lesson for you in that, boy…"

One Saturday morning as we bumped along a dusty track halfway to
nowhere, we noticed something unfamiliar by the side of the road. Old
Fred pulled Chester up and, leaving him to crop the grass, we walked back
to see what it was that had attracted our attention.

It was called, I found out later, an echidna. It was a strange hedge-
hoggy little animal—all spines and a grey, leathery stomach. Though it
seemed improbable, the animal appeared to be either asleep or unconscious. Perhaps a pine cone had dropped from a pine tree (as coconuts
are said to do in the tropics), landed on its tiny bonce, and addled the
contents of its cranium. Old Fred picked up the echidna and cradled it
in his hands. "It's probably been knocked cold by a car," he said, and,
like the considerate old fellow that he was, proceeded to give it what
is known nowadays as a kiss of life. He puffed away for two or three
minutes, forcing oxygen and tobacco fumes into its little body, without
producing any signs of life.

It is written that those of us who are kind, loving and considerate to our fellow creatures reap their reward, and Old Fred's ministrations finally resulted in the echidna responding to the attentions it had received. It gave a bit of a twitch and opened its beady little eyes. Unfortunately, however, its eyeballs were located at the opposite end to that which had received the kiss of life. To me the echidna's gaze appeared to hold a hint, not only of Christian tolerance for Old Fred's activities, but also of sober charity for the idiosyncrasies of others.

Old Fred put the echidna down, right way up, and it scuttled off into the grass—probably to suffer abominably with wind. "Arrr," he said, wiping his mouth on his gnarled old sleeve. "Och aye, and begorrah. Hoots, mon." (All these things are so much better in the vernacular, aren't they?) He spat ruminatively and scratched his mizzen mast. "There's a lesson for you in that, boy…" he said. He paused to marshal his thoughts before continuing. "Always remember as you go through life that it's better to blow than to suck."

I'm sure that was good advice, and that Old Fred was right. I was happy for him that it was an echidna we had happened upon and not a hippopotamus.

A Country Ramble

Police Sergeant Pitt and Constable Morgan lounged comfortably in worn swivel chairs eating lunch just purchased at the takeaway next door.

Outside the three-man station, down the two cement steps, Main Street was busy with Friday traffic—heavy because of the weekly influx of shoppers from outlying settlements. Despite a fine misting of rain, the footpaths were crowded, and proprietors of the shops and hotels could not but be pleased with trade.

Behind the police station, up the slope, three streets paralleled Main Street for eight or nine blocks before petering out; behind them, lightly timbered hills and then the mountains.

Largely obscured by rain and low cloud, the mountains dominated the town which described itself (and not inaccurately) as "Gateway to the High Country" and "The Winter Playground." The brochures also recorded Coombelong's population as 13,406.

Sergeant Pitt was watching Constable Morgan when the telephone rang. Morgan was nibbling at the edges of a very hot meat pie and holding a hand beneath it to catch any gravy that might spill. Pitt shuddered, put his sandwich down on his desk, re-crossed his feet (also on the desk) and picked up the phone.

"Coombelong Police Station, Sergeant Pitt. Can I help you?"

Pitt held the instrument to his ear, nodding his head occasionally. After a few moments he lifted his feet from the desk, transferred his sandwich to his drawer—as though it might be visible to the caller—and sat at attention.

"Yes, sir," he said eventually. "Of course we will, sir. But I'd like to say, sir—if I may—that the pack has not been giving us any trouble lately. I see them around town but I think that one or two of the ringleaders have left the district so they may have changed their ways…"

Pitt listened again, waiting to get a word in. "Yes, sir, I do know the story about the leopard not changing its spots"—he rolled his eyes—"but there has been no repeat of episodes like the river diversion or the landslide and the rest of it…"

Once again Pitt became a reluctant listener. He watched Morgan demolish a currant bun.

Pitt's turn came. "Yes, sir, it is true that I can't be certain that their activities are over… and yes, I agree with you that they have been a major problem… but to infiltrate a mole into the group… a spy… not easy, sir. In fact, it would be very, very difficult!"

Pitt, telephone glued to ear, mimed for Morgan extreme boredom. He yawned silently and made a great display of stretching. Suddenly his demeanour changed, his face reflecting alarm. "Oh, you've chosen a mole already?" His face turned pink with suppressed emotion. "You've what? God, he'll be a disaster!" Pitt collected himself. "I'm sorry, sir… I got carried away… it was just that…"

While Pitt's caller occupied the airwaves, Pitt looked appealingly across at Morgan who gazed imperturbably back over the top of rimless glasses and an apple slice.

Pitt capitulated at last. "Righto, sir. Just as you say," he said resignedly. "I'll book him in at the hotel for an indefinite stay and collect him from the Sydney train next Thursday. And I'll do all I can to help him infiltrate the pack."

Pitt replaced the earpiece and sat gazing out the window at the rain, his lunch forgotten. "God," he said finally, "there's going to be trouble."

"What was that lot then?" Morgan asked through the remnants of a chocolate bar. "You didn't sound too pleased."

"Pleased?" said Pitt. "No, I wasn't pleased. That was Stokes—Inspector Stokes—ringing from Sydney. He's just found the file about the activities of the pack and it's got him all excited. I told him they've been quiet but he's decided to bust them before they do anything else and make a name for himself. He's had the bright idea of infiltrating a spy into their ranks."

Morgan shook his head knowingly. "Let sleeping dogs lie. We don't want them stirred up again."

"You don't know the worst!" Pitt was almost pleased to be the bearer of such awful tidings. "He's already chosen the mole and he's sending him down next week. I have to help him join the pack."

Morgan laughed. "Ha, join the pack? Impossible!"

Pitt, stony faced, said, "It's Detective Shorty Morse."

"Shorty Morse? The dwarf? I don't believe it."

Pitt almost smiled. "The very same," he said. "The awful Morse."

Pitt and Morgan met the Sydney train the following Thursday. Both wore civilian clothes to avoid drawing attention to Morse who was not to be seen as associated with the police. Both knew Morse by sight but neither recognised him among those who disembarked. They were looking for a short, plump dwarf given to making himself objectionable to all with total impartiality; Pitt and Morgan detested him. As it happened, they had not recognised him, and it was Morse who found them.

"Aha," announced a piping, boyish voice. "The spavined old warhorse, Pitt, and the young donkey, Morgan. Did not recognise me, eh? Great detectives you'd make."

Pitt and Morgan stared. Morse was wearing a schoolboy's cap, short pants and long socks; his pudgy knees were the colour of cold spaghetti and could not have felt the sun's rays for many years. A multi-coloured jumper decorated with a Beatles print accentuated his plump little stomach. Above the jumper, and below the cap, a round, ageless face and a pair of bloodshot eyes that looked to have seen all that the world had to offer—twice!

"Well, now that you've taken me in," said Morse, "get me to the pub. I'm dying for a drink."

Pitt and Morgan walked him to the car, Morse carrying a suitcase.

"What have you done about my contact with the pack?" Morse asked in his fluting little voice. Pitt suddenly saw him as the ghastly child he was pretending to be and mentally thanked his maker that he was childless.

"We've been lucky there," said Pitt, voice flat. "You're in! They're holding their first meeting since the powerhouse episode at the back of the park opposite your hotel at 9.00 a.m. on Saturday. I've dropped your name in as being new to the district so you're expected."

Morse was not grateful. "Right," he said, "I'll be reporting directly to the Superintendent, so I hope I have seen the last of you two." He kept his counsel until they dropped him at the hotel.

"And the best of British luck to that little sod." Pitt said charitably as they drove back to the police station.

*

Saturday, 9.00 a.m. The pack had gathered, and its members were being addressed by Mr. Petherill.

"Come, come, boys," he demanded plaintively. "Stop that immediately, Fester, and you too, Smerke, or it will be the worse for you. I should not have to tell you to behave yourselves. Remember that you are wearing the uniform of the Second Coombelong Club Pack. Wear it proudly. The public judges us all by the behaviour of each individual club.

"What is more, lads, we are doubly on our best behaviour today, because we have two surprises. Firstly, a new cub, Reginald... er, Shorty,

Morse. I want you to make him welcome." The troop looked at the raddled choirboy that was Morse with expressionless eyes and reserved judgement.

"And," continued Mr. Petherill, "we will be accompanied on this trek by a visitor who is holidaying in the district. This is Miss Fotherly, boys, and she is, herself, a cub leader in Sydney. In the tradition of Kipling's *Jungle Book* and, in the same way that I, your leader, am known as Akela—the Wolf—Miss Fotherly is known as Baloo. Her name, of course, refers to Kipling's Baloo the Bear."

The second Coombelong Club Pack looked at Baloo the Bear with respect. Their own leader, Mr. Petherill, was pale-faced, short-sighted, two metres tall and pencil-thin. Miss Fotherly was from a different mould. Huge calves knotted with muscle supported a barrel-like body. The khaki shirt which encased her chest and upper, ham-like arms was covered by a motley of badges certifying her expertise at capping fires at oils wells and fighting killer whales. Her scout hat sat incongruously above a face on which a look of baleful menace appeared to be a fixture. As the Coombelong troop gazed speculatively at her, she shrugged on a parka which made her appear larger and even more formidable.

"Crickey," said Slummock in an aside to Midden, "I don't like the look of this Baloo the Bear." Midden was not given time to answer. Miss Fotherly must have had a badge for hearing. In a trice, and with only two fingers, she had picked Slummock up by one ear and was giving him hints and suggestions that most certainly were not in the Scout Manual.

"Please, please, Baloo," said Mr. Petherill. "Put him down. We can't have that, you know. That's not what the cub movement is about."

Reluctantly, Baloo lowered Slummock to his feet. Her face was mottled.

"Baloo," Mr. Petherill implored, "they're only lads… a bit high-spirited, perhaps. Here, I'll call the roll and we'll get underway. Alright, chaps.

Answer clearly when your name is called. We don't want to mislay any of you today, do we? Ha, Ha."

He ticked each boy off as he acknowledged his presence.

"Adder? Bloode? Dribble? Fester? … Fester?"

"Here, sir. I'm here, sir. Present and correct, sir."

"Shut up, Fester, and just answer your wretched name like everyone else."

"How can I, sir, if you tell me to shut up? You told us to answer clearly and now you've told me to shut up? What am I to do, sir? And why me and not the others, sir?"

"Yes. Why him, sir?" said Smerke. "If you…"

"Be quiet, Smerke," said Mr. Petherill.

Baloo the Bear had listened to the interchange with growing amazement. A vein pulsed at her temple.

"Fester, Smerke," she said, "another word and I'll tighten your woggles till your eyes pop."

"Er, thanks, Baloo," said Mr. Petherill nervously. And, to himself, "Oh, Lord, is this thy will?"

"Gloate?" he continued. "Grubb? Grumble? Lurke? Lurke, you look a mess, boy. You'll have to try harder, won't you?"

"I'm sure he has been trying, sir," said Smerke, living dangerously. "I believe…"

"Smerke!" Baloo's voice overrode Smerke's like an avalanche over a daisy. Her eyes bulged ominously.

Smerke subsided instantly and edged back amongst his friends who closed protectively around him.

Mr. Petherill took advantage of the momentary silence. "And I'd better not smell anything like marijuana on this hike either, Lurke. Or there'll be trouble."

"It won't come from me, Akela," Lurke proclaimed unctuously. "It wasn't me last time. I think it was just the exhilarating smell of the bush."

Mr. Petherill sighed wearily.

"McCrobe? Midden? Milldew? Morse… ah, nice to see you here, young Morse. I hope you enjoy the hike. Phewe? Slinke? Slummock? Slyme? Smerke?"

"Oh, I'm here, sir," said Smerke. "Indeed, sir, I…"

"And more's the pity," commented Mr. Petherill, sotto voce.

"What was that, sir? I heard that, sir." Smerke was aggrieved. "Baden-Powell wouldn't have made a comment like that, sir…"

"Oh, shut up, Smerke. You misheard me. I didn't say, 'More's the pity.' I said, 'Poor kitty.' I was thinking of my cat at home all on its own with my mother, that's all. And stop that mumbling, Smerke, or I'll send you home."

Baloo flexed and unflexed her fingers. A trickle of saliva ran down her jowls. Mr. Petherill looked across at her and hurriedly resumed the roll-call. "Stoate? Trashe? Weevil? Worme? Well, that's good. All present and correct. Now, before we, ah, start off, let me say that this should not be a difficult walk. We will be back at the bus stop by five. I want everyone to stay together. Baloo will bring up the rear if she will be so kind."

"There will be no stragglers, Akela," said Baloo ferociously. "Any laggards will get a touch of my hiking staff up their you-know-what's."

Mr. Petherill cast a quick glance heavenward as if hoping for a sign. When it was not forthcoming, he said, "I'm sure that the boys won't lag. We will follow the track up to the reservoir and then along the ridge. There will still be snow on the mountain but it will be well above our route. We're not likely to get another snowfall this year so there is no danger whatsoever. And you, boy, Milldew. I don't know what you have in that rucksack but I need hardly tell you that I can recognise the smell of beer.

We don't have a brewer's badge in the Cubs, Milldew. Your good conduct badge will be on the line today, my lad."

*

From their car, at vantage point across the park, Pitt and Morgan had watched the meeting of the pack. They were interested to see what sort of a reception Morse was given and they were vastly amused when he turned up dressed in the regalia of some Sydney cub troop.

"Mrs. McAuliffe, at the pub, will be glad he's gone out for the day," said Pitt. "They're sick of him already—he's won two jackpots on the poker machines and he's taken out the snooker title."

Pitt might have added to his comments, but when Miss Fotherly stepped forward to be introduced to the troop, he changed his mind. "Quick, give me the glasses," he said.

Morgan took binoculars from the glove box and passed them to the impatient Pitt who clapped them to his eyes. Pitt gave a long, slow whistle, "Well, well, well," he said, and laughed. "Take a look at the female in the scout outfit. The big one."

Morgan took the glasses and inspected Miss Fotherly. "Mm, she looks like a wharfie. A big wharfie!"

"That," said Pitt, "is Detective Hilde G. Schimmelhauser from the Federal Police. I've seen her picture in the Gazette—she could take a wharfie in each hand and polish her car with them."

"Seems to me," said Morgan thoughtfully—and he gave Pitt a quizzical look—"that the state police and the federals have both infiltrated someone into the pack. A clear case of the left foot not knowing what the right hand is up to! I hope they all have a great day."

Meanwhile, the Second Coombelong Cub Pack was making good time to the reservoir. From the rear of the marchers came the occasional shriek of agony as Baloo the Bear caught up with an unfortunate straggler. Among cubs whose raised voices echoed around the valleys was recognisably that of 'Shorty' Morse, whose forty-three years and choice of debauchery over a healthy lifestyle ensured his place at the tail end of those making their weary way up the mountain. One particularly agonising encounter with Baloo's staff and Morse gave forth with a high pitched baying reminiscent of a newly emasculated bison. An impressed Smerke gave Morse a pat on the back in silent commendation.

They ate lunch soon after midday. Baloo took the opportunity to write up her diary: "Dear Diary—am suspicious of Morse, a shifty, villainous youth well-endowed with criminal attributes and rodent cunning. Was probably sent here by the Sydney underworld to take over the pack leadership."

Morse wrote: "Dear Diary. These kids are as innocent as the day is long and do not know their ears from their elbows. This Baloo is the only one I am suspicious of. I am glad I am on the right side in the fight against crime."

Baloo, towards the end of the lunch break added to her notation: "I surreptitiously obtained Morse's fingerprints when he threw away a drink can at lunch…"

Morse wrote: "I got Baloo's fingerprints. Saw her pick up and hide a drink can I chucked away. I pinched it from her bag plus a false Federal Police I.D. card. She is a real terrier."

Akela, a concerned eye on the suddenly threatening sky, urged them to hurry. They got underway quickly, but it was too late. Snow began to fall and, half an hour later, it was ankle deep with visibility greatly reduced. They went more slowly and there was bitter lament from Dribble and

Gloate. By late afternoon, it was apparent that they could go no further and that help was needed.

Akela found a cleft in the rocks where twenty boys could huddle. To thin cheers Dribble drew a large sheet of plastic from his rucksack but there was nothing to use as a ridge pole and the bedraggled group squatted together for warmth with the plastic draped over them to keep off the snow. Morse managed to ensconce himself in the middle of the group where he was relatively sheltered. Under his breath he had much to say about the Superintendent, his parents and ancestry.

Akela and Baloo prepared to go for help. "Don't leave here, boys," Akela told them through chattering teeth. "Remember that the Coombelong cubs are resourceful and enterprising." Baloo wrenched impatiently at his arm and they set off through knee-deep snow, Baloo in the lead. Slyme lit a cigarette and the smoke hung in the still air.

Smerke stared off after Akela and Baloo as they vanished into the falling snow and it was he who asserted that he had heard a yell as if someone had fallen. He argued with Grumble and Adder and eventually the three of them walked carefully down the track.

Smerke was right. They found Akela and Baloo had slipped from the track after a rock had given way under them. Smerke and friends climbed down some ten metres to find that their leaders, unfortunately, had expired—either from the fall or from the cold—and that Akela, who had fallen into an icy creek, had frozen solid.

Adder went back for help and, with the aid of the rest of the pack, they dragged and carried the bodies back to the cleft.

"There won't be any help for us now," said Adder. "We're on our own."

It was mid-morning next day when the Second Coombelong Cub Pack heard the police car. In ones and twos, they emerged yawning and weary from their makeshift tent. The police car stuck in snowdrift at the foot of the hill where the track turned. The engine stalled and there was a distant sound of curses as Pitt and Morgan stepped from the warm car into deep snow. They came trudging slowly up the rise.

"Are you lads alright?" Pitt called when they got to within hailing distance. "Your mothers are worried about you."

"We're fine," Smerke told him. "A trained wolf cub is a survivor." And, as the police reached them, "In the cubs we're taught enterprise and the cheerful acceptance of life's adversities and vicissitudes."

"Yeah," said Fester with a maniacal giggle, "and to make the most of what we've got too."

The two policemen looked curiously at the makeshift tent jammed into the cleft in the rocks. "You were lucky to get a bit of shelter. You would have been cold otherwise," commented Pitt.

"And you were lucky to find yourself a ridge pole for the tent," added Morgan. "No timber around here since the fires." Idly, he lifted the corner of the plastic. His eyes opened wide. "Cor, starve the lizards. That's the Club Master. He's dead."

"That's right," Adder said helpfully. "He and Baloo the Bear snuffed yesterday. Slipped off the track they did. When they went for help."

"Akela froze solid," Milldew said proudly.

"My God," Pitt exclaimed hoarsely. "What's he doing here then?"

"Holding up the tent, of course," said Adder instructively, an edge of contempt for the obtuseness of others in his voice. "No bloody trees around here, are there? Akela was the longest thing we could find. Made a real good ridge pole, he did."

"He always taught us to be enterprising and innovative," Phewe added reflectively. "He would have been proud of us today."

In a whining voice, Grumble said, "A good cub uses whatever material is available."

Pitt and Morgan looked at each other. "Where is Miss Fotherly?" asked Morgan.

"Ah, Baloo the Bear," said Smerke thoughtfully. "Well, as a matter of fact, we ate her."

Pitt's mouth opened and shut. No sound emerged.

"I don't mean *all* of her," added Smerke defensively, noting the effect of his words on Pitt. "Only some."

Dribble edged forward. "We managed to get a fire lit and then Phewe said he was so hungry he could eat a horse."

"Yeah," Midden interrupted, "and then the new kid, Morse, said 'What about a bear?' And that was that."

Midden and Grumble both tried to talk at once. Midden won. "We had some of her last night. That was the grill."

Grumble carried on. "For breakfast this morning we just had the leftovers warmed up and we hadn't worked out yet just what we were going to do for lunch."

Midden pulled a banana from his pack. "I was thinking of fritters," he said.

Pitt fought his stomach for control and, pushed beyond reason, took matters into his own hands. "Look here, you lot—you may as well know that Baloo the Bear, or Miss Fotherly as you knew her—was really Detective Hilde G. Schimmelhauser who was working undercover for the Federal Police!"

The cubs were nonplussed for a moment, and it was Slinke who broke the ensuing silence. "It's jolly interesting her being a policewoman," he said mildly. "She told us yesterday that if she had us in her outfit, she'd chew us up and spit out the chips."

"And we beat her to it!" Gloate was triumphant, "And what did the 'G' stand for? Gristle?"

Morgan remained stony faced while the pack showed its appreciation of Gloate's wit. But Morse belched loudly, and the thought of what part Morse might have played in the affair was too much for Morgan who dived for the bushes and reached them just in time.

Pitt sought to get the investigation back on the rails. "Why did you eat her?" he demanded.

Smerke considered the question. "We might have been here for days. We had to keep our strength up. We were showing enterprise and true grit and self-reliance, just as Akela taught us. We were facing death by cold and starvation, we were lost in the bush, and we were…"

"Yeah, you were lost in the bush—half an hour from the bus stop!" said Morgan, back from the bushes, embarrassed and angry. "Maybe Detective Schimmelhauser's report might not have been to your liking?"

Smerke was surprised. "Were we really being investigated? Why would an undercover cop spend time on us?"

"You should know," said Pitt bluntly. "There's been a lot of concern over episodes like the power grid and the demolition of the town hall and the like. The government has finally decided to put a stop to it."

"Oh," said Smerke, in sudden understanding. "Oh, I see! And you thought it was us?"

"The police have been watching the Coombelong pack for months!" Pitt was uncompromising. "They've got enough evidence to fill a truck!"

"But we're the *Second* Coombelong Cub Pack," said Smerke indignantly. "It's the *First* Coombelong pack that did all that!" He allowed a sliver of a smile that did not reach his eyes. "Cub scouts are taught that it is foolish to follow goanna tracks if you're looking for a fox," he said. "Perhaps that should be included in the police manual."

Blunderbuss for a Butterfly

If 'occupied' is the correct word, Lance Mowle occupied a tree located on the nature strip which fronted the Soviet Embassy in the national capital. Largely hidden by foliage, he sat in relative comfort some four metres above the footpath—his legs astride a major branch, his back against the bole. Field glasses hung around his neck and on his lap a small satchel supported a note pad and a camera.

There were, in fact, five trees—all occupied—in the section of nature strip that fronted the embassy. Lance, as representative of the Australian Security Intelligence Organisation (ASIO), naturally occupied the prime central position adjoining the main entrance.

ASIO took a keen interest in the embassy. It wanted to know who came and went and it liked photographs of visitors. To ensure that Lance was fully occupied during the midday to 6 p.m. summer shift, it also desired an input on events within the embassy grounds which Lance, by reason of his elevated position, could see over the cypress hedge that surrounded the compound.

Lance's embassy duties were virtually duplicated by the occupants of the other four trees. The two trees on the gentle slope below Lance's position were occupied by minions of the CIA (poor Waldo Eagleburger) and MI5 (Nigel Coutts-Peabody). Trees up the slope supported intelligence operatives from France and Israel respectively.

The sharing of an arboreal existence and surveillance of the Soviets had stimulated an esprit de corps within the afternoon shift. It was a boring duty, performed under duress by junior operatives learning the trade.

They shared jokes and relied on each other to fill in if one or another of them had the odd luncheon engagement. On such occasions, details of visitors would be shared and copies of photographs supplied.

The arborealists also shared a keen interest in a developing situation within the embassy between the beautiful Olga, the Ukrainian cypher clerk, and her two admirers who vied increasingly belligerently for her attention. The representatives of CIA and MI5 had money riding on the success of Secretary Burlap. He was blonde and athletic and spent much of his time improving his suntan by the pool where he was able to ripple his muscles for the seeming interest of the desirable Olga. On the other hand, Pierre in tree four (representing France's intelligence agency, the DGSE), and Leon (from Israel's Mossad) in tree five, tended to favour Burlap's rival—Communications Officer Spassky—of the olive skin, the smouldering eyes, the wild locks of black hair—and the quick temper.

Lance did not know enough about love triangles to have a worthwhile opinion on the chances of their amicable resolution. His naivety, regrettably, also extended to the secret service business. His employment, of a few months' duration only, had been engineered by his mother, Mrs. Mowle, a formidable lady of strong opinions who had over-ridden ASIO's protestations that Lance was not quite the recruit they were seeking and had personally supervised his induction.

Lance was the only child of the widowed Mrs. Mowle. She watched over him with a ferocious and consuming zeal. She had shepherded him protectively through kindergarten and school and attended all his sporting and social activities including his first and subsequent dates. When Lance joined the workforce, she saw no reason to alter her ways, and the fact that Lance was now employed by ASIO discommoded her not at all. Their relationship was one in which Mrs. Mowle fought vigorously to maintain her maternal ascendency while Lance fought desperately, if less effectively, to loosen the ties that bind.

The sound of feet scrabbling against the bark and the rustling of branches, accompanied by the exasperated sounds of undue exertion, did not, therefore, come as a surprise to Lance. It was 'Mother' bringing him the 4 p.m. thermos of coffee.

"I'm getting past gallivanting up trees," she said breathlessly, settling herself and her belongings on an adjacent branch. "And I don't like that MI5 chap watching me climb up. It's not decent." She took a thermos from a string bag and poured coffee into a plastic cup. "Here, dear," she said, "and here's an aspirin too. You'd have the sniffles this morning and your chest isn't strong. I'm going to have a word with your boss and get you behind a desk in head office where you belong."

To prevent an unwelcome dissertation on the state of his chest, Lance, with the agility of long practice, changed the subject.

"Olga spent her lunch break beside the pool with Burlap again today," he said. His mother shared his interest in the ongoing saga of Olga's love life and Lance knew that his reports afforded her pleasure and enabled her to assess the significance of each new development. He remained hopeful that, one day, his mother would reveal the secrets of the tempestuous passions that activated Olga and her admirers.

"She seems to be getting very friendly with Burlap," Lance continued. "She let him throw her into the pool and then save her." (Here he blew on his coffee.) "And he knocked the top off her bathing suit. I think it was an accident, but I couldn't quite see because the branches were in the way." He mopped at his lips with a tissue. "Leon, the Israeli, says that Burlap did it on purpose and that Olga didn't mind at all. But I don't believe that." He looked hopefully at Mrs. Mowle for a reaction but she offered no comment, so he continued. "Well, anyway, Spassky was furious. He was on the tennis court beside the pool playing with the embassy's new tennis machine."

Lance, a keen tennis player himself, waxed lyrical. "It's a marvellous machine, Mum. You load it with tennis balls, set the motor going and it fires them out like rockets—one at a time, of course—and it gives you practice hitting them back. Spassky was wishing that it was a cannon and that Burlap was the target. You could tell," he continued, "he was firing them at a post at the back of the court and hitting it most times, what's more."

"Oh, get on with it," said Mrs. Mowle. "I don't care about tennis."

A flash of movement below caught Lance's attention. He clapped the field glasses to his eyes and watched for a moment as the tall figure of the Soviet Ambassador, swinging a walking stick, emerged from the embassy and turned down the footpath towards the nearby shopping complex.

To his mother, Lance said, "That's the ambassador. We call him Igor. He walks to the paper shop down the road every afternoon. Leon says he's into the stock market."

Mrs. Mowle was only mildly interested. "Does he know that all you lot are up the trees watching the embassy?"

"Of course. In fact, Waldo Eagleburger gets on Igor's wick by dropping jelly beans on him as he heads for the shops. Igor gets very testy!"

Mrs. Mowle pursed her lips at Waldo's behaviour but forbore to comment. "What do the others think about Burlap and Olga then?"

Lance was only too pleased to be invited to speak on behalf of the other intelligence agencies. "Oh, CIA and MI5 are pleased. They say that Burlap is home and hosed, but Pierre and Leon are afraid that they may have done their money. Leon thinks that Spassky is going to blow his top if it goes on much longer, and he says that Spassky spent time in Madrid a few years ago and blew his cool over some voluptuous Castilian strumpet… What's a voluptuous Castilian strumpet, Mum?"

Mrs. Mowle had no intention of becoming involved in a discussion on strumpets. "More coffee, Lance?" She proffered the thermos. "What else did Leon say, dear?"

"Well," said Lance, not prepared to give up so easily, "He claims that the Castilian strumpet was…"

Mrs. Mowle interrupted impatiently. "Oh, do stop going on about Spaniards. Get back to the point."

Lance sighed. "Leon said that Burlap and Olga had better watch themselves. He said that another session like that and Spassky will go into orbit."

Accepting that she was up-to-date with events, Mrs. Mowle shifted her substantial hams on the branch, preparatory to returning to terra firma. "Alright, dear, I'll be off, then."

"You didn't tell me what a Castilian…"

Mrs. Mowle chopped him off in mid-adjective. "I'll have your tea ready at six-thirty. What would you like tonight, dear? Apple pie? A nice ro-ly-poly?" Lance licked his lips and his mother repressed a smile. She did not hesitate to exploit her son's vulnerabilities when the need arose.

Over the next several days the intelligence agents in their trees continued to record car numbers and take photographs. Leon got a snap of the milkman while Eagleburger got another of the postman falling off his bike. Pierre won the weekly competition they held with a colour print of two dogs fornicating in the middle of the embassy drive.

Mrs. Mowle dropped in periodically with coffee, clean handkerchiefs and the like. On the Friday, she brought Lance a supply of syrup-of-figs to 'keep him regular.' "All that sitting around on draughty branches is not the best preparation for later life," she said.

Within the embassy, officials and staff went about their business. The weather continued hot and Olga, when possible, disported herself by the pool. While her activities entertained Burlap, they served only to further enrage the rejected Spassky. Unable to set his mind to tasks that may have helped alleviate his suffering, he chose to remain in sight of the pool. The

BOP-BOP-BOP of the tennis balls being propelled at speed from the tennis machine became an irritant.

"That goddam machine," said Eagleburger. "Ah'd like to call in a full scale airstrike on that little 'ole blunderbuss he's playin' with."

Poor Eagleburger little knew that he was to hear the machine fire only once more. His companions were equally unaware as they took up station next day.

It was Sunday and the embassy was largely at leisure. Lance and his companion settled down for a shift much like its predecessor. It was, however, not to be.

Lance, admiring Olga through his glasses, saw it happen. She emerged from the pool and stood, body gleaming with water. She shook hair from her eyes and stretched sinuously, testing her bathing suit to the point of destruction. Then she smiled at Burlap and moved towards the low brick wall that sheltered the end of the pool. It served as a sun-trap for swimmers who wished to extend their tans or who sought a measure of privacy. She crooked a finger at Burlap and there may have been promise in her eyes.

Promise or not, it was enough to send Spassky into orbit as forecast. Perhaps he had reached the end of his tether. In any case, he had come prepared for what he did.

Lance watched Olga and Burlap stroll towards the wall and he watched Spassky, on the tennis court beyond them, take a ball from his pocket and load the machine. Spassky spun it on its wheels so that it pointed towards the wall, and towards Olga and Burlap. He aimed quickly and fired. BOP. Lance's vegemite sandwich—a piece bitten from it and already swallowed—remained clutched in his hand before his open mouth. His eyes flicked to Olga and Burlap. He could still see the tops of their heads as they strolled further into the shelter. Neither gave any indication that anything was amiss and Lance, appreciating that Spassky's attempt at mayhem had failed, breathed a gusty sigh of relief.

At that instant, however, there was a sound of breaking branches and the body of Waldo Eagleburger fell clumsily from the CIA tree to land on the asphalt where it lay unmoving, lifeless.

It was at once apparent to Lance that a line, taken through Spassky's cannon, continued through the spot on which Olga, but a moment earlier, had walked would pass through the Eagleburger tree. "Murder," thought Lance. "Poor old Eagleburger." He made an entry in his notebook, took a photograph of the recumbent agent, and finished his sandwich.

"Spassky fired at Olga, missed—and did in poor old Eagleburger." Lance told his mother when he was finally able to get away from the police. "Knocked him off his perch in the tree with the old tennis machine bazooka," he said.

"How did Spassky come to miss hitting Olga?" said Mrs. Mowle. "I thought he was a crack shot. You can't trust the Russians to get anything right. What do the police think?"

Lance gave a shrug that he had learned from Pierre. "It's all very difficult, Mum. There's no evidence of real witnesses. Remember that part of the crime took place on Russian territory—diplomatic immunity and all that."

Lance sat, lost in thought for a moment until a prod from his mother brought him back to reality. "Luckily for the police, the ambassador agreed that they could talk with Spassky," he continued. "Surprisingly, Spassky admitted to firing the machine but said that he didn't aim it at Olga and had certainly not hit Eagleburger whom, he said, he quite liked. Spassky also said that all the embassy people knew that the trees on the nature strip were jammed with spies, and he said that the Russian secret police could only occupy the trees outside the American embassy in Moscow in the summer because there had been a bureaucratic bungle and all the trees planted had been deciduous."

Mrs. Mowle nodded thoughtfully. "If Spassky agreed to talk to the police, he's either very confident or he's innocent."

Lance shrugged wordlessly.

Next day brought further developments. A round, red mark was discovered on Eagleburger's body, suggesting that the deceased had been struck by some object.

"It must have been made by the tennis ball," Lance informed his mother. "I told you so." He felt reassured by the announcement which supported his own considered judgment.

"Exactly where did Eagleburger get clobbered?" demanded the reporters and TV journalists of the police.

"The abrasion was located on the victim's gluteus maximus," advised the police. "That's BUM to you lot."

Mrs. Mowle sniffed. "I've seen Eagleburger lolling around up in the tree every day for three months. There's no way a tennis ball fired from the embassy could have collected him in the area suggested. There is some other explanation."

A thorough police search of the immediate area turned up the remnants of a pizza (marinara), an advertisement for athletic supports (in colour), assorted (and revolting) debris, a blackbird (defunct) and an old golf ball. These were placed in numbered bags. No tennis ball was found.

There was mounting concern within ASIO as to just how they were going to tell the CIA what had happened to their employee. There was reason to believe that Washington would be miffed that a U.S. citizen, going about his lawful concerns, had been knocked off by a tennis ball from the Soviet Embassy in distant Canberra. It was agreed that the U.S. was likely to take particular offence that a tennis ball, representing a sport in which the U.S. saw its national prestige to be at stake, provided the murder weapon. It was suggested to the Prime Minister that U.S. reprisals were possible, that battle fleets could be put on alert and troops on standby.

At the Prime Minister's behest, ASIO—as the host organisation—convened a 'think-tank' conference of representatives from concerned intelligence agencies, 'involved' Western embassies and government departments.

It was felt that such a conference, of honed and dissective minds, should "within the matrix of events be able to extrapolate the information available," and "come up with the most likely scenario elucidating events that had occurred—premised on the balance of probabilities," and suggest a way out of the schemozzle.

After consultation, the experts agreed that a murder attempt had been made, on Soviet territory, by one Soviet citizen on another but that, through misadventure, an innocent American, minding his own business, had been feloniously slain. Eagleburger, they decided, had been struck by a tennis ball fired by Spassky from a mechanical device aimed at a female employee of the embassy. The point of impact of the tennis ball on Eagleburger's person suggested that the ball may first have ricocheted from a branch before striking the deceased and propelling him from the tree where he had been birdwatching and who, as a result, had fallen to his death.

In announcing the findings of the conference to the media, a spokes-man went on to say that, no matter how cunning and treacherous the Russians, "we can match—and outdo them."

"What did I tell you, Mum?" said Lance proudly. "I saw the whole thing and the 'think-tank' heavies have just spent all morning reaching the same conclusion that I reached in seconds."

Mrs. Mowle looked at her son and stifled a sigh. Resisting an urge to fetch him a clip around the ear, she busied herself with her string bag to keep her hands occupied. "I told you that there was another explanation, Lance—and there is. For starters, Spassky is not a fool. He must have known that a tennis ball travelling at two hundred miles an hour"—Mrs. Mowle had not yet caught up with metrication—"hitting Olga between the eyes, might possibly cause her demise. But he also knew that the tennis machine fires balls at considerably less than that speed so there was no real likelihood of Olga being killed."

Lance looked at her, hoping desperately that the explanation she was slowly unravelling was going to break down.

His mother did not falter. "So he needed something extra, didn't he? He chose a golf ball as being more lethal—the one the police found in the gutter most likely. You saw him take something out of his pocket, but you couldn't see that it was a tennis ball, could you Lance? But then, he missed Olga anyway. And there's no doubt he missed Eagleburger too. The golf ball probably hit the tree, but the mark found on Eagleburger's beam end was not made by a golf ball travelling at speed. The mark was too small and there was no bruising."

Lance made a final effort to recover lost ground. "Ah," he said as the thought struck him, "the old poisoned umbrella in the posterior trick, eh? Like they did in Bulgaria."

"You *are* a dill," said his mother patiently. "I'll tell you what happened if you give me a chance. We know that Eagleburger enjoyed irritating Igor, the ambassador, by bombarding him, symbolically perhaps, with jelly beans. I took the trouble to check at the newspaper shop. The proprietor confirmed that the ambassador always collected his afternoon paper around 4 p.m. before strolling back towards the embassy. My reconstruction of events is that, on his way to collect the paper, he approached Eagleburger's tree—knowing that a jelly bean was likely to drop on him. For whatever reason, he was irritable."

Mrs. Mowle had the bit between her teeth and she was calling the shots the way they fell. "With the walking stick he always carried, the ambassador reached up and gave Eagleburger a poke in the bum—that's gluteus maximus to you and your friends." Ignoring Lance's shocked expression, she pressed on. "Igor is a tall man but there would not have been enough power in the jab to propel Eagleburger from his eyrie and to his doom—probably only enough, in fact, to bruise his dignity."

"What killed Eagleburger, then? How did he come to fall from the tree? You may well ask!" Mrs. Mowle was triumphant. "He killed himself!"

Lance looked at her in disbelief. Yet he knew his mother. The impregnable foundations on which he and the 'think-tank' had built their analysis was under major threat. "But mother—I can't… are you sure? Perhaps…"

His mother gave him no time to air his views. "He stood up and hit his head on a branch in the CIA tree and if that didn't kill him, then the fall did. The police, when they look, will find bark in Eagleburger's hair and an abrasion on the branch above the spot where he normally sat."

At Lance's unspoken query, she nodded. "Yes, I've checked and there seem to be a few hairs still caught in the bark."

Lance's world was disintegrating. He looked at his mother, waiting on further impossible revelations. Nothing loth, she continued. "So the only remaining question, as I'm sure you will appreciate, is why? And I think I can answer that question to your satisfaction.

"I took the trouble to buy myself a copy of Sunday's paper." She withdrew a folded newspaper from her bag and placed it on her lap. "Just picture for yourself," she said, "Igor strolling back with his newspaper. The warm afternoon sun through the dappled shade of the trees. He is carrying his walking stick in one hand and perhaps swishing it idly at the occasional thistle. With his other hand he is holding the newspaper and, because he has only one hand available, he is reading the front page. Igor walks casually beneath the CIA tree. Eagleburger peers down and sees the headline."

Mrs. Mowle was gracious as she approached the denouement. She looked possessively across at Lance. Victory over those who would remove him from her ministrations was almost in her grasp. She unfolded the newspaper and held it so that Lance could see the front page and the banner headline: UNITED STATES AND SOVIET UNION SIGN ETERNAL PEACE AND FRIENDSHIP PACT.

"So?" said Lance. "So what?"

"So, you *are* a ninny, Lance." His mother was exasperated at his obtuseness. "That headline meant that Eagleburger was out of a job! Unemployed! If the Americans and the Russians are friends, there's no work for CIA operatives, is there? He might get work turning nuclear missiles into ploughshares, of course, but no more cushy jobs sitting up trees watching the leaves grow! I bet that footpath outside the American Embassy in Moscow is littered with KGB bodies too."

Mrs. Mowle, tentative earlier, had no doubts now. "Eagleburger got such a shock when he saw that headline and absorbed the implications that he leaped to his feet on his perch—forgetting that there was another branch just above him. He probably knocked himself out or had a heart attack. Anyway, he fell from the tree and died.

"I doubt," Mrs. Mowle continued, "that Eagleburger either saw or heard the golf ball fired by Spassky whistle through the branches at that moment. So, there was no murder—though that was not for want of effort on Spassky's part. The unfortunate death of Mr. Eagleburger was due entirely to misadventure so naval battle groups may remain at anchor and missiles may rest peacefully in their silos."

The evidence was irrefutable. His mother was right. Lance was in shock. The reverence in which he had held his superiors was dissipated. "She's always bloody right," he thought. There was moisture in the corner of his eyes. He wiped his nose with the back of his sleeve.

Mrs. Mowle smiled benignly upon him. "There, there, love." She fought desperately to keep the look of joy from her face. Lance needed her. She waited for his capitulation.

And then Lance said, "Can we have strawberry jam for tea tonight, Mummy?"

"If you're a good boy," said Mrs. Mowle.

The Choreographed Corpse Caper

The Wing Commander was the first to see the body. He came into the mess for breakfast whistling jauntily and, finding the room still darkened, flung back the curtains which protected the room from the searing daylight heat of an outback South Australian summer. He looked out onto the secret defence base which he commanded, through the sliding glass door. His whistling cut off in mid-note.

"I say," he exclaimed, outraged. "Who the hell is that untidy bastard lying around out there on the parade ground? Pickled to the bloody eyeballs, I expect. What a complete bloody shower."

Increasingly indignant at the sheer effrontery of it all, the C.O. raised his voice to attract the attention of the steward. That worthy, interrupted in his laying of the tables, was gazing out at the collapsed figure lying unmoving on the square of dry, packed earth which the C.O. liked to think of as the parade ground.

"You, Smifkins," said the C.O. firmly, "have the goodness to phone the guard and have that fellow collected. Tell them I want him put on a fizzer and paraded before me the instant he sobers up. It's disgraceful. I'll have his guts!"

The making of an executive decision before breakfast mollified the C.O.'s ire somewhat. He ordered bacon and eggs and sat down. He was just beginning his tomato juice when his Number Two, the Squadron Leader, arrived.

"Mornin', Bones, old lad," said the C.O. "A fine day coming up!"

The Squadron Leader refused to be drawn into an exchange of pleasantries. "Sorry to ruin your brekka, Skipper, but we've got a problem. There's a wretched civilian fella out on the parade ground, and he's dead."

"God," said the C.O. "Just my rotten luck to have some selfish bastard ruin my leave arrangements. Blast it." He sighed gustily. "Well, I suppose I'd better go and have a look at him."

The C.O. rose to his feet, drained his glass, and patted his impressive moustache with a linen serviette. He collected his cap from the rack beside the sliding doors and, in the company of 'Bones, old lad,' strode purposefully towards the little group gathered around what he now knew to be a corpse. There was a shuffling and a muttering as room was made for them. Salutes were thrown and returned.

"I'm afraid he's dead, sir," said the Sergeant of the Guard.

"What did he die of?" asked the C.O. "And, what's more, how the devil did a civilian get inside the base again after 6 p.m. last night? The perimeter fence is three metres high, it's patrolled night and day, and there's an armed guard on the gate. Despite all that we've got, bloody civilians popping in and out as if we were a corner store. How did he get in? This is going to involve Security as well as the police. Pretty poor form, the whole damned show!"

The Sergeant was nervous. He fiddled with the buttons on his shirt. "Well, sir, to be frank, it's got me beat. I don't know how he got in. There's no record in the book of a visitor—not that he'd have been allowed in anyway at that hour. He's made an illegal entry for sure. He must have had a heart attack or died of pneumonia."

The C.O.'s eyebrows shot skywards and his moustache bristled as if it had a life of its own.

"What do you mean pneumonia? The bloody temperature hasn't dropped below thirty-five degrees all night and you'll be able to fry an egg on the guardhouse roof in an hour!"

A new voice, a female voice: "Ah, but sir, he's all damp you see."

The C.O. turned to address his new informant. "Just what are you implying, madam? And, for that matter, just exactly who are you? Or"—ruminatively—"is it whom are you?"

"Oh, I'm a civilian, sir. I clean the offices before the scientists come in at 8 a.m."

"Right," said the C.O., his attention returning to the corpse. "What's the significance of his being damp? Is it relevant? A passing shower perhaps?" And then, cunningly, "I suppose it was water and not beer? Has anyone tasted it?"

"As a matter of fact, I did, sir," volunteered the Sergeant sheepishly.

"Well? Come on, what did it taste of? Do I have to drag everything out of you?"

"Er, it tasted of mud, sir."

"Ye Gods." It was the Squadron Leader's contribution to the conversation. "What a complete balls up."

The C.O. screwed his face into a grimace that reflected extreme irritation. "We're getting nowhere." He addressed the cleaning lady. "Just what is your interest in this affair, madam, and what is your name, pray?"

"I'm Mrs. Parples, sir. And I think his being damp may have great significance."

"Parples, Parples?" the C.O. was thoughtful. He resisted an impulse to pluck at his moustache. "Seems familiar somehow… not Emily Parples?"

"No, sir, Enid."

"Hm." (The C.O.) "Well then, what about my rain shower theory?"

"Well, sir, it would have had to have been a very small shower. You can see that the damp area around the deceased is only about half the size of a dinner table, and, sir, if you'll look over there, you'll see another area of curious dampness about the same size." She pointed towards an area a dozen paces distant and waited while the C.O.'s piercing gaze assimilated the view of another vaguely circular area of quite obvious dampness.

Further musings by the C.O. were interrupted by the arrival of an armed guard from the gatehouse. He saluted crisply. "'Scuse me, sir."

"What is it?" said the C.O., annoyed at being interrupted.

"I may have an identification of the *corpus delicti*, sir."

"What's he talking about?" said the Squadron Leader "What's a *corpus delicti*? Don't they teach English at school anymore?"

The C.O. ignored him. "Who is he?"

"Well, sir," the guard retreated a little from his position of, almost, assurance, "there's a lady at the gate, wife of one of the scientists. Claims her husband has gone missing. She has a neighbour with her and I thought you might prefer to have the neighbour try for the identification."

No sooner said than done. The body now had a name. Harry Braunowsky, Scientific Officer Grade II, theoretical ballistics and propulsive algebra. There was a distant sound of hysterics.

The Squadron Leader broke the hiatus. "I might remind you, sir, that your comment about frying an egg in another hour or so is equally true of steak."

"Jesus," said the C.O. "Must you, Bones? But you're right. Well, what have we got—heart attack, murder? What do you think Miss Marples? I mean Mrs. Parples?"

"My opinion, sir," said Mrs. Parples comfortably, "is that we may be looking, if not at murder, at least at a felonious incident."

"Crickey," said the Squadron Leader.

The C.O. made up his mind. To the Squadron Leader he said, "Get on the radio and alert base in Adelaide. Tell them we have an unexplained death and that we need the police—and quickly. Tell them about our little problem with temperature and remind them to warn the egg-heads in

Defence Department of the security implications. If Adelaide get off their wretched butts, we could have them here in an hour and a half."

'Bones' sped swiftly away at a medium saunter. The C.O. watched him go, heaved a sigh, and then directed the guard from the gatehouse: "Cover Mr. Braunowsky with a tarpaulin or something. I want a guard on the body. The rest of you, DISMISS!"

What had originally been a small gathering had grown to a fair crowd. It now dissipated like the leaves of autumn—all except Mrs. Parples.

"What is it, Mrs. Parples?" asked the C.O. resignedly.

"I suggest, sir, that the damp area surrounding the body, together with the other area, be delineated in some way before the evidence disappears."

"Why on earth should we? Oh, I suppose you're right. Guard, mark the circumferences of the damp areas with string or rope and keep everyone away." He lost his train of thought. "Parples," he said to himself. "Where have I heard that name?"

When Mrs. Parples disappeared, the C.O. looked at his watch. "Too late for breakfast," he thought, "and too early for a whisky. Damn!"

As a consequence of an unauthorised and unsolicited body appearing mysteriously on a restricted and classified missile base in rural South Australia, Adelaide was able to act quickly and effectively. Within forty minutes, two police officers and a photographer had embarked on a R.A.A.F. flight bound for the scene of the crime. The three of them were visiting from Scotland Yard on security matters, and so were admirably suited to answer this call.

Superintendent Holmes, Chief Inspector Claude Eustace Deal and Police Photographer (First Class) Hector Porret had an informative journey. Their R.A.A.F. pilot was a mine of topical information both informed and uninformed. He circled the base before landing. "Hope you boys enjoyed the trip. There's Rupanyupna base below us now. We call it Fort Rupture back in Adelaide. Full of boffins it is. Rupanyupna is supposed to be an Aboriginal name for 'home of the wood pigeon.'" He laughed. "The likelihood of a wood pigeon ever having lived down there is zilch. The Aboriginals were probably telling them to bugger off."

There was silence for a moment and then the pilot spoke again. "There now. That's better. You can see all the base from here." The police contingent looked disinterestedly down at the scrubby desert.

The pilot's enthusiasm was not dampened. "The airstrip runs down one side of the base and, over there, where the road from Adelaide comes in, are the facilities and the quarters for the R.A.A.F. personnel and their families. And those buildings there are the workshops and laboratories for the scientists. They're messing about with a new missile and, every now and again, they fire one out into the wild blue yonder. They live outside the base with the public servants and work inside only between 8 a.m. and 6 p.m. With their families, I s'pose there's two hundred of them all up. You can see their quarters just outside the gates. They've got good housing, air conditioning, a great little shopping centre with a tavern, a theatre, swimming pool and a decent gym. They do O.K.!"

The plane landed and taxied towards the control tower where the C.O. and the Squadron Leader, both now resplendent in dress uniform, were waiting. Introductions were made.

"Straight to business then," said the C.O. briskly, and he directed his steps towards the parade ground and towards the body lurking thereon. His visitors followed, Superintendent Holmes tamping tobacco into a meerschaum pipe as he walked while Chief Inspector Deal chewed steadily, if lugubriously, on a well worked-over stick of spearmint.

"The base is entirely surrounded by a security fence," the C.O. was saying. "It's patrolled night and day by personnel in vehicles and by dogs. There is no break in the fence and there's been a guard on the gate all night who swears no one has gone in or out. The deceased could not have stayed on base after six because we have a name and number system of checking them in and out."

"Hmm," said Holmes thoughtfully. "In these affairs, it is often the butler who did it. I don't suppose you have a batman? No? *Hmm.*"

"Y'know," opined the Squadron Leader, speaking for the first time and addressing Inspector Holmes, "you seem familiar, somehow—perhaps it's the pipe. I didn't run into you at the Grimpen Mire Country Club, did I? No? Just thought I'd ask."

They arrived at the parade ground. The guard pulled the tarpaulin from the body. While Porret, the photographer, plied his trade, the two detectives examined the corpse.

"Well," said Holmes, "it would appear that he did not die voluntarily. All that is then left is murder."

"Not a mark on him, sir," said Chief Inspector Deal to Holmes, and then, to the Squadron Leader, he said, "You haven't, by any chance, had a recent visitor by the name of Templar have you? Hyman Templar, that is— though I suppose he could use an alias like 'Simon Hemplar,' perhaps— or similar. A debonair sort of fellow—steely grey eyes, aquiline features, looks like a Greek god, that sort of thing. Anyone like that on base?"

"Only me and the C.O.," said the Squadron Leader.

The Chief Inspector turned back to Holmes. "That looks like a little stick figure with a halo, drawn in the dust beside him. Do you suppose…?"

"No," said Holmes testily, "you ninny. That's a goanna track."

The Sergeant of the Guard was paraded before the detectives and eventually dismissed.

"I suspect that sergeant," said Holmes. "I've been in the business a long time and it's been my experience that anyone who looks you straight in the eye and gives you a firm handshake is up to no good." He sucked contemplatively at his pipe. "Well," he said, "to summarise, we've got exactly nowhere. We have a damp corpse—I don't suppose anyone knows whether he perspired heavily? No? Hmm. There are no bullet holes or stab wounds. He does not appear to have been strangled, garrotted, or bitten by snakes or spiders. Nor are there any signs of a shark attack."

He addressed Chief Inspector Deal. "And make a note that I tried to smell his breath for a whiff of bitter almonds but that he had no breath."

"It's just like the Marie Celeste," said the Squadron Leader.

"Furthermore," intoned Claude Eustace Deal portentously, "his head hasn't been stove in either! It's gotta be natural causes."

"Not quite so fast, young Deal." Holmes was at his best with impetuous young Chief Inspectors. "There are other possibilities. You jump to conclusions too quickly. Have you thought of curare, the venom of the stonefish, or an untraceable alkaloid?"

Deal was crestfallen. "You've done it again, sir. I go along with you on the stonefish venom."

The C.O. had been patient during the proceedings but there was no real progress and he was concerned at the rising temperature—not only for his own comfort but also because of the corpse.

"Gentlemen," he said, "I see that this death has baffled the experts. What is to be done?"

Holmes looked keenly across at the C.O., his eyes avoiding direct contact. A grim smile played across his lean and saturnine visage. "I'm not through yet—not by a long chalk. There's something diabolic here and I'm going to get to the bottom of it. I'll take him back to Adelaide where he'll be sliced into sections like a Bologna sausage and I'll have Forensics examine him slice by slice." To the C.O. he said, "Are you sure you didn't hear the distant baying of a hound?"

"I say," exclaimed the Squadron Leader, impressed by Holmes' single-mindedness, "that's the ticket, old boy. Never say 'die.' That's how we beat Jerry."

"Just one thing before you proceed," said the C.O., teeth gritted. He gave up fighting his inclination and twirled his moustache voluptuously. "I think you should see Mrs. Parples. She seems to be pretty clued up on this whole affair.

"Parples? Parples? The name seems familiar," said Holmes.

"But she's just a bally washerwoman, Skipper," expostulated the Squadron Leader. "She's… oh, blast it, you do what you think best." His jaw jutted doggedly.

Mrs Parples was summoned. She joined them in the C.O.'s office and graciously took the chair held for her by the rotund Chief Inspector Deal. "Yes, sir," she said in answer to the C.O.'s question. "I do have a theory—in fact it's more than that. I started," she continued, "on the premise that, while this may be a secret missile base, it is an ordinary community like any other and its inhabitants are motivated by the same concerns. I've asked around and Braunowsky was a gambler. He seems to have lost heavily on the camel races at Oodnadatta and his family have suffered as a result. Not only did I find out that he had a heart condition, but I also discovered that he suffered a massive attack yesterday just after he got home from work—and, in fact, died."

There was a concerted gasp of astonishment from her entranced audience.

"Then, what on earth was he doing inside the base and how did he get there? It's impossible." The C.O. was icily cool.

"Ah, but sir," said Mrs. Parples, settling herself more comfortably in her chair. "You must remember that this is missile base. Boring husbands talk endlessly about their work and children take in the mathematics of trajectories with their mother's milk."

"Are you saying that someone fired him across the fence like a Guy Fawkes night rocket?" asked the Squadron Leader incredulously. He tittered at the image that crossed his mind.

Mrs. Parples raised a restraining hand. "Let me tell it my way. First of all, the social implications of Braunowsky's death. He'd been a gambler and there was very little money for the widow. But, you must remember that he was a public servant and that, under the regulations, if he died on duty—that is, while at his place of work, which is inside the base—his widow would receive compensation of five thousand dollars."

"A light at the end of the tunnel," said Holmes, breaking new ground with the English language. He tamped tobacco into his meerschaum.

Mrs. Parples ignored the interruption. "Well, it happened that Mrs. Braunowsky was familiar with the Public Service Act and Regulations of 1949, so, while naturally shocked, it crossed her mind that her deceased husband could make himself useful just one more time— provided she could get him over the fence without being seen."

Mrs. Parples took a sip of gin from a glass handed her by the Squadron Leader. "Not easy to get a dead body over a three metre fence that is not only lit at night but is regularly patrolled. She was, however," continued Mrs. Parples, "the wife of a missile scientist and, importantly, she had two strong sons. She also, and vitally, had the franchise for making ice for the village tavern—all that ice you chaps here on base use for keeping your beer cool at the parties comes from the tavern. Remember?"

The Squadron Leader nodded sagely. He, as Officer in Charge of beer and parties, was in a position to know. He was an expert on the chilling of beer.

All eyes were rivetted on Mrs. Parples. She was enjoying herself. "The problem is to get a large and inert body over a high fence. Rocket propulsion was out of the question, of course. That leaves more basic methods. Perhaps something like a ballista which the ancient Romans used to hurl rocks at the ancient Carthaginians, and others, in days long gone. And, speaking of catapults—because that is what a ballista was— what about a trampoline? Yes, Wing Commander, I see you're beginning to get the picture. There is a trampoline at the gymnasium—the rear doors of which are only ten paces from the fence and twenty from the edge of the parade ground!"

Mrs. Parples paused and quenched her thirst with the gin. "The next problem which the newly bereaved faced was how to bounce the inert corpse of her dearly beloved to a considerable height and over a fairly substantial distance. The iceworks, ever to the forefront of her concerns, provided the answer. Braunowsky, if rigid, would bounce quite adequately. Trajectory was not difficult—an object dropped from the gymnasium roof, itself eight metres high, would bounce satisfactorily. When the legs of the trampoline nearest the gymnasium were propped up by the vaulting horse, anything dropped onto the trampoline would then rebound at an adjustable angle. It was then a simple matter to arrange a test run with a block of ice approximately the height and weight of a man. No need for a test pilot for the dummy run, was there?" There was laughter and spontaneous clapping from the Squadron Leader.

Holmes leaned back in his chair and gazed at the ceiling. "The ice melted and became that other damp area," he said. He did not wait for an answer. His rapier-swift mind had made that incredible intuitive leap that distinguishes the really great detectives. That little clue, dropped unwittingly by the cleaning lady, and the whole thing had come together in his mind.

"It's all quite elementary," Holmes continued, the grim smile playing across his lean and saturnine features yet again. "That frozen body bounced over the fence, and the ice melted and…"

"*Voilà*," exclaimed Porret excitedly. "Bravo Monsieur Holmes. You have done it again, *mon ami*!"

"Take no notice of him," said Chief Inspector Deal to the C.O. "He's a Belgian—but he's a good photographer."

Holmes was modest in victory. "If ever that fool Hoyle finishes writing the history of my cases, I'll call this little affair, 'The Case of the Ricocheting Rocketeer.'"

The C.O. and Mrs. Parples stood together as the plane carrying the police and the body taxied away down the runway preparatory to returning to Adelaide. They turned to walk back to the administrative building.

"What put you onto it?" asked the C.O. bluntly.

Mrs. Parples smiled across at him and gave a little skip to put her into step. "The widow hadn't remembered to put the trampoline away. It was still there. Elementary, my dear C.O.," she said.

Class Will Out

There was pride in the old man's voice. "That dog," he said, "has got a pedigree that the crowned heads of Europe would envy. He's a real champion."

He looked across at me from faded blue eyes surrounded by the wrinkles of what must have been half-a-hundred searing summers and more, as if he thought I might deny the truth of his words. Nothing was further from my mind, and I gazed down at the unkempt kelpie that slunk at his heels with admiration and profound respect. I had not met the owner of a champion sheep dog before and it made me feel humble.

A creature of impulse, I had stopped when I saw the notice back along the highway. There were no big towns within an hour's drive so I knew it would only be a small country show but the sign had advertised that sheep dog trials were to be part of the day's entertainment and that was good enough for me. I love to watch trained dogs moving the sheep—the slow, threatening approach with stomach to the ground, perhaps a bark to huddle them more tightly, and the swift circling if any individualist ruminant should contemplate escape. And I admire the relationship and understanding that exists between the dogs and their owners. No, I was not in so much of a hurry that I could not spare a couple of hours to view sheep dogs in action.

I saw the end of the trials and stayed afterwards for a few minutes while the sheep were removed and the hurdles used to pen them were loaded onto a utility by three bored and jean-clad youths.

It was a glorious summer day—the sort of day you can build up a thirst without lifting a finger. There is always time for a beer before the next event at country shows so I vaulted the white-painted wood rail that encircled the ground and cut across the worn, brown, tussocky grass towards the small grandstand that, in winter, no doubt served to shelter the followers of the local football team. I could see the striped beer tent erected alongside it, conveniently placed for its clientele to take advantage of the facilities provided behind the stand.

A quarter-way across the arena, I noted casually that I was on a converging course with a grizzled old fellow who appeared to be in his mid-seventies. His stance was upright and his shoulders square and, despite his years, he looked to be fit and active. He wore twill trousers above scuffed, elastic-sided boots and a faded khaki shirt with the sleeves rolled up over sinewy brown arms. On his head the badge of the countryman, a dusty, broad-brimmed grey felt hat; he wore it tipped forwards to shade his eyes. Just behind him, head down, tongue lolling, trotted a brown and white kelpie dog.

I surmised that the old chap was raising sheep or cattle and that the kelpie had probably competed in the just-finished trials.

"G'day," I said, when we came together.

"G'day," he replied.

"Bloody hot. Isn't it?" I offered casually. "Heading over to the beer tent?"

"Yeah," he said, laconically, and, sensing acceptance, I fell into step alongside him.

It was my turn again. "I've been watching the dog trials," I told him. He did not seem to think that required an answer, so I added, "Is that dog of yours a champion?" and I nodded towards the kelpie.

The old man turned his head and looked at the dog, almost as if he was surprised to see it there. He gave me a quizzical look and I wondered if, perhaps my question had been naive or foolish.

"Oh, him!" said the old man. And then, reflectively, "Ah, yes, he's a champion all right. As a matter of fact, I can trace his bloodline back, oh, must be all of twenty generations." It was then that he gave me the bit about its pedigree being the envy of the crowned heads of Europe. Unexpectedly, he had become quite expansive, and we slowed our pace by unspoken agreement so that he could tell me the rest of the story.

"D'you know," he began, "I'm going back now to the late 1930s. I was only a young fellow then, about sixteen I'd reckon, and things then were really crook. It was the Great Depression and there was no work anywhere in them days. Bloody nothing. I was living out west, way out past Narrabri and Wee Waa, at a little place called Come-By-Chance. Sheep country it is, around Come-By-Chance.

"I had this kelpie bitch," he said. "Her name was Nell. Someone had given her to me as a pup. She was the great-great-great grandmother, whatever, of this dog," and he nodded briefly to indicate the kelpie behind him.

"Well, this day me and my mate were out after rabbits. We used to get sixpence a pair, skinned and gutted. Anyway, we came to this big hollow log and my mate said, 'There'll be rabbits in there,' so we put Nell in at the butt end and we held our big sack over the other end. We could hear Nell working her way through the log so we waited. Then all of a sudden, out came a whole swag of rabbits. Before I could get the sack off the log and close it up, Nell had gone in there too. D'you know, that bitch was a natural. In ten seconds flat she'd sorted those rabbits out—the bucks on one side of the sack and the does and the little'ns on the other."

The old man looked across at me. "My mate saw the whole thing," he said in affirmation of the truth of his story. "And he was so impressed that, when Nell dropped a litter a month later, he offered me a quid for one of the pups. That was a hell of a lot of money at the time, I can tell you. Anyway, my mate had spread the story around town, and I sold the other five pups at the same price.

"Well now," the old man continued, nodding his head sagely, "I had a good head on me shoulders in them days. D'you know what I did?" He did not wait for me to guess. "I borrowed a horse and cart and went off to Coombogolong and Gwabegar and Pilliga and Walgett. Took me six days but I came back with twenty-seven more brown and white kelpie pups that I'd picked up here and there. I sold 'em all off as Nell's pups to graziers as far away as Barraba and Gulargambone. I made a few quid that year alright. I was in the money."

"The year after though," the old man continued, "I got meself organised. That year I sold fifty-seven more of Nell's pups. They were all first rate sheep dogs, naturally enough, and of course they were winning prizes up and down the whole state. By then, Nell's pups were famous and I was getting two quid for each of them. I was on my way to a big future."

The old man ceased talking for a moment while he gazed ruminatively back to those palmy days, and then he said, "So this dog here is a pure bred descendant of one or other of those pups and that's what I meant about pedigree and breeding."

He left me then, refusing the offer of a drink, and he walked away towards a group of men talking and lounging around an old utility in the dappled shade of a peppercorn tree.

I strolled into the refreshment tent and ordered a drink. After the barman had served me, I turned and surveyed his other customers. Alongside me a tall countryman of indeterminate age with a seamed mahogany face pushed a few silver coins across the wet counter in exchange for a beer. He took a long draught, sighed appreciatively, and wiped his mouth with the back of his hand.

"Some good dog handlers in that last event, mate, weren't there?" he said, discerning my willingness to converse.

"Yeah," I was pleased to be talking with someone. "I happened to be chatting with an old fellow a couple of minutes back. He's been breeding champion sheep dogs for the best party of sixty years and I think it was his dog that won the finals."

"Was that the old chap you just walked across the oval with?" asked my new companion over the rim of his glass.

"That was him," I said. "I met him on the way over here."

My new acquaintance chuckled. "That was Old Darbie O'Neal—I noticed the pair of you strolling along while I was moving my car into the shade. And he told you he was a sheep dog breeder, did he? Had the dog to prove it too, eh?" He grinned hugely. "Well, it happens," he said, "that particular dog is owned by the caretaker here and it's not a sheep dog's backside. I'd say it was only having a mooch around when you saw it. Probably followed Old Darbie to take advantage of his shade crossing the oval. And, as for Old Darbie, well," and here he laughed aloud, "he was the postman here in town until he retired ten years ago. I can tell you straight out that he hates dogs. Hates and loathes them, in fact, he's got what you could call a professional antipathy to dogs. Tells a good yarn though, doesn't he?"

Football: The Day of the Powder-Puff

Now that all the semi-finals and the hemi-demi finals and the final-finals of all the football codes are soon to be played, and now that all those doughty warriors of the pigskin are soon to leave us for the two weeks or so before training for next season begins, there may just be time to offer a jaundiced view of football.

It seems to me that the footballers of today are but pale imitations of the footballers of yesteryear. This past season I have watched teams emerge from dressing rooms, all of them upholstered in surgical bandages and long-legged elastic underpants (presumably to protect delicate parts or to hold their trusses in place or, indeed, to keep their wretched groins warm).

I have counted seventy or eighty of such medical aids and appurtenances on the arms, legs and heads of a team as it jogged down the race—enough, one would suppose, to hold them together for at least the duration of the game.

But not a bit of it. From the first blast of the whistle they, and their equally wimpish opponents, were dropping like ninepins—all to remain prostrate whilst registering anguish and suffering until help arrived. Some were carried off on stretchers while others were sprayed with concoctions that enabled them to stagger to their feet (displaying gritted teeth for the TV cameras) and allowed them to remain upright for short periods until someone bumped or pushed them again.

These days, the schools must run courses in the registering of pain and agony (borne heroically) by means of facial grimaces and body language. So skilled are the practitioners of these arts that I doubt not that there are degree courses in writhing and wincing, and doctorates for the portrayal of stoicism in the face of unprovoked violence or the influencing of umpires and referees with death rattles and simulated last breaths.

I watched another team as it took the field and broke into a light trot towards the centre. Within moments, the fusillade from the snapping of assorted tendons and ligaments had sent a number of Europeans and Arabs among the spectators ducking under seats for cover. Only three of that team reached the centre. The rest were scattered about on the grass doing their thing, being attended by medicos, and being carried off to waiting ambulances for further treatment, exploratory surgery, brain scans, therapy and X-rays; some were being hugged and having their bums patted by sympathetic fellow-thespians.

Times were hard when I played football as a youth and none of us ever possessed a cruciate ligament, far less a patella or an Achilles tendon. We would not have known what a groin was, either. In my day, people's legs extended upwards from the feet to the body which they joined at a point known as the lower stomach, and that was that. And we managed very well too.

In our competition (run by the local churches), we never let minor injuries stop us. I remember when our captain, Bristly Dobermann, lost the top of his skull in a mid-field fracas. The game was only delayed long enough for one of the mothers to bring out some sticking-plaster which she attached over the top of his head to each ear. He then continued the game, his enthusiasm unabated.

And I remember our full-back—Motley something or other. I'll never forget him and those dear departed days. Well, on one occasion, Motley was almost bowdlerised by our opponents from the Christian Uplift United. Broke both his legs, they did. Do you think for one moment that Motley would have spoiled the game for the rest of us?

Indeed not! He managed to push most of the bits of broken bone back inside his socks and, with a gay laugh through smashed teeth and a debonair curl of what was left of his top lip, he hobbled back to take his place in the last line of defence. Stout fellow, Motley!

No, things have come to a sorry pass. Football was different in the old days. This preoccupation with trivial injuries is a modern phenomenon. One year knees are the fashion and the next it's hamstrings. This year groins have been all the mode. I believe that, if players insist on having groin problems, they should have them out before the start of the season. Establish a groin bank or whatever it takes and let us get back to an honest day's football where players don't have to be carried off to hospital if they get their knees muddied or their hair mussed.

Return us to the times when men were men. Could you imagine for an instant that the ancient Romans carried on about their groins while they were conquering the world? Why, after a victory over the Sabines, the Roman soldiery ran the fifty or sixty kilometres back to Rome with a Sabine woman over each shoulder! And in those days, the Sabine women were not miserable little shrimps dieting themselves away to nothing—not according to the paintings of that event. Most of them had enough hair to fill a couple of mattresses and they all had shapely and muscular legs, broad lissome backs, strong curvaceous arms and big er… er biceps, but I digress. Anyway, you can bet your embroidered hanky that the Romans did not hang around to whimper about their groins. That would have been the last thing on their minds.

And what about Pheidippides, the Greek, running from Marathon to Athens with news of the great victory over the Persians? Did he fall over halfway clutching a hamstring, moaning and groaning, calling for a stretcher? No fear! He carried on to announce the news and dropped dead like a real winner.

It is obvious that, if men of yore had been like their modern counterparts, history would have been different. In fact, history might not have happened!

What about Henry V—about to mount his charger at Agincourt—and, on his lips ready for utterance, that unforgettable speech beginning, "Once more unto the breach, dear friends…" He gets a twinge in the leg, forgets what he was about to say, and comes out with, "Oooer! Ow! Oh! Sh*$! I've done me cruciate ligament!"

Doesn't have the same heart-stirring ring about it, does it? Not likely to echo down the centuries either! No, the French would have won the battle and rightly so.

So, the football season is drawing to a close and, no doubt, the hospitals are already crammed full of those having their knees reconstructed, ligaments untangled and sprained backs and tendons being treated with lasers. Some of them are probably being cossetted and spoonfed with chamomile tea by nurses, some of whom, most likely, will have blonde or red hair and ruby lips and shapely torsos and big… but I digress.

The Goat Caravan

From behind his uncluttered desk, Bellowes watched Martin Rigby settle himself in the soft leather of the visitor's chair. Rigby was of medium height; he looked lean and fit. His dossier listed his age as thirty-six and his marital status as single. It evaluated him as capable and intelligent. Bellowes noted his composure, despite what must be, for him, a very stressful appointment.

It was easy for Bellowes to imagine Rigby as the competent army captain that his military record indicated him to be and to envisage him leading the Goat Caravan operation. Bellowes already knew something of Rigby's version of the strange events that had brought him to this appointment, but he was unable to discern in him any suggestion of a man seeking to exorcise the trauma that had ended his military career.

Bellowes was sixty-plus, greying, overweight, florid, well dressed. He gave the appearance of amiability and his disarming smile invited confidence. The Defence Department, which was paying his consultancy fees, was not, however, doing so because of his avuncular attributes but in recognition of an excellent analytical mind and a capacity for incisive judgment. He had been asked to look carefully at Martin Rigby and to "discover if he knows anything about the body that someone left so untidily on the Plain of Jars in northern Laos." Of that terse directive, Bellowes could make what he chose but his intention was, as requested, to take a very careful look.

Bellowes smiled professionally at Rigby, leaned elbows on the desk and steepled his fingers. "Well, I'm glad you could come, Mr. Rigby. They will have told you, I'm a consulting psychologist for the armed forces. Despite your anticipated discharge from the army on medical grounds, the service remains concerned for your health and your total recovery. It—the army, that is—has retained me in the hope that, by examining the reasons for your feelings of guilt about the Goat Caravan mission, we, together, can put those events into some sort of perspective. That sounds pompous, doesn't it?" Bellowes chuckled. "What I'm trying to say is that the service wants to help and is reluctant to sever its connection with you in case your judgment and your health remain affected by your experience in Laos."

Rigby nodded, neither concerned nor greatly interested. He leaned back, crossed his legs and straightened the creases of dark grey slacks.

Bellowes spoke again. "Let me hasten to add that I will need all your candour if I am to help you."

Rigby shrugged in a gesture that reflected his wish to be elsewhere doing something else. "You'll know, then, that I'm not here by choice." His voice held irritation. "I just want to be totally finished with the army and I want them to forget I exist."

Bellowes waited, not offering comment.

Rigby thought about it for a moment. "Alright, so I'll go through the whole bloody story again if that's what it takes!" He looked at his hands, gathering his thoughts. His fingers closed slowly into fists and then relaxed. And he started to talk, his eyes—after a time—no longer appearing to see Bellowes—or his consulting rooms.

"It's not so long ago that Australia's military forces were involved in Vietnam and Thailand and, before that, there was Malaysia and Borneo and Korea. All those neat little South-East Asian wars were really nasty little affairs if you were there. You could get dead! They all spilled over international borders into places like Laos and Cambodia and even China.

"In 'Nam, one day, the C.O. sent for me. There was a civilian in the tent with him, but I wasn't introduced. He was Australian. They wanted me to lead a group of eight American Special Forces troops into the tri-border area, in Laos—way to blazes north of Vientiane—into Golden

Triangle country where Burma, Thailand, Laos and China all meet near the headwaters of the Mekong. The back of bloody beyond!

"The civilian told me that two Englishmen had been in there for a couple of years—spying for someone or other, I expect—he didn't say. They were in there, supposedly, as part of a French missionary station to the Hmong and the Shan tribes. The civilian wanted them brought out quickly and *very* quietly."

Rigby spoke cynically: "American interests were going to land me on the Plain of Jars in northern Laos in one of their little Beechcraft. I was going to rendezvous with their men at the strip and I was told that they would be looking after the supplies.

"God, if only I had known!" His smile was rueful. "I would have said, 'No thanks, Colonel. Find yourself another sucker—sir!' Anyway, that's water under the bridge." Rigby resumed his narrative and Bellowes, fascinated, listened.

"Rough country up there and, as I guess you know, the Golden Triangle means the drug warlords and, in that area, Khun Sa, the biggest of them all. He's raised a bandit army from descendants of Kiang Kai-Shek's Kuomintang forces which fled to Yunnan and beyond in the forties after their defeat by Mao's commies. I wasn't wrapped in the deal, but I agreed.

"We had no official presence in there, of course, and we'd have been on our own in the event of trouble. So, re-supply was a problem and air drops that might have drawn attention to us were out. But it was the end of the wet season, and the terrain was so rugged that we couldn't carry more than our M-16s and a small backpack. Some character had dreamed up a real doozy to handle re-supply. You wouldn't believe! The Americans said it was typical transport for the Hmong tribes in the hills above Luang Prabang, but I've got my doubts. It was a bloody goat train!" He shook his head in reflective wonderment before continuing.

"The Beechcraft took me in to the Plaine des Jars and I was met by the eight Yanks and two Hmong tribesmen with their herd of twenty scrawny goats. I had maps of our route, and someone had done their homework from old French colonial maps and aerial photographs; the tracks north to the mission were marked with distances and gradients.

"The transport expert had allowed us five days to walk in and four days to come out. It had been worked out—and by God they were spot on too—that the goats could carry provisions for the Americans and me, the two goatherds and the Brits when we brought them out. The goats each carried twenty pounds, even through the hills, with ten of them carrying fodder for all the goats. As the goats ate their way through what their mates carried, we were then able to eat two goats between the eleven of us every night going in, and two and a half goats on the way out. According to logistics, we'd eat the last goat the night we got back to the airstrip where the Brits and I were to be collected."

Bellowes muffled a gust of laughter at the thought of the goat caravan wending its way over mist and rain-shrouded mountain tracks with the goat numbers diminishing in accordance with a mathematical formula as they, freed from carrying fodder for their fellow ruminants, themselves provided fodder for the carnivorous component of that little band.

Rigby acknowledged Bellowes' amusement. "It worked. It was bloody brilliant. The hills were steep and muddy. We couldn't have carried more than our M-16s and a light pack. The goats were sure-footed and reliable, and they handled the hill tracks like Sherpas. We'd all be hungry by dusk and the two goats just fed us all. Goat stew for midday and evening meals and those who could keep it down had it for breakfast. We ate the last goat on the last night. Any delay going in or out and we'd have run out of food."

Outside Bellowes' office, Sydney's autumn winds rattled the old-fashioned wood-frame windows of his consulting rooms. Beyond the small unkempt garden, which he always intended to look after when he found the time, he could see the leaves scudding along Blues Point Road towards the harbour. He shivered.

"Well," said Rigby. He was more comfortable than he had been earlier and seemed to be telling the story for himself as much as for Bellowes. "We reached the Mission, eventually, and the two Brits were waiting. Wilson and Kemp they called themselves. Might even have been their right names. They were scared and in a hurry to move. Must've been running from something.

"I wouldn't have minded a feed; we were sick of goat—it needs hanging—but we were under orders to turn around immediately and, besides, the French didn't want us around the Mission even for five minutes.

"Late that afternoon, we came out of a gully to find a group of Chinese preparing an ambush: a military platoon they were—Khun Sa's lot. They weren't happy to see us. We were too early! We hefted our M-16s and I think they knew the Yanks were Green Berets. They let us through.

"That episode made us twitchy and I planned to double the watchkeeping that night. That was when it happened." Rigby's voice had risen. He leaned forward, feet splayed as if to rise. He took a deep breath and waited a long moment as his tension dissipated.

"I never discovered who did it," he shook his head, "but that night someone spiked the goat stew. We all ate from the dixie, of course, and, whatever it was, it zonked the lot of us.

"When we woke, just before dawn next morning, the Brits had gone. Disappeared into the drizzle! The Chinese must have followed us and doctored the stew while we were butchering the goat. And they kidnapped the Brits.

"When we finally accepted that there was nothing we could do about it, we packed up and headed for the rendezvous. We finished off the goats on day nine and, next morning, paid off the goatherds and waited for the mist to lift so the Beechcraft could land; I could hear it circling. The Yanks were going to make their own way back to their operational base and I eventually got on the plane—alone.

"While I was waiting for the pickup, I was thinking about those two poor bastards. I had gone to get them out and failed. And I realised too that I was only a tiddler in a big deep pool. It's no secret that the U.S. is trying to close down the drug scene in the Triangle, and they don't mind who they lean on. So I suppose that Khun Sa grabbed the Brits as bargaining chips.

"Maybe it was reaction but all I could think of was, 'Stuff the Army... I'm finished with it... I want OUT!' My nerve snapped when we got airborne. The pilot got concerned, cancelled the run to Saigon and diverted to Ubon where there was an Australian base and hospital.

"Next thing I was on the flight to Bangkok and then to Sydney for the shrinks to look me over. I bet I missed a lot of heavy interrogation, but there was nothing I could tell anyone that the U.S. Specials didn't know anyway. So I had a breakdown. I'm finished with the Army and the sooner it is finished with me the better."

Bellowes had listened without interruption. Occasionally he had used a green pen to jot briefly on a small notepad. Now, as he collected his thoughts, he straightened the pad so it exactly paralleled the edge of his desk. He stretched and sat forward in his chair, facing Rigby directly. He put the pen down.

"Yes, you're right, Mr. Rigby. That is why you're here—to resolve a problem. Your story is one of guilt for failure to rescue two people for whom you had been given responsibility. Such feelings are standard textbook reactions and are usually resolved by the passage of time. The sub-conscious works to enable you to rationalise events and accept the inevitability of developments over which you had no real control. All gobbledegook, I know—but true, nevertheless."

Rigby, his story told, leaned back, relaxing as he read acceptance in Bellowes' pontifical words.

Bellowes, affable and expansive, said, "Well, that was some story!" He tapped the green pen against a thumbnail and picked up the pad. "I would like to clear up a few points. There are some elements that I find interesting and, indeed, curious!"

Rigby shrugged. "There's nothing more I can tell you. I don't care whether you find my story curious or not. I have no faith in psychologists or psychiatrists, anyway. I just want to finish here and be off."

Bellowes nodded briefly. "If I am not satisfied then the Army is not satisfied. If that happens, you will continue to be hassled for answers."

Rigby was irritated. "Oh, ask away!"

"Right," said Bellowes, and suddenly he no longer appeared either amiable or harmless. "You did say that the food situation depended totally on the goats and that the sheer logistics of that operation could not have been tighter?"

"Yeah, I said that. It was true."

"Then why did the situation not fall apart after Wilson and Kemp were kidnapped, disappeared or whatever happened to them?"

Rigby thought about it. "Yeah, I see what you mean. It is odd." He furrowed his brows, eager to help. "There were the eight Yanks and me and the Hmong goatherds, of course..."

"And just exactly how many Hmong were there?" Bellowes was insistent.

Rigby shrugged, put his elbow on the desk and cupped his chin in his hand. "Oh, I suppose there were two or three of them. I don't remember, particularly."

"But you said there were two when you met up with the goats on the Plain of Jars!"

"Did I say that?" Rigby was not too concerned. "Well, I'm not sure… there may have been one or two more. I seem to remember… maybe a couple of cousins or an uncle joined up with them."

"I do not think that such was the case," Bellowes said confidently. He drew a circle on the pad with his green pen. "I think you had two extra Hmong with the caravan from the night of the so-called kidnapping.

"Those two Brits. You said yourself, Mr. Rigby, that they were anxious to be on their way when you collected them. I wonder why? After all, they had been there for several years. Why the rush? Why would Khun Sa suddenly see them as useful pawns? More likely they offended him. Were they treading on his toes? And, in view of the business he is in, it follows that they must have become a nuisance or a threat to his operations. They must have realised that the military rescue mission had not been mounted without a good reason and they were not likely to be left to their own devices on arrival back in Saigon—given a pat on the back and a wave goodbye."

Rigby laughed. "You've got a great imagination…"

"You think so? Well, let me see if my reconstruction of events holds up. If I follow that line of thinking, our friends must suddenly have found themselves under threat and they must have thought hard and quickly. Your being tasked to get them out was fortuitous and unexpected in their timeframe. They had planned to do a runner, but they would not have got far in European clothes would they? No," Bellowes answered himself, "but if they could merge with the local tribesmen, they might get away with it. They would know the Hmong through the French Mission and may have spoken the language. What better cover? Let me say, for argument, that they had their disguises ready—tribal vests, black Hmong trousers, cloth for those turban things and, vitally, skin dye."

Bellowes continued with increasing assurance. "You said yourself that the food rationing did not break down and that the tight rationing worked out exactly. So, the numbers of your party did not change after the supposed kidnapping.

"I believe that Wilson and Kemp got one hell of a scare at the ambush and that forced them into making their move earlier than planned. They doctored the stew and staged the vanishing act. All they did, in fact, was ditch their European clothes and become Hmong. The two herdsmen were not going to say anything to you and the Americans, they had just been tribals anyway… invisible people. None of you realised that two had become four and Wilson and Kemp successfully merged with the scenery and the numbers in the caravan did not change."

Bellowes made a spare gesture with his hands. "How am I going?"

Rigby shrugged, exasperated. "An interesting theory. Surely one of us would have recognised them—even with blacking on their faces? I take your point about the rations, but one thing about the Hmong is their belief in the extended family. If relatives arrive, they are fed until they go. A couple of tribal hunters probably dropped in and stayed a day or so. Big deal!"

"Nice try," said Bellowes. "But let us go back to your Saigon briefing. You were told at that meeting that the two men you brought out were involved in the drug trade and that Wilson, at least, had shipping connections that were bringing drugs into Australia. That, I think, explains the ambush incident and the subsequent disappearance of the two men."

Bellowes did not wait for a reply. "And then," he said, "there is the problem of the body of a European on the Plain of Jars. Can you help us with that?"

Rigby's face reflected shock as he sought to mask his emotions, and Bellowes did not miss the whitened knuckles. "I don't know about a body. It couldn't have been either of the Brits… we walked three days after we lost them…"

Bellowes glanced out the window at the oleander bowing in the blustery wind. "He was found two weeks ago near the airstrip after you were collected by the Beechcraft. The body was in a washaway covered with brush. We are expecting identification within days."

Bellowes continued, didactically. "Europeans are inclined to forget that even the Plain of Jars for example is, after all, someone's backyard. Bodies, unless well buried, do not stay hidden."

Rigby paused, calculating. Suddenly he was on the defensive. "And?"

"And," Bellowes repeated, "according to my theory, the body would seem to be yours, or rather, that of a Martin Rigby, late captain of the Australian military forces."

Rigby's eyes clouded and he rubbed a hand across his face. He spoke quietly. "Your conclusions have been reached on very little evidence. Flights of fancy may be the stock in trade of psychologists but the courts demand facts. You might remember too that there are courts that deal with slander!"

Bellowes had watched Rigby fighting for his life. He nodded, acknowledging Rigby's defiance.

"I admire your nerve. You claim to be Rigby and your impersonation has been impressive. But you are not quite him—a little slip here and there.

"For my money, you are Kemp. And either a murderer or a party to murder. You chose to stick with the rescue mission, and you and Wilson became Hmong goat herders for the rest of the trek to the rendezvous."

Bellowes raised his eyebrows interrogatively. "Rigby" did not react and Bellowes continued: "The last morning, for some reason you—or

Wilson, or both of you—murdered Rigby and you assumed his identity. You both had the military background, were the same size, and I know Kemp had Australian parents so the accent was not a problem. But you did not board the Beechcraft alone! We checked the Americans and were told that, when the mist lifted, the Beechcraft landed and collected two men who introduced themselves as Captain Rigby and Max Wilson. Rigby was in uniform and Wilson was a civilian. No doubt Wilson made a point of calling you 'Captain Rigby,' so who was the pilot to argue? He took you at face value. You staged your breakdown and the pilot dropped you at Ubon. Wilson went on to Saigon with the aircraft and disappeared at the airport. And, yes, the C.O.—and others—were annoyed because, by then, you were on your way to Sydney. They managed to round up a couple of the Americans and their story largely supported your version because they knew nothing of Rigby's death, Wilson's resurrection, or your impersonation."

Rigby stood and walked to the window to gaze across the park to the sweep of Sydney Harbour.

"You did well, Mr. Bellowes. I won't pretend any longer. You've worked it out and I know you can blow my story sky high with a photograph or an army acquaintance of Rigby. But I'd like to set the record straight.

"Yes. Khun Sa *was* after us. Wilson was a drug-runner and he was a nuisance to Khun Sa who probably thought I was Wilson's partner. But I was not involved in drugs at all—I had been a Weapons Officer in the army and the mission had hired me as a security and protection.

"Rigby and I got on well—we'd been on a course together in 'Nam a few years back. He told me about the caravan and how it had come about, and made it easier for me to become him.

"As for the murder. I'm deeply sorry it happened. All I wanted was to reach Australia and vanish. Wilson had a criminal record. On the last morning, after the Yanks headed out, I went down to scout the landing place. When I got back, Rigby was dead. Wilson had been arguing with him and, when Rigby told him he was to be arrested when we landed in Saigon, Wilson shot him; he always carried a pistol. I had no choice but to say I boarded the plane alone; Wilson was supposed to have vanished.

"The goat herdsmen had been hanging to collect anything we might leave behind, and they'll clear me of any murder charge. I'm only sorry I wasn't there to prevent it happening.

"The pilot was expecting an army captain and a prisoner or two, so I took Rigby's jungle greens and his I.D. card and became a captain: the game had changed but we were still at risk.

"I thought I'd do a runner at Saigon, but the breakdown was a better idea and I had no problems at Ubon and I had seen the last of Wilson. I knew he'd disappear the minute he arrived—he was afraid of Khun Sa's long arm."

Bellowes nodded. "That fills in the gaps. Your version of the murder will be checked. You might have got away with it, but the Army was uneasy… something not quite right…"

Kemp's lips quirked in a wry smile. "The matter of the goat stew made you suspicious. In theory, with two less mouths to feed we should have had a goat or two over. I might have guessed those bloody animals would be trouble."

A Small Matter of Honour

I was shearing with Jack Johnstone's gang in the New England area, to the north of Tamworth. It was my third season with Johno's gang but most of the rest of them had been together, through the shearing season that is, for eight or ten years.

There were seven of us in the gang: five shearers, a young fellow who was a nephew of Johno, and another bloke, Acka Wilson, who did the cooking. Acka and the young fellow yarded the sheep and did the pressing and the rouseabout work and anything else going.

The gang worked four months or so each year, starting in mid-August and going through into December. When the season ended, we'd all go back to fruit picking or digging spuds or whatever everyone did with the rest of the year.

Shearing is hard work, and when you finish for the day, all you want is a bite to eat, a couple of beers and your bed. So there is neither the time or the inclination to get involved with the locals except maybe to say g'day if you see them. We just mind our own affairs and they mind theirs. And time is money for us, so, while the work is there, we get stuck into it and that's that—except if it's raining and the wool is wet or if we're travelling between jobs. We work seven days a week from dawn to dusk. We live together, eat together and drink together. You learn the names of each other's wives and kids, the size of the mortgage on the house—if you've got one—and what sort of a dog everyone's got, even. You come to know them all like your own brother and, by the same token, they come to know you too. I guess you could say that a shearing gang becomes a tight little family that thinks and acts as one. The question, of course, is, "One what?"

A few years ago now, a decent gang would go through just about all the properties in the district. On the small places, there might be a couple of days work here and a few days there, while at the big places, you might be set for a couple of weeks. Nowadays, only the big properties contract for a proper team and the small places mostly do their own or help each other, though in some areas, the graziers, as they like to call themselves, combine and a gang of shearers will shear for a dozen properties in the one shed.

Anyway, we hit this property sometime in September. We'd been there before because, if you're a good, reliable gang, they'll use you every year and you can build yourselves a regular route. It was a good station of a few thousand acres of real nice sheep country. The place was owned and run by a middle-aged widow, a Mrs. McCabe. She ran sheep and some cattle, and she was breeding horses which she was breaking to the saddle to sell in Sydney. She had one permanent hand on the place and he was an old chap who'd been there all his life. He told us that he had first worked as a 'rabbiter' for Mrs. McCabe's grandfather seventy years earlier. He said that they had casual help in for the lambing and for fencing, but that Mrs. McCabe did most of the work herself. She was doing a damn good job.

The station had once been part of a bigger property and there was a decent shearing shed. Mrs. McCabe was pleasant to us, and the shearers quarters were clean and comfortable. We were quite happy to be there.

As I said, it was September and that's school holiday time. Mrs. McCabe had two of her brother's kids staying up at the house with her. There was Mitch, about fourteen years old, and Glen, a year younger. They were from a property outside Walgett, and they were a couple of tough, cheerful country kids who could ride, drive a tractor, round up cattle, chop the wood, and do anything else that needed doing. They knew how a shearing shed was run and they made themselves useful. After work, when they were not larking about or away at the dam having a swim, they would be around the shearers' quarters listening to the yarns that were told with the evening beer. One day the pair of them would be running properties of their own if their father had enough money and, if not, they would be managing places for someone else. We all liked them.

Three or four days of that and another boy arrived. Mrs. McCabe collected him off the bus in Tamworth and brought him back in the ute. He was the son of some old friend of hers who lived in Brisbane, and he had come up for a holiday in the country. He was about twelve and his name was Noel. He was a skinny sort of a kid with a pale face and long hair. He did not know much about country life, and it showed. I don't think he'd ever seen sheep before and he'd never ridden a horse either. At least he tried with the horses, but Mitch and Glen had been riding all their lives and they made the kid look a real beginner which, of course, he was.

Mitch and Glen did not take to him. I expect it was part of the reaction that a lot of country children have for those from the city. They think that the city kids laugh about them and think of them as being a bit thick. So, when that pair had a city boy as raw as Noel on their own home territory, they were contemptuous of him, and they did not bother to hide their views. You could see that Noel wanted to be friends. He told the two of them to call him Ned but they preferred not to call him anything until a day or two later when they reckoned they had summed him up. Then they called him 'Nelly.'

Glen began to take the mickey out of him; the gang laughed. I told myself it was none of my business but I felt sorry for the boy and I hoped he would ask Mrs. McCabe to be sent back to Brisbane where he belonged. Apparently, he said nothing to her though, and he kept on trying to make friends. The brothers began to make his life a misery and, without meaning to be cruel, the gang encouraged them.

Shearers have a reputation for being a rough, hard-living lot and I guess our gang was fairly typical—two real hard cases and none of the rest of us had ever taught Sunday School. We liked Mitch and Glen, and the other boy, Noel, was as alien to us as he was to the brothers.

There had been a shower of rain on the Saturday night and, because we hadn't many sheep under cover, we decided on the Sunday morning not to start shearing until midday or thereabouts. We were lounging around in the shed drinking cups of tea from the big pot on the baize-topped table where we ate, filling in time. Mrs. McCabe told the three boys to give the shed a good broom out and get rid of some of the dust and dirt. Noel was pushing the broom while Mitch and Glen were laughing and horsing about. I could see they were planning something. Next minute, Mitch had grabbed Noel from behind and Glen used an old pair of hand shears to chop off a bit of his long hair. The brothers thought it was funny—and the gang laughed too. Noel's face was white. When the laughing died down a bit he said, "I'll fight both of you outside." Mitch and Glen were taken aback for a moment and then they laughed at him. The shearers were surprised too, but a fight is a fight and Sunday mornings are dull if you're not working.

They did not give the boy time to think better of his rash decision. "Outside," said half-a-dozen voices. "Fight," said someone and the old fellow came through from the back room.

Outside everyone went, down the ramp, and the three boys in front. There was only the yard—hard trampled dirt with no grass and a few sheep milling about in a pen in one corner. The shearers lounged back against the fence rails and lit their cigarettes. "Come on," they said. "Have a go. Have a go."

Noel took off his pullover and rolled up his sleeves to show skinny arms. Mitch looked him over and was not impressed. "I'm not going to fight you, Nelly. You're too little for me. Glen can have you."

Glen grinned cockily and threw his jumper to Johno. Then he stepped forward and squared off. In a moment they were at it, hammer and tongs, as the saying goes. Glen had the reach, and he was fit and the heavier of the two. The gang expected the fight to last about half a minute and they gave Glen noisy encouragement. The kid, Noel, surprised everyone. He just fought, and when Glen gave an inch, he stepped forward. Five minutes and Glen found he had bitten off more than he could chew, and the shearers had stopped their barracking. When Glen went down Noel was onto him—sitting on his chest and bang, bang, bang with knobbly fists. Glen rolled onto his stomach and covered his face. The kid got off him and stood up. No one said anything. "Now you," he said to Mitch. The shearers were silent and the smoke from their cigarettes circled up lazily in the still morning air.

Mitch said, "I'm four inches taller than you, Nelly." The kid hit him in the mouth. Mitch was older, bigger, stronger and he gave the smaller boy a lacing. The only sound was the shuffle of feet and the thud of fist on flesh and the laboured noise of their breathing. The dust from the sheep droppings hung over them like a grey cloud.

When the kid got knocked down for the third time, the cook said, "That'll do. We'll call it all square."

Johno called across, "Had enough, kid?"

The boy shook his head and got up again. There was blood on his face and his shirt was mostly ripped off, but he never took a step backwards and he never stopped fighting. In the end it was Mitch who flopped down onto the sheep dirt. "I've had enough," he said.

One of the shearers clapped but no one joined in. The boy picked up his pullover and turned to go. Johno walked over towards him. "Hey, hold on a minute." The boy turned towards him, but there was no expression on his face. "I'm saying sorry to you, Ned," he said. "You've got more guts than anyone I know, and I reckon we all owe you an apology."

Shamefaced we followed suit. Mitch and Glen shook his hand, and the kid was pleased when they called him 'Ned.' The three of them were good mates after that. Ned—Noel—was just the same as before. There was a difference though. It was in us. We all knew we hadn't given the kid a fair go, and we knew he'd proved himself a better man than any of us.

It's funny but that was the last year that the gang was together. Everyone seemed to wander away. We didn't even finish the season.

A Policeman's Lot

"Hullo! Hullo! Hullo, Beryl! Sorry I'm late down for breakfast. My handcuffs fell into the toilet."

"No, Beryl, you don't have to say, 'Good morning, sergeant.' Yes, I know you are only a police constable and that I am a sergeant, but I keep telling you that we can be informal at home. We are married after all and are, therefore, equal partners off duty. Now, spring to it, Beryl and see what you can furnish in respect of the aforementioned breakfast."

"No, I won't remove my truncheon from the table. In my old training days, we were told never to be separated from our truncheons. Just as well I had it with me on the day of the bikie incident. Did I tell you about that? Oh, I did! Well, I arrived just as this huge bikie was winding up and I could see he was about to go berserk. So I gave him a very light nudge with my truncheon; he tripped on his push bike and knocked himself out. It was then that the other lads began calling me "Thumper"—after the head rabbit in that kids' story, y'know soft and cuddly but really strong and fearless! How we all laughed together over that! They saw me as a cult figure by then, of course."

"Yes, Beryl you may sit down now. Straighten your back, constable—I mean Beryl—your shoulders have slumped, and you've got lint on your uniform. That's the sort of sloppy attitude that will get you an adverse report, my dear!"

"Mmm. The eggs and bacon do look good! Though the tomato looks a bit suspect. Of course, it may have suffered malicious damage in the fruit shop. These days the retail outlets are full of miscreants about their nefarious and unlawful business—spreading moral turpitude among the law-abiding citizenry.

"Perhaps the interests of the other tomatoes would be best served if you were to apprise the fruit shop proprietor of the possible existence of the potential felons already referred to and of their suspected malice and hostility to tomatoes in general. We may have uncovered something here, Beryl. It could be that we are looking at the work of a psychotic tomato hater or even a tomato fetishist."

"Yes, alright, Beryl! I know my eggs will get cold. I think I'll let the tomato resolve its own problems. You are quite right, dear, I am too enthusiastic. But it is difficult to turn off a mind fine-tuned to the detection of crime, a mind in overdrive, so-to-speak. And, speaking of overdrive, I believe we should depart for the stationhouse in about ten minutes, if that meets with your concurrence."

"Perhaps while I am putting on my jacket you could park the vehicle out on the road—which is, of course, a public place and thoroughfare within the meaning of the Act—so that I can shut the garage door. As always, we will proceed in an easterly direction. And remember that the vehicle should be parked not less than three metres from the corner and alongside and parallel to the curb with the front of the said vehicle not obstructing, in any way, direct access to mailboxes and fire hydrants."

"I BEG YOUR PARDON, Beryl! A pox on the aforesaid mailbox? I'm shocked! That's no way for a constable to speak to a sergeant. Were we outside the front door, we would be officially on duty and about our lawful business and subject, therefore, to the obligations thereof in terms of regulation nineteen slash four. And I would have to put you on a charge, Beryl! And, furthermore, your suggestion in regard to the fire hydrant is improper, to say the least. It could be seen as an incitement to a misdemeanour under the Summary Offences Act of 1912 and would probably lead to more serious charges!"

"Hey, stop that, Beryl! You got me in the eye with that tomato! That alleged vegetable might have proved to be an important breakthrough in our endless war against crime. Destruction of evidence can be a serious matter! Ow! Ow! Stop it, Beryl! Ouch! Ouch! Ouch!"

The Great Sedan Chair Robbery

(A whimsy in which some historical licence has certainly been taken.)

It was a typical summer day in seventeenth-century London—intermittent rain, cold and foggy. And it was Friday. So, as he did each week, Mr. Bertram Fogg emerged from the portals of Brown's Gaming and Cards Club for Gentlemen at exactly 9.00 a.m.

Mr. Fogg, the club's manager, had learned to be prepared for eventualities and he carried two identical soft leather bags with leather drawstrings. One contained a mess of torn-up paper and a medium-size river stone and the other, which he kept hidden in a fold of his coat, contained the week's takings from the club of just under two hundred English pounds, some of it in gold sovereigns.

Mr. Fogg paused to examine the weather before taking a pinch of snuff and duly sneezing. He raised a hand displaying four fingers to summon a sedan chair from the rank across the road. The number of fingers indicated his preference for a 'king size,' four-bearer, family model sedan chair as opposed to the two-bearer 'standard' model.

When the sedan chair arrived, Fogg gave a cursory glance at the stalwarts who were to carry him and, as he got in, announced his destination as Figgin's Bank in Carp Street. After seating himself he placed the bag containing the money beneath the bench seat and retained the other one on his lap.

The sedan chair was lifted unevenly, jolting Fogg forward, and he shouted a remonstrative oath to the bearers. They mumbled an apology and set off at a rolling trot that moved the sedan chair along marginally faster than a brisk walk.

Fogg's departure from the club had not been unobserved. Waiting outside on this occasion was one Wee Willie Moody III (WWM to his friends), a small, upwardly mobile businessman in the robbery industry. WWM was a ladies' man and the possessor of bright brown eyes in a round, nut-brown face with an ever-present and cheerful smile. He had watched Fogg emerge from the club and order his transport from a position further down the street where he leaned casually against a railing. He had smiled at the total predictability of Fogg's unchanging routine and, reassured, had taken off by way of a short cut which would enable him to reach an address in Chestnut Street ten minutes or so before Fogg's sedan chair would arrive at that point. The house, which possessed a balcony overlooking the street, was owned by a lady friend of WWM. He intended to leap from that balcony onto the roof of Fogg's conveyance and hold up Bertram Fogg at pistol point.

The business in which WWM was engaged, to wit the robbery of coaches and sedan chairs, had been handed down from his grandfather to his father and, finally, to him, Wee Willie Moody III. Like his father before him, he had been destined for the trade since birth and, as a consequence, his early schooling had been undertaken in ancestral Glasgow, a city with an outstanding reputation for education of those with occupational plans for non-lawful pursuits. Thereafter, WWM III, like his forebears, had robbed the Oxford coach, the Brighton coach, the Bath coach and the Cambridge/Bedford coach together with half a dozen other inner-London coaches and, of course, sedan chairs (which he thought of as minicoaches) and which were often used by people like Fogg to deliver money to banks. Over a period extending through three generations, it is not surprising that coach robbing had become somewhat repetitive for the Moody family and, although he did not realise it, WWM III had also, like Fogg, become a creature of habit.

Because his activities had prospered, WWM III, with other 'Captains of Industry,' had been forced to modernise. After completing a small-business diploma, he invested in time and motion studies, accounts management and workplace incentives which resulted in the re-organisation of the firm's enterprises. Under the new regime, he robbed the Bath coach (for example) every fourth Thursday, the Brighton coach alternate Wednesdays, and so forth. Mr. Fogg had been fitted in for attention every second month; WWM was pleased with the new efficiency.

Recently, the time had come for Wee Willie to withdraw his son, WWM IV, from Harrow, reasoning that, while Harrow had produced a great number of robber barons, there was nothing like on-the-job training. He had originally decided that WWM IV could have the pleasure of robbing Mr. Fogg on the next appropriate Friday, and he had promised a pre-operation briefing.

"Oh, thank you, Pater," WWM IV had said. "'I'm looking forward to it terrifically! Absolutely ripping show!" True to his word, WWM III thoroughly briefed his son on the proposed robbery, taking him through the whole routine step by step. His last duty was to take him around to meet Rachel (an attractive and pliant lady friend) who owned the balcony from which the robbery was to be effected.

Wee Willie III had used the balcony on other occasions and had a mutually satisfactory arrangement with Rachel that involved him arriving early on such days and which gave them the opportunity to fill in the time quite pleasantly. While this part of the plan was not spelled out to WWM IV, the boy had not entirely wasted his time at Harrow and he showed great enthusiasm for that part of the plan.

"I could get here an hour early," he enthused. "Two hours!"

Rachel tried delicately to explain, "Your father, Big Willie and I..."

She was interrupted by the presumptuous youth. "His name is Wee Willie..."

Rachel fixed him with a steely glare. "I should know!" she said.

WWM III had listened to the exchange with growing irritation. He looked at his seventeen-year-old son—his own image, apart from more hair—and changed his mind. "I've been thinking, my boy… that letting you rob old Fogg, this time, might be a bit premature."

He went on to suggest that the lad's resemblance to his father had persuaded him that the boy could better be used to establish an alibi by passing himself off as WWM III and calling on the Bow Street Runners at the time of the robbery!

"They could well have suspicions about me," he said, nodding his head. "I sometimes visit their office in Bow Street to tweak their tails and I've had a funny look or two recently. They have no evidence, mind you, but if you're there pretending to be me at the time of the deed, well, it'll confuse them no end."

WWM would not have been so complacent had he known of developments in nearby Bow Street at the Runners' headquarters. His name had 'come to the attention,' as the saying goes, of the Runners who (at that time) comprised London's rudimentary police force.

The force had been concerned at the endless coach and sedan chair robberies and had tasked Psychological Branch to produce a profile of the type of suspect they should be seeking. To their amazement, the best match among those they had dealings with appeared to be a Mr. Wee Willie Moody, the biggest nuisance to the Runners in all London. This gentleman (the Runners did not call him that) would appear at H.Q. with infuriating frequency to complain about the robberies, the inability of the force to do anything about them and to enquire where their next preventative action was to take place.

In charge of the investigation (Operation Dick Turpin) was Detective (First Class) Ezekiel Jorrocks (one of the force's finest). He was big and strong, black of hair and square of jaw, with quick, pink ferret eyes and one too many chins.

While WWM was certainly on Jorrocks' list, he appeared to be a respectable businessman and, in any case, Jorrocks had no good opinion of the Psychological Branch which he knew to be packed with the Commissioner's useless relatives. Besides, he had a strong lead from a wizened old coachman who remembered seeing the same person in the vicinity of two of the robberies. It had been cold and the person had been dressed in a loud tartan overcoat that had certainly not been bought in Savile Row. Unfortunately, the old coachman had died and Jorrocks thought he had lost the trail but, lo, he happened across just such a garment on the coat rack at a coffee shop in Bobbins Road. Unhappily, the owner departed while Jorrocks was ordering coffee but, with the help of the proprietor, the table used by the gentleman had been identified and Jorrocks had been able to retrieve a piece of black sausage, left on the plate, and on which remained a fingerprint!

The coffee shop proprietor certified the remnant, and it was thereafter enshrined in a glass case which held pride of place on Jorrocks' desk. All that remained, then, was to match the print. The chances of that happening had been greatly enhanced the previous week when a trainee detective, practising with the finger-print equipment, had turned up a matching print in the front office of Bow Street H.Q. itself! Jorrocks and staff planned to begin finger-printing all future visitors beginning in a week or so in the hope that the coach robber, whoever he was, would make another visit.

And then, in an incident which brought several strands of his investigation neatly together, Jorrocks had a revelation. He had been sitting (feet on desk), gazing blankly at a whiteboard over the beginnings of what seemed likely to become a large stomach and on which (the whiteboard, not the stomach) he had recorded details of stage and sedan chair robberies over the last financial year. Unexpectedly, he discerned the glimmer of a pattern. He saw that the robberies were not the random events he had supposed but instead were as predictable as Christmas and Bank Holiday. He ran a shaking finger down the almanac, momentarily chewed at a lip, and then announced excitedly to his cat, "Barker, old girl, the next robbery will occur this Friday about 10.00 a.m. It's all here, by God! It'll be Brown's Gaming and Cards Club's weekly take and that whinging old Fogg… but, this time, I'll be there too!"

Unable to sit still in the light of his momentous discovery, he filled the cat bowl with Meaty Bitz from a packet he kept in a desk drawer and departed whistling. It is noteworthy, here, that Jorrocks had always wanted a dog so that he could call it after Hamilcar Barca, father of the great Carthaginian general, Hannibal, whom he held in high esteem. Someone had given him a cat but he had called her Barker anyway; she showed no resentment, however, and, as you will see, will have the opportunity to play a vital role in the events that were unfolding.

*

At 9.00 a.m. on the Friday, WWM IV arrived at Bow Street to give his father an alibi. He pushed open the door, taking pleasure in letting in a draft of cold air and a swirl of leaves.

He wore an overcoat and scarf—partly to keep out the chill and partly to disguise his youthful features. On his head was a shiny topper (left over from Harrow) tipped forwards.

A pudding-faced young Runner, sitting at a desk, put down the quill pen he had been using to pick his teeth. "G'mornin', sir?"

WWM IV deepened his voice and gave the counter a thump with a closed fist. "As a citizen and ratepayer, I have come to complain about the number of coach and sedan chair robberies and I demand to know when you are going to catch those responsible!"

The young Runner sat forward eagerly. He knew that a Mr. Wee Willie Moody was a suspect and, like everyone else, sought to impress by implying a greater knowledge than he possessed. "Well, sir," he said unctuously, "you will be pleased to hear that we expect an arrest this very day. We think we know the perpetrator—or 'perp,' as we call them in the trade. In strict confidence the villain's name is Wee Willie Moody and he seems to have cornered the coach and sedan chair robbery market. And, I might add, he's a very ugly and nasty piece of work!"

WWM took exception to the slur on his father and his eyes flashed. "I say there, that's my pater you're maligning!" Fortunately, the Runner had not had a Harrow education and did not know what a pater was or what maligning meant either, so he ignored the interruption.

"Our own Detective Jorrocks expects to catch this Moody fellow in the very act and"—he pulled a fob watch from a pocket and examined it—"he should be making the arrest within the hour!" Then the Runner went on to tell WWM IV about the tartan overcoat and the fingerprint. WWM listened. He was very glad he had not given his name. He knew that overcoat! He struggled for inner calm as the Runner pointed to Jorrocks' desk and the glass case holding the incriminating piece of sausage.

WWM IV realised that there was a strong likelihood of his father's next visit to Bow Street being in a different capacity from the one he usually adopted. He was shocked and suddenly full of trepidation; but then he remembered that his father had never been caught and took heart. He tipped his topper forward a trifle to shade his face, thanked the Runner for his help, and made a dignified exit.

Once outside, however, WWM IV's short-lived confidence evaporated. Things had gone very wrong! He had not been able to provide the alibi his father had expected and, in fact, he had discovered that the Runners knew far more about his father's activities than WWM III would have believed possible. How did they obtain the fingerprint on the sausage? How did they know that Fogg was to be robbed that very morning? WWM IV shivered. The more he thought about it, the less he liked it and the more he worried about doing nothing while his father continued to act as if he had not a care in the world.

Passing a butcher's shop, he came to his senses and the cunning bred into generations of Moodys re-asserted itself. He entered the shop, purchased a piece of black sausage about the same size as the piece he had seen on Jorrocks' desk and asked the butcher to examine its quality. In so doing he obtained a good thumb print! He then returned to Bow Street H.Q.

Peering through the window, he could see the young Runner, feet on desk, and still picking his teeth with the pen. WWM IV picked up a cobblestone and threw it through the skylight, visible at the rear of the Runners' premises. There was a sound of breaking glass, and a glance through the window showed the young Runner's chair slam to the floor as that gentleman activated himself. As he scurried off to investigate, WWM entered through the front door. He removed the piece of sausage from the glass case, fed it to Barker the cat (who had been dozing on the window ledge—and, as it happened, dreaming of black sausage), placed the new piece of sausage in the case and departed.

*

WWM arrived at 14 Chestnut Street. He paused at the door to gather his thoughts. He had no concerns at the prospect of robbing Fogg—after all, it was only another day at the office!

The view he held of his professional activities was tinged with romanticism and nostalgia. The feeling that he was upholding a tradition was central to his thoughts and a consequence of experiences during his formative years.

Those Wild West movies he had watched at the Saturday matinees at the Odeon Theatre in Glasgow—the masked men in their black cowboy hats dropping from a tree branch onto the roof of the Tombstone stagecoach... the mandatory fight with the stagecoach driver... the sheriff and his posse intercepting the fleeing robbers at the pass... The similarity with robbing stagecoaches and sedan chairs in London was inescapable. "Nothing changes," he thought and breathed a sigh at treasured memories.

And any suggestion that movies had not been invented in those days would have brought a very stiff rebuttal from WWM. "Films," he would have said dismissively, "were developed in Glasgow before Hollywood had even been stolen from the Indians. And as for cowboys, why"—he would have affirmed—"the Highlands have been full of cowboys since Bonny Prince Charlie! And dear old Glasgow had its share of villains, even if they all wore two-pint tam o'shanters instead of black ten-gallon Stetsons!"

He looked up at the balcony. "And here I am," he soliloquised. "From that spot I will shortly hurl my small but perfect body onto the roof of the thundering Tombstone stage!"

His imagination soared: "Soon it will swing around the corner... uh, through the pass, I mean... drawn by four black stallions and pursued by masked outlaws intent on stealing the gold being delivered from the mine to the McWells and McFargo bank in Edinburgh! No doubt the driver, old Fogg in this case, is lashing the horses to further efforts while, simultaneously, and at the same time, firing off a shotgun over his shoulder... BOOOM!... and one of the outlaws bites the dust—in this case, mud!"

WWM III disappeared inside and, on this occasion, cut his entertainment to a mere five minutes (claims were made of a headache). He re-appeared thereafter on the balcony, declaiming to the quite voluptuous Rachel (and, to himself), "So here I am, the famous Wee Willie Moody III, daring coach and sedan chair robber, ready for yet another intrepid feat. Admired by all, sought after by the bumbling sheriffs and rangers, but in vain!" He mounted a small stool behind the balustrade without really pausing in his monologue. If Rachel had been listening to him, she was no longer in evidence.

"Ladies and gentlemen," he orated, "you are about to witness the gallant and fearless Wee Willie Moody perform a death-defying leap onto the roof of the Tombstone stage, which is transporting one, Bertram Fogg—a perfidious and wealthy saloon gambler, despoiler of women and forecloser of mortgages. From him"—he paused for breath—"from him I will wrest the gold he has stolen from the poor and downtrodden for re-distribution to the needy—namely me!"

The sedan chair turned the corner, interrupting WWM's flight of fancy. He raised a licked finger to estimate wind speed and, after using the 'V' between thumb and forefinger to judge the angle of the jump, threw a leg over the balcony. Idly, he turned over a few thoughts as he waited. "When leaping from the balcony, show teeth in a devil-may-care smile to impress Rachel. Also throw out chest, hold stomach in, and land lithely for benefit of any interested party!"

WWM arrived on Fogg's sedan chair with a thump. He carried credentials with which to introduce himself in the form of a loaded pistol. The bearers flinched a trifle at the sudden additional weight. "Must've just eaten his morning sandwich," surmised one of them. But there was no animus in the remark for they knew from experience that Fogg would pay them adequately.

With some difficulty, WWM wrenched his mind back to the task in hand. He donned a black mask taken from a pocket, seated himself carefully, and then hammered on the roof of the sedan chair with both fists.

"Hullo in there, Fogg. It's me again! Your friendly neighbourhood dispossessor." WWM used fingers on the roof to imitate a drum roll. "You, my friend, are about to be pillaged by the coach and sedan chair robber extraordinaire to the crowned heads of Europe."

Fogg, however, apprised of WWM's arrival by the thud on the roof and the scrabbling noise as his visitor sorted himself out, moved quickly. He took the leather bag containing the money and pushed it beneath the seat. Then, from the folds of his coat, he withdrew the duplicate bag containing the rock and the paper and placed it on the seat beside him.

Mr. Fogg answered his guest. "I know you're up there, you noisy little Scottish pillock. I recognise the voice. But we'll see about the 'extraordinaire.'"

"Well then," replied WWM loudly. "Hand over the money and let's get on with the rest of the day. I've got a dentist's appointment at eleven!"

Fogg was unfazed. "You're up on the roof, you little berk—and I'm content to keep it that way." Quickly, he pulled the latch holding up the window blind and then repeated the process on the other side of the sedan chair.

WWM drew his pistol and leaned over the side of the vehicle preparatory to inserting it into Fogg's ear. He got an excellent view of the blind and nothing else. Reluctantly, he settled himself on the roof as a prelude to implementing Plan B.

Bertram Fogg, meanwhile, had begun implementing his own Plan A. Drawing a double-barrel pistol from his coat pocket, and cocking it, he fired—one after the other—both barrels.

The first shot sent a ball of lead up through the roof. It travelled parallel to Wee Willie's spine and about a finger breadth from it; the ball punched a hole through the back of Wee Willie's hat brim, pushing it forward over his eyes. The second ball pierced the roof between his parted legs. This time, the ball passed so close to a vital and valued piece of Wee Willie's anatomy that the organ referred to, like a frightened kitten, retreated into the innermost recesses of Wee Willie's pelvis. There, in fact, it remained for three days despite all blandishments of its owner including the offer of half a tin of cat food left temptingly nearby.

The would-be robber thereafter sat nervously on the roof of the sedan chair (sphincter clenched), while it travelled over the cobbles at a brisk walking pace. He had not fired his own pistol (and, indeed, had not expected to), but he knew that, inside, Bertram Fogg would be feverishly re-loading his own state-of-the-art double banger. He knew too that, in short order, he was likely to be the recipient of an ounce or two of lead in the tripes.

WWM leaned carefully over the edge of the conveyance to check the other window, but it was shut. He sat down again, exasperated and aggrieved.

WWM's morning was being spoiled. "Bloody hell," he thought, "those Wild West movies made it all look so easy! But there's always bloody problems." He raised his voice. "You're wasting my valuable time, Fogg. And it was jolly unsporting of you to fire at a sitting bird!"

"Open season on gaolbirds, old cock," was Fogg's cheerful rejoinder. "And I hope it's not raining out there because I'm about to puncture the roof again—and you too, if I'm lucky!"

Appalled at the thought, WWM leaped to his feet. The roof of the sedan chair, however, had been constructed of light material sufficient only to keep out the weather, and he fell through it to land untidily on the seat opposite Fogg.

Elated at his change of fortune, WWM aimed his pistol and Fogg, with seeming reluctance, relinquished his pistol and the leather bag from alongside him, deep dejection on his face.

"Well, now," Wee Willie said. "You may stop the coach and I'll get off. And you can tell the sheriff who—as is traditional, will appear too late—that the masked man has foiled him yet again and has vowed never to be taken alive!"

Fogg, only too happy to comply, had opened his mouth to give the command that would relieve him of WWM's company, together with the bag of paper and the river stone, when there was a development.

A shot sounded in the distance and an almost-spent pistol ball thudded against the back wall of the sedan chair. There was a noticeable increase in speed, initiated by the suddenly galvanised rear bearers. "Faster, faster!" came their plaintive lament.

Neither Fogg nor Wee Willie were hit but the latter dropped to his knees in order to lessen the likelihood of that occurring. Looking between Fogg's feet, he espied another leather bag.

"Oh ho!" Wee Willie forgot about the danger of being shot. "So there's a real bag and a fake bag?" He pulled the new bag towards him, keeping Fogg covered with his own pistol. A quick glance apprised him of its contents.

"You rotten crook," he said, horrified at Fogg's duplicity. Then, back on his feet and holding the bag with the money in one hand, he leaned out of the window. Behind the sedan chair, and following it at a brisk trot, came four uniformed Runners in tight formation. They were led by Acting Detective (First Class) Ezekiel Jorrocks, who had intended catching the robber much earlier but who had got lost on the way to Mr. Fogg's club.

"God a'mighty, it's a bloody posse," said Wee Willie. "I might've known there'd be one!" He aimed Fogg's pistol above their heads and fired both barrels. "After consideration," he added, "I have decided to stay aboard!"

WWM took a moment to reassess the situation. His face was troubled, but he was not about to give up. "I think we'll lose them on this next hill. And, just over the crest, there's a lane off to the right that we'll use."

To his concern, the bearers slowed to a walk at the slope, and he breathed a gusty sigh of relief as the Runners too dropped back to a plod at the incline.

Two more pistol shots were fired by the Runners, and Fogg was relieved when Wee Willie called, "Hard a' starboard," to the bearers as they reached the turn-off.

They swung into the lane and the bearers jogged a dozen steps, blowing like grampuses. Then they lowered the sedan chair to the ground and, as one, took off at a fast clip.

"It feels as if we've got a flat tyre!" Wee Willie observed. He looked out the window and noted that the sedan chair had run aground and that the crew had deserted.

"Gawd," he exclaimed, aghast. "Come out here, quick, Mr. Fogg," and he gestured with the pistol. Fogg emerged just in time to see the Runners trot past the head of the lane, gathering speed as they hit the downslope.

"Mr. Fogg," Wee Willie reflected civilly, "I suspect that I'm in trouble. I thought that we could elude them, but the Runners are going to wake up in a minute that we are no longer ahead of them, and they will come back."

Mr. Fogg nodded affably.

"So, I will be caught, Mr. Fogg, sentenced and possibly sent to Australia as a convict and felon." Mr. Fogg nodded agreeably.

"But," Wee Willie spoke with less civility, "your employer won't be too amused at you being robbed again, will he? No, it will probably mean your job, Mr. Fogg."

"I'll just make myself scarce, then," affirmed Fogg. "You ain't going to shoot me and I'll think up something to tell them." He stepped back and fell over the handles of the sedan chair and wrenched his ankle.

"Goodness gracious," Wee Willie commiserated. He exuded concern: "Maybe we can help each other! I'll give you back your money"—and he passed over the leather bag—"and I'll tell the Runners that you and I were in the sedan chair when an argument developed between the bearers and several drunken layabouts and that they all took off down to the next corner where there was more room to fight."

At that moment, the Runners appeared at the corner. Fogg looked at WWM and hefted the leather bag. Slowly, he pursed his lips and then nodded agreement. "Yes, my employer would not be amused."

WWM wasted no time. He threw away his mask and dropped his firearms into a drain. He picked up two marble-size stones and gave them a quick wipe on his sleeve. "Part of my disguise," he told Fogg. One he put in his shoe to give him a good limp and the other he put in his mouth. The bulge in one cheek distorted his face and, thereafter, he had much difficulty speaking.

And it was WWM III who confronted the Runners. Jorrocks, while he knew of Mr. W.W. Moody, had not met him and when, as requested, the suspect gave his name, Jorrocks was not able to guess how it should be spelled. Nor could Jorrocks resolve whether he should be delighted to have captured the stagecoach robber or, as the story unfolded, whether there had, somehow, been a mistake. He listened to WWM's story, with considerable difficulty, and a great deal of scepticism, but Fogg—with his own employment prospects in mind—supported the story and, here and there, even embellished it!

Realising that he was getting nowhere, Jorrocks reached a decision. "Alright," he said at last, and he placed a hand on WWM's shoulder, "for a start, you're under arrest… though I'm not quite sure for what, at the moment. We'll take you back to Bow Street for interrogation while you, Mr. Fogg, are free to go for the present. I'm not happy, mind—no, I'm not happy at all! And I may need to call you again!"

Fogg, relieved, pointed out that his bank was nearby and that he would repair there without further ado to complete his business. He took leave quickly and hobbled off.

WWM's gammy leg ("an old war-wound earned in the service of the Queen at the Battle of Sebastapol," he told Jorrocks) caused him so much trouble getting into the sedan chair that the Runners had to lift him in with much cursing and exertion; nevertheless, they eventually completed the task and locked the door. So, as the bearers were nowhere to be found, a reluctant and suspicious Jorrocks decided that the only way to get their prisoner back to Bow Street was for the Runners to serve as bearers.

Thus, it was that an embarrassed foursome of Runners set off back down the hill, retracing their steps to H.Q., where, Jorrocks told himself, he was going to extract the truth from his captive (Mr. Wiwmilmodiz?) by means legal or illegal!

WWM sat comfortably inside, hoping it would rain on the Runners, pondering his prospects. As he did so he fondled the twenty sovereigns he had been able to extract from the bag before he returned it to Fogg.

He looked out the window, wondering idly what it would be like in Botany Bay and whether he would ever get the chance to rob the Tumba-bloody-Rumba coach on its way to Wagga Wagga!

The Runners swung around a corner and WWM sat forward, senses suddenly alert. They had turned into Chestnut Street and, further down the road, he could see Rachel's balcony from which he had leaped not long before. He looked up at the hole in the roof through which he had earlier fallen and made a decision.

He spat out the stone that had provided his facial disguise, pulled off his shoe and, after discarding the stone that had given him the limp, slipped it on again.

They had almost reached the balcony when WWM acted. He stood on the seat, head and shoulders through the hole in the roof, and tossed the twenty sovereigns so that they landed at the feet of the Runners before rolling off in all directions. The Runners, seeing the coins, dropped their burden to scramble over the cobblestones. It was regrettable that even the redoubtable Detective Jorrocks succumbed to greed and chased the coins as eagerly as his men. WWM climbed through the hole and stood on the roof. He reached up, pulled himself onto the balcony and disappeared inside No. 14.

*

WWM IV had been very worried about WWM III to the extent that he decided to retrace his father's planned route in case he could be of assistance.

He was surprised, therefore, to see a sedan chair coming towards him in Chestnut Street. He then watched, with increasing astonishment, as the four bearers dropped the chair and ran in all directions to scrabble in the gutters. Yet another wonder unfolded as he watched his father rise through the roof of the vehicle, like Venus from the waves, ascend the balcony and vanish. It was almost a religious experience! WWM IV, however, immediately deduced that his father was escaping from custody.

He broke into a run and arrived at the scene as the Runners finished retrieving what coins they could find and were realising that their prisoner had escaped.

Jorrocks' face was apoplectic. WWM IV addressed him. "Sir," he said respectfully, "I saw your wretched prisoner escape and, with your permission, sir, I think I'm quick enough to follow the fellow and, perhaps, apprehend him! Give me a minute or two…"

With that he leaped onto the sedan chair, up to the balcony of No. 14, and vanished inside. He ran down the hall, noticing that his father was in bed with Rachel, down the back steps and into the tiny yard. From there it was out the gate, left down the lane, left again at the first corner and out into Chestnut Street.

The Runners were still arguing among themselves where he had left them. "Quick! Quick!"

WWM IV called at the top of his voice. "He's gone down the back lane. Hurry! Hurry! We can cut him off on the next block before he reaches the crowds in Fleet Street and is lost."

The urgency projected by WWM IV galvanised the Runners and they took off after him as he turned back into the laneway. Wee Willie kept ahead of them, maintaining his exhortations for their utmost endeavour, and managed to harry the Runners to exhaustion.

Eventually, the posse reached Fleet Street but found no sign of the escapee. Wee Willie and the Runners stood in a little circle, red-faced and panting. Wee Willie recovered first an addressed Detective Jorrocks. "At least I got a good look at him, sir! He's taller than I am with lots of hair!" Knowing his father's standby disguises he continued confidently. "And he has a bad limp which I suggest is the result of a misplaced scapula bone in his left leg." (He had sat for a biology exam in his last term at Harrow and had failed but saw no reason to restrict his diagnosis on that account!)

Jorrocks looked at WWM with increasing interest. He was impressed! "And," Wee Willie added, "he had a lump on the side of his upper-right jawbone. I could sketch him, and you could have a flyer out on him in no time… I'd offer a small reward and he'll be back in custody in an hour or two! Furthermore, he speaks English poorly and I think I detected a Swedish accent!"

Jorrocks was *very* impressed! "Detected is indeed the word, young man—and I believe that it is an excellent detective you'd make! I'm offering you a position as Apprentice Detective with the Runners. It's a great opportunity for rapid promotion in an expanding business—never likely to be a shortage of crime, is there? Ha, ha!"

Wee Willie had already come to the conclusion that stagecoach robberies might be getting too dangerous a profession and the suggestion that he become a detective appealed. "Father will be pleased," he thought wryly. "His only son fully employed hunting villains." He accepted.

Jorrocks gave him no time to muse further. "And what's your name then?"

WWM IV started to say, "W… W…" but he was a quick-witted youth, and he finished the word without pause. "William," he said firmly (mind ticking over desperately), "William Little." (Thus establishing a new dynasty!)

"Right, then, Junior Detective W. Little, welcome to the Runners," said Jorrocks, clapping the new recruit on the back. "Superannuation will start immediately, Worker's Compensation will apply plus generous annual leave, sick leave, motherhood leave and time off for prostate operations after you've been with us for a while."

After becoming a junior detective with the Runners, William Little moved quickly to deal with loose ends. He confiscated WWM III's tartan overcoat (and destroyed it) and persuaded his father that retirement was better than transportation to Australia, even if it was quite nice at Bondi Beach in the summer. And he sought out Mr. Bertram Fogg and repaid, with sufficient interest to settle ruffled feathers, the twenty sovereigns that WWM III had stolen.

He lost no time in putting the new skills Jorrocks was teaching him into practice: he removed the butcher's thumb print from the black sausage in the glass case and replaced it with one of Jorrocks'. The glass case disappeared next day and William Little, on his way to his desk, did happen to notice Barker, the cat, enjoying something that looked very like black sausage.

No more was ever heard of Wee Willie Moody—whoever he was!

There is a footnote to this story: WWM III, to fill in the time after his enforced retirement, decided to write the family history.

He discovered that his Scottish ancestors had been so prominent (and pestiferous) among the cross-border raiders that an early English monarch was said to have remarked that the Moodys had "irritated like a flea in his codpiece."

Buoyed by this compliment from the Royal Family, WWM III sought approval for the granting of a family coat-of-arms and sent an illustration of his suggested design based upon the King's words.

The official reaction to that request was such that WWM's descendant, WWM IV, opted for a swift departure to Australia, where he decided to adopt a new Christian name and family occupation, thus bringing the noble WWM line to closure.

Lucky Sam

This is the story of an underprivileged youth whose faith in himself enabled him to rise from the bottom of the heap to, well, if not the top, at least the top of the bottom.

The morning sun bathed the small room with light. Sam stretched, luxuriating in the warmth. "Lucky Sam," he thought, and smiled.

Sam's room lacked even basic amenities and, furthermore, seeing it was on the fifth floor of a building with no lift and that he was confined to a wheelchair, there were those who may have believed that the place had its drawbacks. His eyes, however, glistened with perpetual appreciation of the few minutes of sunshine that his room received on three days each year (providing those days were not wet).

Sam, a pygmy, had been born in Africa. He was also an albino, a condition that ensured endless sunburn. "Lucky ol' me," he would tell himself. "Better than frostbite!"

He was also very deaf and wholly dumb, ailments which were not helped by his blindness. He had, however, been taught to write at the mission school using a pencil held between the toes of his right foot (did I tell you that he couldn't hold a pencil because of bad elbows?). Unfortunately, the mission was unaware that Sam was left-handed and therefore, left footed. Ah well!

It will not surprise, then, that Sam did not have an active social life. Nevertheless, he saw his own problems as trifling and remained cheerful; he felt guilty at his own good fortune as compared with that of others.

An incident illustrative of Sam's attitude to life occurred when Sam was standing beside the great, greasy Limpopo River watching the crocodiles. His crutches, riddled by white ants, collapsed precipitating him into the water to roars of laughter from the villagers. Sam re-surfaced, smiling beatifically. "O, ha ha," he thought, "I must be blessed to be able to amuse my fellows without being vulgar!"

One of the missionaries, laid up with a disease that missionaries are not supposed to catch, instituted a conversation with Sam.

"What is your dearest wish?" he asked in Swahili, tapping out the words in Morse on Sam's noggin.

"Beg pardon," wrote Sam with his foot, using a Bantu dialect. The missionary repeated his query.

"To get rid of my acne!"

"Brave little fellow," wrote the missionary on Sam's bonce. "We'll send you to Australia… there's a place in Wagga Wagga that makes the Mayo Clinic look Third World!"

Sam was packed off to Australia for doctors to look at his acne and maybe stretch him a little. He was delighted as it would give him the opportunity to fulfil his ambition of becoming a concert pianist and play at Carnegie Hall. He also suspected that an albino might be better off in Australia.

Sam was confined to a wheelchair and the Welfare Officer visited with food and Braille lessons. When he did not appear for five days, Sam was concerned. After nine days, he was hungry and after eleven, ravenous. The smell of new-baked bread from the Wagga Wagga bakery decided him. He did not realise that the Welfare Officer had died and that it would be months before a successor was appointed. It was a stroke of luck for Sam.

He decided to visit the bakery and buy two sticky-buns to tide him over. He locked the flat and, after feeling his way along the hall, arrived with his wheelchair at the top of the stairs.

Five floors! But, if he were very careful, and kept a firm grip on the banister. Like so! BUMP! Then BUMP, BUMP, BUMP! The ten flights were traversed in a flash with Sam's wheelchair ricocheting off the walls in the comers. He shot through the door into the busy street. He felt fresh air on his face and swung the wheelchair in the direction of the glorious aroma.

Despite his disabilities, Sam did not lack confidence, and he proceeded at speed, rattling his stick along the buildings and passersby to get his bearings. Little did he know he was about to pass the premises of Finkelstein and Son, manufacturers of the famous Finkelstein grand pianos and that, long drawn to that instrument by some inner force, he was about to become inextricably involved with that company.

By an oversight, the basic components of the Finkelstein piano were assembled on the ground floor of the factory. The next process took place on the first floor and so on until the finished pianos—objects of great beauty—were finalised on the eighth floor. The building was old and had only a small passenger lift. It was necessary, therefore, for Finkelstein senior and son Abdul to lower completed pianos, prior to their dispatch, to the footpath using a block and tackle.

On this occasion, Finkelstein senior, an old gentleman of eighty-seven, let go of the rope to scratch his bottom at the very moment Sam was rolling down the street, virtually out of control—and heading for a busy junction. The beautiful piano, its walnut panels and ivory keys shining in the morning sun, fell from the sky. It landed on the front of Sam's wheelchair, breaking both his legs.

Sam was doubly appreciative of his good luck when young Finkelstein (who had hurried down in the lift) told him that the accident had been fortuitous because Sam would surely have been run over by a bus at the next intersection.

"I am sorry," said young Finkelstein, "it slipped!"

Sam decided to write a note in Braille saying, "Apology accepted… anyone can make a mistake…" Something along those lines. But when he felt for his writing materials, he realised he had left them at home. Unable to pen a 'thank-you' note, but in order to express his gratitude, Sam nodded his head vigorously. To his astonishment, the sudden movement of his head dislodged the brain cell which had been responsible for cutting off his vision for all those nineteen years.

Suddenly Sam could see! Overcome with joy he held out his wristwatch and read the time. "Nine twenty-four," he thought. "I could have sworn it was later."

His joy was marked by sadness, however, as he realised that he would never get his money back on the Braille lessons. Nevertheless, it was a day he would never forget because his favourite team, the Walruses, were that day to beat the Penguins in the play-off for fourth place in the local under-sixteen stickball competition.

Young Abdul Finkelstein was impressed by Sam's manly demeanour and had noted the flow of emotions over the lad's strangely coloured face. Correctly interpreting Sam's longing look at the remnants of the piano, he offered him a job. Sam twinkled both eyes gratefully and intimated pleasure by signs and twitches and that he would start work next day providing his legs were better. He also advised that, although he supported Home Rule for Ireland, he remained an Episcopalian at heart.

Sam reported for work as promised. His legs had not quite healed, but he made light of splintered bone poking through his socks and adopted a devil-may-care attitude that won him respect and affection from his workmates.

By midday, he had fathomed the intricacies of piano-making and offered a suggestion—attach four castors to the bottom of the piano instead of the customary two! With a few deft signs and movements from his now-functioning eyes, he conveyed his idea to the management.

"Yes," said Finkelstein senior slowly, and then, enthusiastically, "YES! With four castors we will be able to push them whichever way!"

Sam was promoted and his salary tripled, a move which brought him into contact with Esmeralda, a young Spanish girl of thirty-nine who worked in the kitchen. The pair got on famously and she taught Sam tricks learned as a cook and others from an earlier profession. Many the wink, wink, nudge, nudge brought guffaws from their workmates. Their friendship blossomed and Sam found it easy to overlook her small peccadilloes (he preferred large ones); he winked at her suggestively in Spanish, drawing cries of "Ole!" and "Barcelona!"

Abdul Finkelstein learned of Sam's ambition and noted his long fingers. "Potentially a master pianist," he decided.

Next day, it took two minutes to discover that Sam was about as musical as the office cat, so that was that. As recompense, Abdul appointed him foreman of the Piano Wire section.

"My cup runneth over," Sam told himself!

Sam's rapid rise in the firm had attracted the notice of Abdul's sister, Fatima. She gave Sam opportunities in the soft-pedal room which had an inside lock.

Sam had become firm and nubile and, although Fatima's white skin reminded him of wet tripe, she was the boss's daughter. When Esmeralda discovered his turpitude (which is a nice way of saying he was also getting it elsewhere), she was annoyed.

She found him dozing in his wheelchair, a lecherous smile on his face. Enraged, she grasped its handles and ran it across the room and into the wall. Sam was catapulted from his seat and his head punched a hole through the bricks which, luckily, were painted buttercup yellow, a colour he liked.

Painfully, Sam withdrew his head from the cavity. "Godamighty!" He smiled querulously. "What bloody idiot did that?" He pushed himself up the wall and, to his astonishment, stood unaided. He clasped his hands and gazed ceilingwards. "Lordy," he said in a ringing voice, "you've done it again!"

He turned to discover Esmeralda and addressed her with his new voice: "Your assault seems to have shoved all my vertebrae back into alignment! Thank you. D'you want to buy a wheelchair? Cheap? And, furthermore, I am suddenly able to speak. He's cured my hearing too. That other brain cell must've been jarred loose from its lair in my frontal lobe!"

Sam's brown eyes were lambent with emotion. He spoke again, "Sorry for the interruption, LORD, you've done me proud and I'm sure I've had my share of good fortune. Thanks a bunch, and let me know if I can do anything for you. Over and out!"

Now that Sam's faculties were in order, he was able at last to defend himself in the cut and thrust of married life and there was nothing to delay his marriage to Fatima. He gave his collection of rabbits' feet, wheelchairs, hearing aids etc. to Esmeralda for her church bazaar and she, reconciled to Sam's nuptials, served as flower girl and best man.

Eventually, Sam became a partner in the firm and extremely wealthy. Increasingly, as he aged, his mind returned to those dear, happy days by the waters of the grey, greasy Limpopo and his multitude of tribal friends.

Before the end, he commissioned the building of a two-hundred-bed clinic on the spot where his crutches broke so long ago and precipitated him into the crocodile-infested water. The tribe had gathered to see and hear one of their number who had made good in the outside world; their nakedness contrasted sharply with Sam's exquisitely tailored suit (in which he was sweating profusely).

Slowly, Sam mounted the podium and held up a gnarled old hand of indeterminate colour.

"I dedicate this clinic," he said, using the Bantu sub-dialect of his forebears, "in grateful memory of times long past"—his voice strengthened, carrying even to those at the very back of the throng—"to assist my fellow pygmies who, like myself, were born deaf, dumb, blind and albino, with bad elbows."

Educating the Kid

I am sitting on the wooden verandah of the pub with Stoo, having a beer. Two steps away, beyond the shade, the sun is beating down on dusty asphalt. It is about forty degrees out there. The beer is cold and there is a film of moisture on my glass.

We are sitting comfortably, not talking, when the taxi pulls up in front of us. Who should get out but the kid and we all knew where he had been. When he saw me, he turned away to get his bag. Stoo picked up his glass from the rickety table between us. "Hey, kid!" he said. The kid looked up and went red. I could see the sweat on his forehead and his eyes crinkle up. "D'you want a run at the weekend?" Stoo added. I couldn't believe my ears and then the kid sort of straightened up.

"Yeah, I'd like to, thanks," and he walked past us into the pub.

Stoo looked at me and winked. I didn't say anything because Stoo wasn't likely to give me an answer. He is no talker. He says what needs to be said and does what needs to be done and that's it.

Stoo is forty-three—not tall but big around the chest, red-faced with cropped hair, going grey. He is a good bit older than me and he kept me out of trouble until I got enough sense to keep myself out, so I made a point of taking notice of what he said. I'm not too old to learn.

Taking the kid out again was beyond me. I still feel guilty for dragging him along last time. I would have thought a bust on the nose would have been better.

The trouble with the kid started a couple of weeks back and it was my fault. Stoo and I run a funeral parlour. There is not a lot doing in our line of business in a small town and, on the side, I cart wood, run a book on the city races, and help out in the bakery. Stoo and I are keen fishermen and we head out every Friday afternoon about four and we're on the river before seven ready to fish until dusk on Sunday. We take Stoo's panel van, as the only wheels I have are on my half of the hearse. There is a weatherboard shack by the river with a wood-fire stove and a couple of bunks.

Stoo knows the owner of the property and he has a key for the gate which is kept locked to keep the shooters out. There is never anyone else there as the place is way out in the sticks and the owner spends his time in Sydney. The few sheep that graze on the hills running up from the river look after themselves.

The river is a beauty—big deep pools edged with eucalypt and casuarinas, joined by white water, and the fat rainbows and browns fight for our lures. I have a deal going with the barber, and the fish I take back usually keeps me in cigarettes for the week. Stoo uses his for trade at the pub and the travelling salesmen stay there because there is always trout on the menu.

Stoo and I are mates and we like to be off on our own when we are not working. He took his brother from Wagga with us once but it didn't work out and, since then, we knock back anyone who asks us.

There is this kid in town, about seventeen, and he's keen on fishing. His old man runs the pub and I cart wood for him often enough. The kid had been at me for months to take him fishing and I had always put him off. A couple of weeks back he laid the word on me at the right moment, so I put it to Stoo and he said yes. I knew 'yes' meant that we would give the kid a run and that would square us for the time he took his brother. I told the kid to be ready at four and to bring a bit of tucker.

On the Thursday, an old codger who did a bit of rabbit trapping out on Goonya Station up and died. Mrs. Mullins from the post office passed a message on Friday morning that his boss would pay for the funeral and would we collect the body. As it happened, the hearse was having its brakes done, so we went out after lunch in the panel van to collect him. The van was packed up ready for the fishing trip and we had two containers in the back full of ice for the fish; the manager of the iceworks owed me a few favours. We got a puncture on the way back and it was four o'clock when we hit town again. The kid was standing outside the pub with his rod and a rucksack, so we stopped to pick him up. He put his gear on the coffin in the back and got in with us. Stoo did not bother asking me—he took the road for the river: neither of us liked being on the track to the hut after dark as there were washaways, wombat holes and other hazards. We were keen to get in while the light was good.

As a matter of fact, we had taken a body with us before and we reckoned that the deceased might well enjoy a last fishing trip. What the relatives did not know would not hurt them!

We reached the shack at dusk and started off-loading the van.

"What did you bring the coffin for?" the kid asked.

Stoo was casual. "We keep our grog in there," he said. The kid gave a grin and started dragging out his rucksack. The strap caught the lid of the coffin and pulled it sideways. We had not screwed the top down and the kid let out a yell when he saw the old codger lying there. He jumped back and fell over my kit-bag. Over the edge of the track he went and I could hear him rolling down through the scrub. When he got back, his face was white.

"That's old Griffiths who snuffed it out at Goonya."

Stoo told him that old Griff was alright where he was and that we had plenty of ice around him. The kid was upset, and I thought he might have knocked his head on a rock when he went over.

We got him inside and got the fire going and water on for a brew. The kid dug some cocoa out of his bag and some little cakes his mum had made him, and he ate those. He seemed to pick up after he got that lot down and he was telling jokes in a loud voice and laughing at all of them.

We let him carry on. We decided not to fish that evening and that we would make an early start in the morning.

About ten the fire was dying down and I said I'd turn in. The kid asked whether we were going to bring the old bloke inside and Stoo told him no and that no one was going to pinch him from us. When we were in bed the kid kept on telling jokes until Stoo told him to shut up.

An hour or two later, I woke up. The kid was having a nightmare and he was talking in his sleep and throwing himself about. I got up and woke him and went back to bed. The wind was coming up outside and a branch was banging on the roof. There was a dingo howling in the scrub somewhere. I hoped it was not working up to a storm as the trout seem to sulk when there is thunder, and they won't take anything but maybe woodgrubs on the bottom. I don't like to do my fishing sitting down.

I was no sooner asleep than all hell broke loose. The kid was it again and yelling this time. "He's coming through the door. He's knocking on the wall. He's alive. He's alive!" I got up cursing and fell over the stool trying to find the lamp. Stoo did not get up and I saw him light his pipe and lie back. I took half an hour to quieten the kid and got wearily back into bed.

At three in the morning the storm broke. The thunder came rolling down the valley and the rain started drumming on the tin roof. I rolled over drowsily. Next minute, the kid was off again. I got out of bed. The roof was leaking, the floor was awash, and the kid was in a proper state. He said that old Griff had been calling to be let in out of the rain and I don't know what else. The kid said that he was not going back to sleep and that he was off home in the morning.

Stoo was still lying back puffing his pipe. Dawn was beginning to break and I was worn out. Stoo agreed that we would have to take the kid back home and that the weekend was a wipe-out.

We cooked eggs and bacon for breakfast, packed the van, and started back without having wet a line. The sun was just coming up. The leaves on the trees were glistening from the rain and there was a sparkle on the river. I saw a fish jump just as we topped the rise near the gate. The road was wet and muddy and, when Stoo let the clutch out, the van slid back down the rise. He swung the wheel and the back of the van rammed into the low earth bank by the side of the track. The back doors swung open and the coffin slid down the van floor, over the edge, and came to rest almost upright. The lid fell off and Griff sort of stepped forward and fell slowly out. I've never seen anything like it. The kid got out of the van, walked through the gate, and then started running like mad up the track.

We got the old bloke back into the coffin and gave him a brush down. We shoved some wattle saplings under the wheels and the van came up the rise again, no trouble. Eventually we caught up with the kid along the road and he got in and sat, puffing and blowing. He didn't say much.

After we dropped the kid at the pub, Stoo said. "We'd better hurry, just in case!" We hurried around to the funeral parlour—in the back way—and got old Griff out of the van. We worked like mad for ten minutes and had him laid out in the chapel with the artificial flowers and the candles, and all the mud and grass off him. We shoved the empty coffin back in the van and opened a bottle of beer on the back step.

We were just in time. Murphy, the kid's old man, and Drozzo, the local cop, came in the gate. The kid's old man was a surprise. He really had his fandangoes in tangle and he was going to have us lumbered for desecration and molesting the dead, and blasphemy as well.

Stoo refilled our glasses and asked what the song and dance was about. When Murphy finished listing all we were supposed to have done to his boy, Stoo lit his pipe and said, "I knew we should have dropped him off at the hospital. He's off his rocker."

Stoo said that of course we hadn't taken a corpse with us on a fishing trip but that the kid had fallen and hit his head. "He was peculiar after that," Stoo added.

I took Murphy and Drozzo and showed them old Griff lying in state, all nice and clean, and I showed them the empty coffin in the van. Stoo sat on the step, having the occasional sip and puffing smoke. Drozzo had a look around and agreed that the kid must have got concussion. He quietened Murphy down and got Stoo to see the publican to the gate. Then Drozzo turned to me and gave a bit of a wink.

"You might need these," he said. "I found them in the van." And he handed me the bottom half of a set of teeth.

Next thing I heard was that they were going to keep the kid in hospital for observation. And now, here he was out on the loose again and the first thing Stoo does is offer to take him fishing again. It was beyond me.

I lit up a cigarette. Stoo was watching me with a grin on his face. He just looked at me for a moment and then he said, "When you've cuffed a good pup to teach it a lesson, it doesn't hurt to give it a pat later."

Morte d'Stanley

My Uncle Stanley had been sluicing huge quantities of alcoholic liquor down his throat for most of the seventy or so years that had been allotted him. His family had been aware that the demon drink would catch up with him sooner or later and his demise, therefore, was not entirely unexpected.

Of those who felt a sense of loss at his passing, none would have had more reason for regret than the shareholders of the brewery that manufactured his favourite beverage. It would certainly be necessary for his name to be removed from the list of company assets.

Surprisingly, Uncle Stanley had found time to sire a largish family which he had presumably begotten between quaffing the contents of glasses, pots, middies, schooners, bottles, flagons, casks, demi johns, barrels and sundry other containers. So his departure from this vale of tears was not to go unnoticed or without due ceremony and mourning.

Mother, who was Uncle Stanley's only sister, telephoned Aunt Audrey, his wife, to ask details of the 'arrangements,' which was as near as Mother could come to referring to the funeral.

"Two o'clock," said Aunt Audrey, "At the cemetery." Then she hung up. She was a woman of few words.

Mother and I took a taxi to the cemetery. The taxi driver seemed to be new to the trade and I offered no comment when he took us the long way around because we were far too early anyway.

We came down Calvary Drive from the wrong direction, so far as I was concerned, and we turned in onto a rough dirt road, some distance short of the big stone pillars that marked the cemetery entrance. I supposed the old cemetery to have been filled up and that a new area was now being used. Nevertheless, the state of the entry track surprised me as the taxi bumped over it.

"Strange," I said to myself as I paid the driver.

Because we were early, Mother and I strolled across the grass to where the rows of headstones commenced. We passed two or three and, though I thought some of the inscriptions a little odd, I offered no comment, feeling that Mother should be left alone with her thoughts.

It was Mother who opened the conversation. "My goodness," she exclaimed in amazed tones. "Just look at this!"

She was gazing at a black marble tombstone on which a message had been inscribed in gold lettering. Over her shoulder, I read, "'T'was a lump of German sausage that upset her little liver and my Trixie (I regret) has been rowed across the river. On her little woolly bed she lay suffering, in pain, and it's very sad to know she'll never lick my hand again!"

Mother rolled her eyes to indicate disbelief. "What a bloody chauvinist pig her husband must have been," she said. "She'll never lick his hand again… of all the nerve."

I moved a few steps along the path. "What about this one then?" I asked.

Mother peered at the inscription, this time on a brass plate affixed to a column of pink granite.

"In memory of Big Tom. I bet the pussies for miles around are enjoying the rest."

"Well, I never," said Mother, blushing.

The next grave was surmounted by a life-size statue of an angel nursing what could have been a celestial musical instrument or, perhaps, a tortoise with mumps and its leg in traction.

"In memory of Danny," it reported blandly. "Died of fur balls, January 1981."

"I think that's what your father had," Mother announced, dabbing at her eyes with a handkerchief. "I don't believe they should use tombstones for medical reports."

Our activities were unexpectedly interrupted by a young man in corduroys and a yellow singlet on which 'MOSCOW LIBERALS CLUB' had been stamped. He seemed to have materialised from nowhere.

"G'mornin," he said cheerfully, and gestured towards the row of gravestones. "Most of these are my own work," he told us. "I'm a stonemason and a poet as well so I've really got it all together, I reckon. I rather fancy that an appropriate little sonnet, or whatever, dulls the grief, as it were." He scratched frantically at an armpit. "Lost a loved one, have you?'

We made appropriate noises.

"A lot of them pop off in the hot weather, you know. The old ones get the wheezes and flatulence, then their bladders go and, before you know it, KAZOOM, they've had their chips."

Mother's jaw had dropped, but our new acquaintance, like any good salesman, was in full flight. "What was the name of the deceased?"

I deferred to Mother, but she appeared to have been struck mute. "Stanley," I told him. "It was Stanley." I was about to add Uncle Stanley's surname but the poet was too quick. His eyes went blank and he cupped the back of his head in one hand and his chin in the other. It was readily apparent that he was communing with his muse.

"We can do you a stone alright," he told us after a moment or two. "It's hard to find something to rhyme with Stanley, though. A pity you hadn't called him something else. I've got lots of things that go with 'Rover' or 'Prince.' Still, I suppose I could put the name first. How does this strike you?

"Poor old Stanley," he declaimed, "died of choller. GOD came down, and reclaimed his collar."

Mother burst into tears and the poet looked mildly pleased at her recognition of the poignancy of his verse and at his own ability to strike the right note.

"I'm sorry, lady. You must've been real fond of him. How's about: 'Your place by the fireside is empty and your bowls are gathering dust…'"

Mother sobbed aloud. "I don't like that bit about his bowels gathering dust."

The poet cast me a glance full of sympathy for the extent of Mother's sensibilities. Placatingly, he asked, "What was he? A Great Dane? A German Shepherd?"

Mother emoted more loudly than ever.

"No," she sobbed, her voice going up an octave. "He was an Australian pastrycook."

"Oh, dear," said the poet, abashed. "Was he indeed? He's not one of us then. I'm afraid you're in the wrong place. You'll have to go through the gate in the hedge over there and I think you will find yourself among your own."

He seemed a bit miffed at losing our custom.

Through the gate we went and there was Aunt Audrey and all the cousins. We joined them just in time to partake in the burying of Uncle Stanley.

"I think, perhaps, a nice memorial in marble…" Aunt Audrey suggested to Mother. "I thought that we could…"

"So long as there's no poetry on it," Mother said firmly.

On the Training of Cats

Our three cats are all refugees from somewhere or other. They chose us, in fact, rather than us choosing them. Personally, I prefer dogs, though I can put up with cats, if only just.

Our cats do not like to be confined indoors. Nor, for that matter, do they like to be confined to the outdoors. What they do like is the right of free and unobstructed passage throughout the house to the great outside where they can loll on the sun-heated plastic garden table on the patio or doze in the dappled shade provided by the rhubarb. To meet this requirement, it has been our custom to leave open the sliding glass door to the patio to the extent that a cat can just ease through. While this system worked admirably through the winter, with the onset of summer the blowflies found the gap without trouble and they joined us inside in large numbers.

We started shutting the sliding door, a move that had a traumatic effect on the cats. If they were inside and the door was closed, they came to believe that the outside was infinitely desirable. If they were outside, they developed an inexpressible longing to be inside. Of course, with three cats, all with minds and opinions of their own, we could have employed a fulltime doorman who would, inescapably, have developed tenosynovitis within a week or two.

It was worst during meals. A cat would sit at the door making plaintive noises for it to be opened. Often one of them would be seeking to come in while another was seeking to go out and the third pondering its options. With practice, I came to be able to withstand their demands for as much as ninety seconds at a time but, as my wife could hold out for as long as four minutes, it invariably fell to me to leave the table, walk the thirteen paces to the door, and supervise an entry or an exit. As this sequence of events could occur any number of times during a meal, I was greatly wearied by mid-summer. I decided to build an entry flap for the cats in the fly-wire door that connects the patio with the laundry.

I wanted the cat door to last, so I constructed a frame from some good solid timber I had been saving against the possibility that I might, after retirement, add an upstairs level to the house. I attached a substantial wood flap by means of steel hinges, but when my wife noticed me giving the whole thing a coat of paint, she threw herself about in simulated horror and said that she could not permit me to affix such a monstrosity to the back door where it might offend the neighbours. She said that it was far too heavy for the cats and, in a fit of hyperbole, claimed that it would prove an impassable barrier to a charging rhinoceros. She also conjectured that the fly-wire door itself would become so heavy with the addition of my cat flap and frame that, were we to use it ourselves, we would have to install some heavy equipment in the backyard to winch the door open and shut.

It had been my intention to ignore her jibes and incorporate the cat door despite her protestations. However, to occupy the time during her diatribe, I had been idly holding the cat door against the place on the wire door where I intended locating it. To my horror, I found that my measurements had been wrong and that it would not fit. The discovery enabled me to accede graciously to her demand, thus putting her under an obligation which I could store for future use.

I purchased some light pine wood, a wafer-thin piece of ply and two tiny aluminium hinges. I then built and installed a magnificent cat flap. The frame, surrounded by new fly-wire, sat squarely in the middle of the door and was firmly fixed at top and bottom. The flap itself was so light that a gnat could have pushed it open with its proboscis.

We put the cats outside and stood back to watch them use the flap. They sat in a little huddle looking in at us and making the standard plaintive noises.

"Go outside and put one of them through it," my wife said. "The others will follow."

I went outside, picked up the nearest cat, put its head against the flap and pushed gently. The cat got a surprise when the flap moved. It clawed my hand and disappeared over the back fence. The other two had watched with moderate interest and had not taken flight. I wiped off the blood and very carefully pushed them through, one at a time. Success!

They both walked around to the sliding door and made plaintive noises to be let out. Patiently, and one at a time, I carried them back to the cat flap and, gently, pushed them through.

Since that time, I have shown all of them how it works, a hundred, nay, five hundred times. They steadfastly refuse to use the flap and, at one stage, in fact, managed to tear a hole through the wire gauze at the side of the flap, thus implementing an entirely new route and doing the blowflies a great service.

Instead of walking the thirteen steps to open the sliding door, I now walk twenty-nine steps to help them either in or out of the cat flap; in the meantime, my wife has increased her resistance time to 4.3 minutes.

I fixed the hole in the fly wire and put bars on either side of the cat flap to prevent them going through the wire again. I don't think they mind, actually, and their patience is infinite.

I have considered an electronic eye that opens the cat door as they approach. I have thought about adopting the principle of the pedal bin so that when they step on a little plate their weight opens the door. The idea I like best involves an oil-fired boiler on the patio from which runs a copper tube that comes up through the cement exactly one cat length from the back door. My plan is that when a cat stands just outside the flap making noises to come in, the sound of its whinging actuates a valve, and a jet of boiling steam emerges from the copper tube and strikes the cat on a spot where it will be encouraged to move forward without undue delay or further complaint.

Such ideas are, perhaps, a bit impractical and I am working on a more realistic solution. I am adapting an old possum trap that has been lying around home for years. The possum trap is to be placed in front of the cat door. The cat will approach closely to the wire door so that its snivelling lament will be heard more readily by those inside. The cat will enter the trap, thereby releasing a catch. The back door of the trap will drop and shut the cat in. A time-delay switch will then operate so that the back and front of the trap will drop away, leaving the cat firmly held by the two sides which have moved in on a spring. Eleven seconds after the operation is put in train, an electronic bell will ring.

When I hear the bell, I rise from the table, let myself out through the sliding door and approach the cat door from the rear. Then, very carefully, I line the cat up with the cat flap, making allowance for wind velocity, elevation, and moisture content of the atmosphere. Then I take a short run and boot the cat so that it passes through the cat door at the speed of light.

I am very much looking forward to completing the project.

Squaring the Series

He was already in the compartment when George boarded the train and George assumed that he had come from further up the line. He was a big strong chap, somewhere in his forties, with 'medium successful grazier' written all over him. George and he had the compartment to themselves, and they said "G'day" to each other, as country people do. He went back to reading a newspaper and George took the window seat opposite. The whistle blew and away they went.

They had been travelling for ten minutes or so and Medium Successful had turned over a couple of pages of his newspaper when he suddenly burst out laughing. Eventually, he transferred the paper to one hand so that he could wipe the tears of laughter from his eyes with the other. He looked up finally to find George gazing curiously at him.

"There's a funny thing in this paper," he said, and he proceeded to tell George the story that had so amused him. "There is this miner who works at a coalfield in England. He lives in one of those streets where there are fifty or a hundred terrace houses all exactly the same. It seems that this night he finishes a shift at the mine at ten o'clock, comes home and everyone is in bed asleep. He lets himself in, takes his boots off downstairs in the kitchen so as not to wake the wife and, after he's cleaned up, goes up to bed. Well, it's a Thursday night so he exercises his conjugal rights as is his custom and falls asleep. He's on the early shift next morning so he's up again by six. He goes downstairs, dresses and puts his boots on, grabs his hat and he's off to the mine."

George looked mystified but his companion shook with laughter before he could continue. "The funny bit is, that when the miner gets home after his shift, his wife asks, 'Where the hell were you last night? Why didn't you come home?' Of course, he realises that he must have slept in the house next door by mistake and that his neighbour, who is also a miner, must have been on the night shift. So his own wife is now wanting a divorce and he's in all sorts of trouble with the chap next door in whose bed he slept and, what's more, he's in trouble with his wife as well."

George did not have a newspaper to while away a dull train journey. He was pleased to be talking to someone and he did not wish the companionable interchange to end. He therefore threw himself about laughing and agreed with Medium Successful that it had been an excellent story, excruciatingly funny, and exceedingly well told. To keep up his end of the conversation, regrettably—as it turned out—George said, "As a matter of fact, something rather similar happened to me not so long ago."

George's fellow passenger folded his newspaper and sat forward in his seat so that he could listen more easily over the noise of the train.

George then told his story. "A while back," he said, "I went onto a property for a month as Manager. Sheep country it was. I won't tell you where it is but, originally, it was part of a very big property owned by one of the meat companies. The company began to feel the pinch and it cut the place into ten smaller properties, five on either side of the track. They were still quite large though and they all had frontages of twenty kilometres and all the houses were set back five kilometres or so from the front gates. The houses were all the same too because the meat company bought them as a job lot from a mining company that had gone bust."

A strange look had come over the face of George's companion while that worthy had been telling his story, but it was not often that George had an appreciative and attentive audience and he carried on his story without giving Medium Successful's appearance a second thought.

"Well," said George, having finally set the scene. "One night in town I really hung one on. You wouldn't believe it but when I drove home that night, I missed my turn-off which, as it so happens, was the second on the right. So, down the track I went another twenty kilometres and then another five kilometres up the drive to the house. The missus was in bed asleep, but," said George (proudly), "she soon woke up when I got in. I planned," George continued, "to move a couple of hundred ewes from one of the front paddocks next morning, so I was up at dawn. Down to the front gate I went in the ute. Couldn't find the bloody sheep though. I scouted about a bit and then I noticed a big gum-tree by the gate that shouldn't have been there. I went up and had a good look at it and, by jingo, I realised that I was on the wrong property."

Medium Successful Grazier's face had gone a brick-red colour, but George assumed that his story had been so amusing that it was all his travelling companion could do to stop busting out laughing again.

"It so happened," George continued innocently, "that the lady I had thought to be my wife and I had not exchanged a word. Just where her husband was I'll never know. Anyway, I can tell you that on realising my mistake, I didn't waste any time taking off for home. I moved my ewes up to the sheds ready for the shearers and told my wife I'd been detained in town overnight."

George sat back, a big grin on his face, waiting for signs of appreciation for what he felt certain had been a good yarn. It quickly became apparent to him, however, that his story had not gone over at all well and that his fellow traveller was not amused.

"I know those properties that were cut up by the meat company," said Medium Successful, spitting out each word through clenched jaws. "It happens that one of them is mine!"

George's face paled. "My God," he said aghast. "You didn't come from further up the line at all." And then he said, accusingly, "You must've only got on the train just ahead of me."

Silently, George berated himself for being such a prize imbecile, but time for soliloquy was not to be his.

"You said your turn-off was second on the right," said Medium Successful. "Well, I'm third on the right."

"What's that got to do with me?" George said defensively.

Medium Successful stood up and started taking off his jacket. "I'm going to knock your bloody block off," he said.

George, who had once wanted to be a jockey but had been told he was too light, looked up at his one-time neighbour who was at that very moment depositing his folded jacket on the seat. He noted, for the first time, the width of his friendly travelling companion's shoulders and the size of his arms.

"Wait a minute," urged George, his mind turning over in desperation. Then he had one of his all-too-rare touches of genius. "Don't you have any faith in your own wife?" he asked triumphantly. That stopped Medium Successful for a moment, but George could not think of what to say next and the initiative was lost. After a pause, he resigned himself to having his block knocked off and he said, "Anyway. Any man worth his bloody salt wouldn't've left his wife at home on the night they were celebrating Little Chester's big win at the Korrobolong race meeting. First time a local horse has won it," said George, and he added virtuously, "If my wife hadn't been waiting on a call from her sister in Sydney, she'd have been there with me, and I wouldn't've hung one on and I'd have got home to the right bloody bed."

Medium Successful, on the point of knocking George's block off, paused. "Hold on a minute," he said. "Me and the wife were there that night. Down at O'Rafferty's Wheat Sheaf Hotel."

"Oh," replied George, forgetting his predicament for the moment. "I was at O'Gorman's."

Medium Successful scratched his head. "Then either you weren't at my place at all or… I've got it, I've got it," he said. He sat down and roared with laughter again and slapped his thigh. "Now I remember. Yeah, we stayed in town that weekend. My wife's old granny came up from Melbourne and she minded the place for us—feeding the chooks, you know." He was convulsed with amusement.

George was not amused. "He's like a bloody chameleon," he thought. "One minute he's raging on and about to do me a mischief and the next he's falling about laughing at my expense."

Medium Successful was still mopping at his face with a handkerchief and trying to control his mirth when the train pulled up at the junction. George, who was continuing his journey, slouched unhappily back in his seat, but his companion stood and took down a battered leather case from the rack. Medium Successful put his jacket over the arm holding the suitcase and, with his free arm, gave George a punch in the eye.

"Sorry, mate," Medium Successful said. "That was the best joke I've heard for years. I'm not too fond of the old lady's granny and she certainly hasn't complained but, after all, she is family so that's one for the road." Medium Successful got down from the train onto the platform and shut the carriage door behind him.

George was nursing his eye and moaning gently to himself. He was very irritated. As the train started up again, he rallied. He stood up and opened the window in the carriage door. "Hey," he called as he passed Medium Successful. The train was gathering speed. "Now I remember, too. I don't think it was the Korrobolong race meeting after all. It could have been Anzac Day or Christmas or Easter. I forget."

George had the satisfaction of seeing the smile vanish from Medium Successful's face before he sat down and picked up the newspaper and began reading it with one eye.